BUNHEADS

BUNHEADS

a novel by
Sophie Flack

poppy

LITTLE, BROWN AND COMPANY
New York   Boston

Poppy

Hachette Book Group
237 Park Avenue, New York, NY 10017
For more of your favorite series, visit our website at www.pickapoppy.com

Poppy is an imprint of Little, Brown and Company.
The Poppy name and logo are trademarks of Hachette Book Group, Inc.

The publisher is not responsible for websites (or their content) that are not owned by the publisher.

First Edition: October 2011

Library of Congress Cataloging-in-Publication Data

Flack, Sophie.
     Bunheads / by Sophie Flack. — 1st ed.
         p.   cm.
     Summary: Hannah Ward, nineteen, revels in the competition, intense rehearsals, and dazzling performances that come with being a member of Manhattan Ballet Company's corps de ballet, but after meeting handsome musician Jacob she begins to realize there could be more to her life.
     ISBN 978-0-316-12653-3
     [1. Ballet dancing—Fiction.   2. Interpersonal relations—Fiction.   3. Competition (Psychology)—Fiction.   4. Dating (Social customs)—Fiction.   5. New York (N.Y.)—Fiction.]   I. Title.
     PZ7.F594Bun 2011
     [Fic]—dc22   2011009715

10   9   8   7   6   5   4   3   2   1

RRD-C

Printed in the U.S.A.

For all of the unsung heroes in the back line
of the corps de ballet

FALL SEASON

1

My name is Hannah Ward. Don't call me a ballerina.

Ballerinas are the stars of the company. They dance center stage under the spotlight, and they get their own curtain calls. Their head shots are printed in the program, with their names in large print. Me, I'm a dancer in the corps de ballet, just one of the dozens of girls who dance in graceful unison each night. My mother thinks I'm a star, but she's biased.

Besides, the word ballerina *sounds too pink, too froufrou. Yes, we wear tutus and tiaras, but only when we perform each night. We spend most of our time hidden from the audience, working as hard as we possibly can to strengthen and control our bodies so that when we step onstage, everything we do looks perfect and effortless.*

We rehearse in old leotards, threadbare tights, and torn leg warmers. We rarely buy new dance clothes because we know that most ballet careers are short-lived. Today, for example, I'm wearing a faded navy cotton leotard and black, slightly less faded leggings. There's nothing pink or froufrou about that.

"Throw yourself into your dancing now," one of my teachers once said, "because the life span of a dancer can be as short as a fruit fly's."

٩◦ ٩◦ ٩◦

"Five minutes to curtain, ladies. Let's shake a leg!" Christine, the stage manager, stands in the doorway with her hands on her hips. Her headset crackles, and she hastily barks something into it, then turns back to us. "Adriana, you don't even have your shoes on. Am I going to have to hold the curtain?"

Adriana wrinkles her pointy, powdered nose and holds up her shoes, plus the needle and thread she'll use to sew herself into them. "See, I'm doing it," she responds. "Anyway, there's plenty of time. I have the whole overture."

Christine smiles then, looking affectionate but also a little tense. It's her job to make sure that every performance of the Manhattan Ballet goes the way it should. This means worrying about everything from the placement of the spotlights to the egos of prima ballerinas. With one last glance at us, she turns and scurries out, her short, platinum blond hair sticking up in all directions. "Places," she calls.

I sympathize with Christine: It looks chaotic in here. We're backstage in the Green Room before a Friday night performance, and all around me dancers are being fastened into their pristine white tutus. The room is a tangle of satin, tulle, and long, lean limbs. Some girls look deep in thought, while others chat loudly

2

with one another. On the floor are discarded bits of clothing, lone pointe shoes, leg warmers, and half-empty water bottles.

"I took, like, eight Advil today," a dark-haired dancer named Olivia says as she smacks her gum. "I hope I don't die before the curtain comes down."

"You'd better not let Christine see that gum or she'll grab it right out of your mouth," Adriana says as she sews into her pointe shoes. Her legs are long and almost skeletally thin.

But as I step into my own circle of ridged white tulle, I leave the chaos behind. It happens every time I dress for *Waltz Variations*: I feel as if I've time-traveled to a past, more glamorous era. Fake diamonds drip down my sternum, and my false eyelashes seem as large and as dark as butterfly wings. Laura, one of the dressers, fastens the hooks on my bodice as I pull on my ivory gloves.

As soon as my costume is secure, I scurry out through the Green Room curtain and into the hands of the hairdressers. My friend Zoe is already there, impatiently tapping her foot in its pink pointe shoe.

"Hurry," she growls as a flustered hairdresser attaches a diamond headpiece to Zoe's pale blond bun. "No, that's not it!" She pushes the hairdresser's hand away.

Because there's hardly any time, I decide to secure my headpiece myself. And apparently Zoe has decided to do this as well, because she shoves the hairdresser out of the way and steps in front of me, blocking my view of the mirror.

"I'm on before you," I tell her, but she's too busy with her bobby pins to listen. I place the diamond-encrusted tiara around my bun while trying to peer around Zoe, who refuses to relinquish her place before the mirror. I stab myself in the scalp with a bobby pin. "Ouch," I yelp. Then I sigh loudly. "Z," I say, "you know, you're totally in my way."

"What? Oh, hi, Hannah." Zoe whirls around as if she's only just noticed me. Her green eyes feign surprise. Her mouth, like mine, is full of clips and pins.

"Hi," I say, putting my hands on my hips. "Do you mind?"

Zoe grins, turns back to her reflection, and scoots about a quarter of an inch to her left, so now I can *almost* see myself in the mirror.

Just as I get the tiara fixed, I hear the intro to my music. I run down the dark hall toward the stage, a piece of loose blond hair trailing behind me. I tuck it up into my bun and cross my fingers that it stays. My partner, Jonathan, is waiting for me in the darkened wings, a reassuring smile on his strong, handsome face. I lean back into his arms and allow him to support my back as he lifts me into the bright lights of the stage.

There I join the dozens of corps dancers, and as we swirl together, it seems as though we are an undulating sea of white. I am lifted off my feet, and it feels like flying.

"Whee!" I exclaim to Jonathan, who giggles.

Above us, chandeliers illuminate our twirling bodies, and I wonder if this is what a prom must be like. I didn't go to my prom, because I was already performing with the Manhattan Ballet. I've seen *Pretty in Pink* and *10 Things I Hate About You*, though, so I can imagine it well enough: There would be limos to ride in, and hidden flasks of liquor; the girls would be dressed in strapless satin gowns, and the boys in rented tuxedos. They'd slow-dance under spinning multicolored lights and make out in dark hallways.

Sometimes I think I must have missed something great. But then I tell myself that things experienced onstage are usually more exciting than things experienced in real life anyway.

The music swells, Jonathan lifts me again, and there's a surge of applause as Lottie, the aging star of the Manhattan Ballet, enters stage left, her auburn hair in a slick, tight twist and diamond studs sparkling in her ears. I can't see the audience members in the darkened house, but they're out there in their velvet-cushioned seats, watching us with anticipation and delight.

And I don't feel like a teenager onstage — I feel like a princess waltzing with her prince.

I wanted to be a dancer for as long as I can remember. When all the other little girls in my neighborhood were riding around on their pink-tasseled bicycles or comparing the latest fashion accessories for their Barbies, I was taking ballet classes at the local studio and fantasizing about dancing the role of Marie in *The Nutcracker*.

Every day after school, my mom would pick me up and drive me to dance classes in Boston. I'd change into my leotard in the backseat of our minivan and do my bun in the mirrored sun visor. I didn't fit in with the other kids at school, but when I got to the studio, I felt completely at home. I loved the discipline of the practice: There was always some step to improve upon, some position to perfect. And the adrenaline rush I got from dancing — it was intoxicating.

When I was ten, I told my mom that I was going to be a professional dancer. Instead of smiling and patting me on the head, as if that was just another silly idea from a headstrong fifth grader, she took me seriously. Maybe that's because she's an artist herself — a pretty successful ceramicist, to be specific — and so she values the creative impulse over just about anything else.

We began taking road trips to New York City so I could train with some of the best coaches in the country. The summer I turned fourteen, I studied at the Manhattan Ballet Academy, and when August came I was invited to enroll full-time. It was an amazing opportunity, a dream come true. The hitch? It meant moving to New York — alone.

My parents weren't thrilled at the prospect: My mom worried that I was too young, and my dad worried that I'd get mugged. They had qualms about the academy dorms — *were the doors locked at all times, were the floors coed?* — and they wondered whether the high school I'd attend, the School of the Arts, offered classes in creative writing, my favorite subject. They realized that, even after I'd made it so far, there was still no guarantee that I'd actually become the professional I wanted to be. That's why I had to tell them, over one of my mom's hippie dinners of baked tofu and mashed yams, that this was the chance of a lifetime and that I was willing to take the risk.

I could see them struggling with the idea as they chewed (though my dad may have been struggling with his dinner, too;

he'd never liked tofu). They understood that I'd be miserable if I stayed home in Weston, Massachusetts—that every day I'd wish I were at the academy, working toward a chance to be a part of the Manhattan Ballet, which was one of the best companies in the world.

After a few moments I saw my dad nod his head, ever so slightly. My mom turned to me, and her smile was happy and sad at the same time. "All right, then," she whispered.

Today, five years later, I'm a senior corps member with the Manhattan Ballet. We perform three to four ballets a night to packed houses in New York City, and when we go on tour, our audience can fill five-thousand-seat amphitheaters.

I'm a ballet dancer, but I'm not a *ballerina*. And it's the most amazing, wonderful, and crazy life I ever could have imagined.

2

"Monique's dress was so busted," Daisy says as she pulls her silky dark hair into a bun. "It would make Gisele Bündchen look like Susan Boyle."

I laugh as I sip a venti drip. It's nine forty-five in the morning, and I'm in the dressing room — my home away from home — listening to two of my three best friends in the company dissect the most recent episode of *Project Runway*. "Was it really that bad?" I ask.

"I mean, it was a total potato sack," Daisy says. She leans toward the mirror with her mouth agape as she applies mascara.

"Well, you would know about potatoes," I smirk, pulling on my black Repetto leotard.

Daisy rolls her eyes and sighs. "God, Hannah, for the last time, it's *Idaho* that grows all the potatoes."

I grin because of course I know that; I just like to tease Daisy because at sixteen she's the youngest in our dressing room and she's been in the company for only six months. She's a total bunhead: She lives and breathes ballet. "Idaho, Ohio, Iowa," I say, waving my arm dismissively. "They don't call it flyover country for nothing."

"I'm from *Nebraska*," she says, her dark eyes flashing. Even though she's from the Midwest, Daisy looks olive-skinned and exotic because her mother is Jordanian. She's five foot three, with tiny bones, knobby elbows, and a wide, infectious smile. "Nebraska is known for its corn."

"Oh, *riiiight*," I say, smiling. "My bad."

She sticks out her tongue at me.

"I thought the dress was all right," Bea says as she pulls her bright red hair into a high ponytail. "I mean, it was kind of baggy, but what she did with the pleating was interesting."

"Oh, Bea," I say, "it's just like you to find something nice to say."

Beatrice Hall—Bea—is from Maine. Like me, she's nineteen, and she's been my best friend since we roomed together at the Manhattan Ballet Academy. She was brought up ultrareligious (as in going to church all the time and praying before you eat and all that), and she's the youngest of eight kids, so she had to learn patience and diplomacy early on. But Bea has a wicked sense of humor, too. She has huge, beautiful blue eyes and pale, freckled skin. Her ears stick out slightly, and she has incredible coltlike legs that seem to go all the way up to her armpits.

"My mother raised me right," she says, nudging me with her toe.

I giggle and push it away. "Get your gnarly foot off of me."

9

"*My* gnarly foot? Have you looked at your bunions lately?"

Then the door bursts open and Zoe Mortimer leans in the doorframe, a Diet Coke in her hand. She's wearing her new cropped Prada blazer and skinny jeans. She looks haughty, as usual, but it's not on purpose; it's just the way her face is. She grew up on Park Avenue and is as rich as anyone I've ever met. That kind of privilege just shows.

She puts her hands on her narrow hips and grins, looking like the cat that ate the canary.

"What?" Bea demands as she braids her ponytail. "Are you going to tell us why you're smiling like that?"

Zoe tosses her long blond hair and steps delicately over Bea's clothes, which are scattered on the floor in piles of tights, leg warmers, sweatpants, and leotards. "Yes," Zoe says. "Just a sec, I've got to get changed." She slips off her jeans and very slowly roots around in her theater case for a fresh pair of tights.

"Take your time," I say sarcastically. "Keep building the suspense."

She grins slyly at me but doesn't say anything. Then, after she's changed into a gray Lycra leotard and shell-pink tights, she turns to face us. "Adriana heard that Otto's going to start rehearsing his new ballet."

Otto Klein is the director of the Manhattan Ballet, the man who selects the ballets and decides who will dance them — in other words, the man who determines our futures.

"Whoop-de-do," Bea says, sounding bored. She puts the finishing touches on her hairdo and opens one of Zoe's old issues of *Vogue* magazine. "Does Gumby think that's news?"

"Who's Gumby?" Daisy wants to know.

Bea smiles. "Adriana! Because she's freakishly flexible. Gumby—that green rubber guy who can bend...oh, never mind, you're too young."

I giggle. "Yeah, but we dance, like, forty different ballets a season. So what's the big deal about this new one?" I yawn and twist my hair into a high bun.

Zoe raises an eyebrow as she continues. "Adriana said Otto wants to cast a corps girl in the lead, and that's why he's been watching class."

Now, *this* is news. Daisy puts down her eyebrow pencil, and Bea closes the magazine and sits up a little straighter. I take another sip of coffee and wait for Zoe to continue. Now that she's mentioned it, I realize that Otto has been around a lot more lately. Usually we see him only two or three times a week, but he's been slipping into the studio during our center work nearly every day recently. He lingers at the back of the room, along the mirrored wall, his jaw clenched as he taps his fingers on his thigh.

"I saw him giving you the up-down in class yesterday, Hannah," Bea says. "The day before, too. Maybe you've got a shot at it."

"You think?" I ask, feeling a little shiver of excitement.

"I doubt it," Zoe snorts under her breath. She leans toward the mirror, retouching the lip gloss on her full, pouty lips.

"Excuse me?" I say.

She turns to me and gives me one of her special Zoe smiles, the kind that's only about 10 percent sincere. "No offense, Han, but I wouldn't get my hopes up," she says. She carefully lines her lipsticks up in a neat row. "There are a lot of corps girls for him to choose from. He might have someone else in mind. Like Adriana herself, say. Or like . . ."

"Or like *you*?" I ask.

Zoe nods. "Yes, like me. I mean, I'm just trying to protect your feelings, Hannah."

"Yeah, right," I say, suddenly annoyed. "Of course, you're only concerned about my feelings."

"Absolutely!" Zoe replies. She blots the corner of her mouth with a tissue and then makes a kissing face at her reflection.

Daisy and Bea pretend to be absorbed in whatever they're doing. They've learned to stay out of it when Zoe and I have one of our occasional spats.

I meet my gaze in the mirror. Staring back at me is a hazel-eyed teenager with high cheekbones and dark blond hair that sometimes, on rainy days, gets a bit frizzy. I set my jaw and straighten my shoulders. I can feel Zoe looking at me from across the room, but I ignore her. Each of us knows what the other is thinking: *That part is going to be mine.*

Otto encourages competition between his dancers, as if there weren't enough already. He likes to put Zoe and me together because we're both blond and tall, and no doubt he'd get pleasure out of causing a rift between us over a new part. Otto's of the Nietzschean "what doesn't kill you makes you stronger" school.

"Anyway, I'm going out for a puff." Zoe gets up and throws on a loose cable-knit sweater over her leotard. She's headed up to the roof, where the smokers like to gather. "Don't miss me." The door slams behind her.

"We won't," Bea mutters under her breath as she throws a pair of pointe shoes into her theater case. Bea has no patience for Zoe's attitude; she tolerates her mostly out of loyalty to me. "God forbid someone suggest that Otto was looking at something other than Zoe's bony behind," she says when Zoe's safely out of earshot. "Her ass is so concave, I could eat soup out of it!" She mimes ladling soup into her mouth, and Daisy succumbs to a fit of giggles.

I laugh so hard I nearly spit out my mouthful of coffee, but there's a part of me that wonders what gets said about me when *I* leave the room.

"I don't care what you say," Daisy sighs, starry-eyed. "I would love to look like Zoe."

I rest my head on my hands for a moment. Even though she's kind of a brat, I never like fighting with Zoe. I still have ten minutes before company class, so I decide to go clear the air with her.

I take the elevator to the top floor and hurry up the stairs to the roof. The heavy metal door that says EMERGENCY EXIT ONLY groans as I push it open. There aren't any windows in the theater — not in the studios or the dressing rooms or anywhere — so the bright September sun makes me squint.

I look around for Zoe, but for some reason she's not up here. An empty Starbucks cup rolls toward me in the slight breeze. The building's huge air-conditioning unit makes a loud humming noise and spews hot air over the flat black roof.

I walk to the edge and look down over the plaza. Below me

is the vast courtyard of Avery Center. There are clusters of tourists here and there, and I think I see Jonathan, late as usual, hobbling toward the theater because he pulled his ACL in rehearsal yesterday. Behind him the fountain at the center of the plaza sends up sparkling jets of water.

I close my eyes and breathe in, and all thoughts of Zoe vanish. The first autumn bite is in the air, and it marks the beginning of another year with the company.

Is Otto really looking for a corps girl to dance a new lead role? If so, then maybe he's looking to promote one of us to soloist.

The life span of a fruit fly. "What am I waiting for?" I ask aloud. "This is my year." I look up at the sky, and the wispy clouds seem to dance overhead. "This year," I tell them, "I'm going to be promoted."

I walk to the other side of the roof and look out over the traffic on Broadway. Two taxis are having a honking war, and on the corner of Broadway and Sixty-Fifth, a man in jogging clothes is doing jumping jacks as he waits to cross the street. A yellow school bus disgorges a group of high school students on a field trip to Avery Center. I watch them walk single file up the steps to the plaza, their mouths open in awe at the grand architecture of the buildings.

I spend most of my waking hours in the building directly below my feet, but beyond that lies a whole bustling world. I think of all the neighborhood sights that I never actually *see*: the lights and crowds of Times Square, the restaurants and bars of Hell's Kitchen, the galleries of Chelsea, the tree-lined streets of the West Village, and the shops and rock clubs of the East Village. If I weren't a professional dancer, maybe I'd feel more a part of New York City. But for now this theater is my entire world, and I don't miss the outside one bit.

I turn and walk back toward the door, scattering a flock of pigeons that had settled on the roof. My pledge will be my secret. "You can do this," I whisper.

3

"Hannah, you on next?" a low, gruff voice asks.

It's Harry, one of the stagehands, lingering in the backstage area where I wait for my entrance. He's about six foot three and probably weighs almost three hundred pounds, with kind eyes and no visible neck. Harry has worked at this theater longer than I've been alive. His grandfather and his father were stage-hands, too. At this point in his career, Harry knows as much about ballet as anyone I can think of.

"Hey, you," I say, rolling my neck to give the muscles a final stretch. "I'm on in a few minutes."

"Break a leg." Harry smiles. His nine-year-old daughter, Matilda, appears from out of nowhere, wearing a half-torn tutu and a battered pair of Nikes.

"Hannah!" she says breathlessly, her chubby cheeks bright pink with excitement.

Matilda doesn't come around the theater often—backstage isn't the best place for a kid—so I'm always surprised that she remembers my name and that she seems so excited to see me. I guess she's what they call precocious.

"Hey," I say, "I see you've got your tutu on. Are you dancing in one of the ballets tonight?"

She giggles. "I wish! But I have a recital coming up. Do you know the Delancey Dance Academy? That's where I take lessons." Her voice is proud, and her little chest puffs out.

Harry ruffles his daughter's curly dark hair. "Mattie wants to be a ballerina, too, when she grows up."

I look down at this smiling little girl in her pigtails and dirty tutu. Her face shines with delight. The theater must seem like a magical world to her—I know it did to me. When I first became an apprentice, I wanted to sleep on the stage, under the rows of lights that glittered like far-off planets. Sometimes when no one was around, I'd sit on the edge with my legs dangling into the orchestra pit and look out in awe at the vast, empty house with its carved, gilded ceiling and crystal chandeliers.

"I want to dance in *Swan Lake*," Mattie informs me.

"Good for you," I say. But I can see already that she has her father's body, and this does not bode well for Mattie's future ballet career. Harry is not built like a dancer; Harry is built like a Mack truck. "That's wonderful."

"We're going to do *The Nutcracker* this year, though," she adds.

"Wow," I say. "You know, we're rehearsing *The Nutcracker* now, too? We dance it every year starting the day after Thanksgiving."

17

Harry smiles indulgently. "It's not the real *Nutcracker*," he whispers. "They're just going to have Sugarplum Fairy costumes. My wife is slaving over the damn thing already." He laughs. "But Mattie loves to dance. Don't you, girl?"

Matilda nods happily. "I want a costume like yours some-day," she whispers. Her pink cheeks flush even pinker.

I glance down at the silvery satin costume and touch one of its hand-sewn pearls reverently, protectively. "I hope you get one," I whisper back.

Then Luke, my partner in *FourWinds*, appears, wanting to prac-tice the pirouettes we do together in the first section. He doesn't acknowledge Harry or Matilda but reaches out and grabs my hand. To a lot of dancers, the stagehands are simply invisible, like familiar pieces of furniture. Those dancers don't appreciate that without the stagehands, nothing—and I mean *nothing*—would work as it should.

"Please," Luke says. "I'm nervous." He blinks at me with his large, slightly watery green eyes.

I feel sorry for him, and so I nod. "All right, come here. Hold your arms out." I've danced this ballet dozens of times, but it's not easy, so I can sympathize. I step into his arms.

Matilda's eyes grow even wider. Now she'll get an impromptu performance.

I count off four counts, just to give Luke time to prepare, and then I start to turn. I fall to the right on the first pirouette, though, because Luke has me off my supporting leg.

"Hold me more firmly," I tell him. "You won't hurt me."

The second time he keeps me on my leg, and I rotate three times. Matilda applauds.

"Good! You'll be fine," I say reassuringly.

But right at that moment, Otto Klein glides by, frowning slightly as he sips from a bottle of Evian, and Luke visibly pales. "Is he watching tonight?" he whispers.

"I doubt it," I say, shaking my head, because I know Otto's presence will only make Luke more nervous, and then he'll forget what I told him about holding me right.

Of course, Otto probably *will* watch, and the thought of it makes my heart beat a bit faster.

I wave to Harry and Matilda, and then Luke and I go to join handsome Jonathan and gangly Adriana, who are waiting in the wings. The lights from the stage stream through the wings in pink, yellow, and blue beams that look like the sun shining through the clouds. We count our eights to make sure we come in on time. It might be overkill, but I like to count them on my fingers so I don't lose track.

On the end of the ninth eight, we walk onto the stage in unison and into our formation. As soon as I make the transition from wing to stage, I grow about two inches. I listen to the music and it cues my muscle memory. I tombé-glissade-piqué into Luke's arms. Then, preparing for the pirouette, I take a breath. On the first rotation I'm off my supporting leg, but I use my core strength to put myself back over my toe for the second turn.

"Sorry!" Luke whispers.

"Don't worry," I whisper back, even though I'm annoyed at him.

We run into formation and he lifts me high and quick for the pas de chat as we cross with the couples on stage left. I pose on the side in B-plus (one leg gracefully crossed behind the other) and then curtsy to the couples on the right and the left of us as if to greet them: "Hello, Adriana. Hello, Olivia."

Onstage we're all on the same team; worries about competition, casting, and promotions vanish, and we revel in the dance itself.

When the music stops, the audience erupts in applause. As I curtsy, I feel the adrenaline coursing through me.

"Thanks for not dropping me," I whisper to Luke as we take our bow.

"Anytime," he says with a grin.

Still trying to catch my breath, I walk backstage to check tomorrow's schedule. The schedule tells us which ballets we're dancing in, which ones we're rehearsing for, and which roles we might have a chance of getting. Dancers study it as if it's the word of God. If your name is printed under a soloist or principal part, it means that Otto sees potential in you, and your career is in the ascendance. Continually being cast in smaller corps parts, though, means the opposite. Since we perform so many different ballets in a season, each ballet is, in theory, an opportunity for a great part. So we're always hopeful—even if we're often disappointed.

All the lights are off except for a single blue bulb that burns dimly above the bulletin board, barely illuminating the schedule tacked there. I scan the paper for my name, and when I see it, my breath catches in my throat: I've been called to understudy Lottie Harlow for the lead in Otto's new ballet — the part that Zoe and I were angling for.

I feel a rush of excitement. Okay, so I didn't actually *get* the part, but Otto wants me to learn it! If something were to happen to Lottie, he trusts me to carry the ballet in her place. I smile and give a happy little hop. This could be a sign of good things to come.

Bea hurries up next to me, still breathing heavily from her performance, and looks for her own name. "Are you serious? I'm dancing *Unraveling in G* again?" Her red lips look black in the dim blue light, and her pancake makeup covers her freckles completely. "It's like I'm still an apprentice," she says grimly.

"That sucks," I say. Then, unable to help myself, I blurt, "I'm understudying Lottie in Otto's new ballet."

"Really?" Bea immediately brightens. "Good for you." She reaches out and gives me a quick squeeze. "See? Otto *was* watching you."

Then Daisy and Zoe come over, eager to find their own names. Zoe pushes past us, knocking Bea off balance.

"God, Z," Bea says. "Shove much?"

Zoe ignores her and two seconds later gives a little yelp. "I'm understudying Lottie," she says, turning to us and smiling, her teeth white and perfect.

Immediately my heart sinks a little. Of *course* Otto put us together again.

"I guess Otto was giving me the up-down, too, huh?" Zoe says slyly.

"Uh, yeah," I mumble.

"Hey," Daisy says. "You guys? Where am I?" She tries to catch a glimpse of the schedule, but we're all in the way. She jumps up and down, attempting to look over Zoe's shoulder.

"Looks like you're in *Symphony in G* and *Haiku*," I say.

"Yes!" Daisy pumps her little fist. "I've always wanted to dance *Haiku*."

Zoe leans over and whispers in my ear, "What a dork. That's, like, the lamest part in our rep."

"She's oblivious," I whisper back. "But at least her delusion will keep her happy. You know how she stress-eats when she freaks out."

Zoe giggles.

"It's so cool you guys are learning Lottie," Bea says loudly, trying to make sure Daisy doesn't overhear us calling her a dork for being so excited about an apprentice ballet.

But Daisy doesn't even notice; she bounces off toward the Green Room, her dark hair unraveling from its bun.

Zoe turns toward me and speaks with deliberate casualness. "You know, Otto will probably rehearse a second cast, which means one of us will dance it." She thrusts her shoulders back and gives me a little smile. "I *wonder* which one of us he'll choose. . . ."

I shrug and turn away, although inside I'm practically seething. We all want bigger and better parts. It's ingrained in us — the drive to succeed is as natural to us as breathing.

Behind me I hear Zoe snickering. I guess she thinks she's funny.

Honestly, I don't think Zoe and I would have been friends if she hadn't sought me out when I first came to the Manhattan Ballet Academy. Like me, she was one of the youngest girls in Level C, and she stood next to me in class. I was too shy to talk to her much, but I was happy to have an almost-friend.

Over the course of a few weeks, we started talking more, and eventually Zoe invited me to dinner at her apartment. Since I'd been surviving on the slop they tried to pass off as food in the dorm cafeteria, I was thrilled at the idea of having a home-cooked meal. And I was also — though I would never admit this to Zoe — aching for a mother figure, even if it wasn't my own. I was fourteen and on my own in New York City. It wasn't easy.

As I entered Zoe's Park Avenue foyer, a yappy Pekingese nipped at my ankles.

"Hello, Hannah," Zoe's mother cooed as she leaned against the doorframe. "I'm Dolly. Zoe has told me so much about you." Dolly's hair was a darker shade of gold than Zoe's, but mother and daughter had the same striking green eyes. Dolly wore a crimson velvet robe wrapped snugly around her tiny frame. When she reached out to hug me, holding me tight to her bony sternum, her perfume overwhelmed me. Then she stepped back and craned her neck.

"Zoe!" she shouted down the hallway. There was no answer. "She is *so* lazy." Dolly sighed. Then she smiled broadly and picked up a martini glass that had left a circle of condensation on the hall table. "Her room's the fourth on the left." She rested her elbow in the indentation of her hip and swirled the liquid in her glass while looking me up and down. "If you'll excuse me."

As I later found out, Dolly was the daughter of a Texas oil tycoon and, according to Daisy, a big donor to the Manhattan Ballet. Her partying and bed hopping made her a regular on Page Six. Dolly was hospitalized for stress twice, but everyone said it was anorexia. Once, and only once, I saw her eat. It was a single stalk of celery that she retrieved from her Bloody Mary.

I remember walking down the hall to Zoe's bedroom and knocking hesitantly.

"Come in," Zoe called. She sat on the floor blowing on her freshly painted toenails. A music video blared from a wall-mounted flat-screen TV. "You want to order some sushi?" she asked. She tossed a menu at me. "It's the best in the city. I like the spider rolls."

I looked around at her huge bedroom, with its expensive furniture and its modern art (I saw one of Andy Warhol's panda screen prints by the window). Zoe fit in perfectly there: Even her upturned nose and pronounced cheekbones seemed like evidence of a genetic predisposition for wealth.

I picked just a few things off the menu, but still I could see that I was ordering more than sixty dollars' worth of food. "I've got Mom's credit card," Zoe said. "Order more."

"Should we order something for her?" I asked.

Zoe shook her head. "She's going out. Robert De Niro is having a party at Ago."

"Oh . . . okay." What else could I say?

As we waited for our sushi delivery, we heard Dolly clattering around, getting ready to go out, but she never knocked on Zoe's door to say good-bye. It was as if they were roommates rather than mother and daughter — roommates who didn't even like each other much.

We ate in Zoe's massive living room, with the lights of Park Avenue twinkling far below us. We left a pile of sushi trays and soy sauce wrappers on the coffee table. "Don't worry about it," Zoe said. "Gladys'll get it in the morning."

"Who's Gladys?"

"The housekeeper," Zoe said matter-of-factly. "Can I have some of your salmon skin roll?"

Obviously, I didn't get my family dinner that night. And I never did, even though I went to Zoe's house dozens of times and sometimes even spent the night.

I haven't been invited over in a long time, but then again, we're not kids anymore. I don't need a mother figure. I just need to dance that part in Otto's ballet.

4

In celebration of being selected to understudy Lottie, I decide to go downtown after Saturday night's performance. I forgo my usual post-dance body-maintenance routine and just rub arnica gel on my bunions. Then I slip into a pair of boots and a wrap dress that my mother used to wear in the seventies. The cab takes me south on Seventh Avenue to Gene's, which is my cousin Eugene's West Village restaurant. I skipped lunch and I'm starving.

It's raining, and the streetlights seem to bleed yellow-and-white streaks on the windows of the cab. I see a few people hurrying along the sidewalks, their black umbrellas hovering above them. Puddles gather at the curbs, gathering little boats of newspapers and coffee cups.

When I first came to New York City, it was impossible for me to think that someday it might feel like home. Though I put on a brave face, during my first few weeks of school at the Manhattan Ballet Academy, I was scared to leave the Upper West Side or to go outside after dark. Still, New York was thrilling. Sure, people on the sidewalk were sort of pushy, and they rarely made eye contact, but that was because they were ambitious and driven. The city's energy was palpable. Just to be outside, to walk down Broadway, was like drinking a shot of espresso.

It's probably how all the new kids at MBA feel right now. They're fresh enough to look around themselves in amazement and awe. And I envy that.

But I envy Zoe, too, who was born to all this. She grew up practically around the corner from the Met, and she started at the MBA when she was eight years old. She's as ambitious and as jaded as a nineteen-year-old possibly can be, and the attitude seems to be working for her.

I wonder if it's the city or the ballet world that toughens you up. It seems that either could do the job.

"Seventeen forty," says the cab driver, jolting me back to reality.

The receipt prints out noisily as I fumble for a twenty. "Keep it," I tell him, and dash into the warm dimness of my cousin's restaurant.

Trudy, the bartender, waves in my direction and starts pouring me a glass of red wine, even though she knows I'm two years away from being legal. I look around nervously, just in case there's someone who might ask for my ID, but there's only a group of silver-haired old men drinking wine and arguing about baseball in the corner and a young, laughing couple in the back.

I sit down at the bar and take out my copy of *Frankenstein*, which I've been trying to finish since July. But I'm still amped from the performance, and I can't concentrate. I'm watching the couple without thinking, and then suddenly the guy turns and catches my eye. He has dark hair and pale skin with the shadow of scruff along his jawline, and he's incredibly cute. He holds my gaze for a moment as his blond date texts on her phone, and then he smiles at me — a big, warm, surprising smile.

I duck my head and feel the blush climb up my neck to my cheeks. I'm too embarrassed to smile back.

"Here you go," Trudy says, passing me a large goblet of wine. "Drink up."

"Thanks." I take out a few dollars to tip her, but I don't pay for the wine. Eugene gets mad if I do; this, plus his laxness around the matter of drinking age, is one of the reasons he's my favorite cousin.

I want to look at the young couple again. Because I wonder, are they actually a couple? They seem like they should be — they're in a romantic Italian restaurant together, after all — but the look the guy gave me would seem to suggest otherwise.

"Haven't seen you for a while," Trudy says, interrupting my thoughts.

"Yeah, it's hard to get away," I say. "Otto doesn't approve of 'field trips.'"

"Field trips?"

I laugh drily. "It's what he calls any sort of activity that takes place more than ten blocks from the theater."

"Yikes," Trudy says. Then she eyes my clavicle as she sets a plate of breadsticks in front of me. "Eat, eat. You're too skinny, my dear."

"Really?" I ask. Actually, I've been feeling sort of bloated lately, but I haven't weighed myself because I don't own a scale — and because I don't really want to know.

"Well, compared to me you're skinny," Trudy says. She pinches her stomach. "I've got enough gut for both of us."

"Oh, don't be ridiculous," I say, smiling. "Can I have a bowl of the pesto rigatoni?"

I tell myself I won't eat the whole thing — and anyway, I missed lunch, so I need some calories.

"Sure thing," she says, giving me a little salute. "Coming right up."

As I sip my wine, I look to the back corner of the restaurant, but the guy and girl are gone. I can't help feeling a little disappointed; even if he was on a date with someone else, he was good scenery. I open up *Frankenstein* and stare blankly at the pages. Then I open my journal, which I always have with me, and do the same.

I'm still sort of spacing out when I hear the strumming of a guitar. I turn around and look to the small stage that Eugene installed against the far wall of the dining room. Sitting on a stool, holding a battered old Sigma acoustic, is the cute dark-haired guy.

From this angle I can see him better, and I can tell that he's my age, or maybe a year or two older. He's wearing faded Levi's, a V-necked sweater, and a pair of Adidas sneakers that has seen better days. His fingers move quickly over the frets of the guitar, and then, a moment later, he opens his mouth and sings. He has a deep but breathy voice that reminds me of Nick Drake's.

"*Saw you at the Guggenheim / shivering outside in line / wondered if you'd have the time / to turn around and see me,*" he sings.

The blond taps her foot and mouths the words along with him. She's moved to a closer table so she can take pictures.

"*Across the park the leaves are red / the hawks have put themselves to bed / The snow will come the old man said / So please be with me . . .*"

The melody — or maybe it's his voice — gives me shivers. I stop trying to pretend I'm not staring.

"*Here I am so far from home / and I don't want to be alone / Do you want to be my own / my lovely girl . . .*"

As he finishes, he looks up, and our eyes meet again. I feel a flutter in my stomach that is not unlike the one I feel the moment before I step onstage. It's like a surge of nerves and anticipation. *Hello*, I think, *who are you?*

He sings half a dozen more songs as I sip my wine. I don't pretend to read my book or do anything but watch. Sometime during his set the blond vanishes.

He comes to the last verse in a song about California and then sets down his guitar. There's a smattering of applause from the table of old men. A moment later he's coming toward me, and then he's sitting down next to me at the bar. "Can I have a Brooklyn Lager, please?" he says to Trudy.

I can feel my heart thudding in my chest and a blush creeping into my cheeks. *He's sitting next to me*, I think dumbly. *He's sitting right next to me. What do I say to him?*

30

Trudy raises one tweezed eyebrow and says, "Done already? Because I didn't hear that song I like, about the river."

"I'll dedicate it to you next time," the singer says, flashing her a grin.

"It's a deal." Trudy reaches for the tap and nods in my direction. "Her name is Hannah. She's the owner's cousin, so if you plan on hitting on her, you had better have the best of intentions, or else he'll hunt you down and break your legs."

I laugh, in part because I'm mortified and in part because Eugene is about 110 pounds soaking wet.

"Duly noted." He grins.

Trudy gives the cute guitar player his beer and then slides my pasta down the bar so I have to catch it before it careers off the end. She always does that.

"That looks good, too," he says to me with a smile. "Is that pesto?"

I nod as I grind some pepper over it.

"That's a lot of pepper," he observes, watching the dark specks cover the top of my pasta.

I look down. In my nervousness I've ground way too much pepper onto my dinner. "Uh, I really like pepper," I say, and surreptitiously try to push some of it off onto the bar.

He smiles again, revealing a row of straight white teeth and two matching dimples. His eyes are blue, with lashes as long as a girl's. I have no idea what I should say to him. He seemed perfect from far away, but now that he's next to me he's just making me nervous.

"I'm Jacob. I understand you're Hannah."

31

He extends his hand and I shake it, and in doing so I nearly spill my wine on my lap. "Oh," I gasp as I catch the glass just in time.

"Excellent reflexes," he says.

I can only nod. I don't know how to flirt with guys — I've been insulated inside a dance studio for the last twelve years of my life. When was the last time I had a conversation with someone who wasn't a dancer? Does the cashier at my corner deli count?

I stab the rigatoni with my fork while watching Jacob out of the corner of my eye. He's lanky, tallish. His hair is tousled, and there's a tiny cut on his chin where he must have nicked himself shaving. I have to repress a sudden urge to reach out and gently touch it.

He eyes my book, my journal, my pen. "So, do you go to NYU?" Jacob asks, looking at me over the rim of his pint glass.

I shake my head for a long time, long enough to get my vocal cords working. And then I say it. "No." I think, *Come on, Hannah, is that really the best you can do?*

"Okay," he says. "The New School? That's where Sasha goes. She was here earlier? She's my brother's girlfriend, and she's more loyal to me, apparently, than my own brother, who called five minutes before my set to say he couldn't make it. But anyway, do you go there?"

I say no and shake my head again. I've become virtually unable to speak. Thank God no one else is here to see this humiliating display; Zoe would never let me hear the end of it. But at least the blond isn't his girlfriend.

"All right, then," Jacob says gamely. "We can make this twenty questions. So, you're not a student."

I shake my head.

"Are you a spy?"

And this is so absurd that I'm shaken out of my vocal paralysis. I laugh and say, "Nope, not a spy."

Trudy shoots me a look—*is this guy bothering you?*—but I smile. Jacob is definitely not bothering me. I hardly even care what he's saying; sitting next to him is making me feel giddy.

"Okay, then," he says. "Let's get to the bottom of this." Jacob gets a serious look on his face and leans closer as he goes through a number of other occupations. He guesses au pair, actress, and yoga instructor, all of which I suppose are plausible, and then, when he strikes out with those, he goes on to professional skydiver, mountain climber, and hit man. The whole time he's talking, I can't stop noticing just how cute he is.

"No, no, no," I say, laughing and shaking my head. A piece of hair comes loose from my ponytail, and he reaches up and gently tucks it behind my ear. I flush and feel a tingling where he touched me. My heart begins to race.

"I give up, then," he says.

"I'm a dancer with the Manhattan Ballet," I say finally, and watch as his eyebrows lift until they're hidden under his bangs.

"No way," he says. "That's so cool. I haven't been to a performance in a while, but I've totally seen your company. I got those cheap standing-room-only tickets."

I look at him in surprise. I can't imagine there are many

33

nineteen- or twenty-year-old guys out there who've ever seen a ballet, let alone more than one. "Really?"

He nods and his fingers tap an excited beat on the bar. "Yeah, I was taking this class about modernist music, and there was all this stuff about Stravinsky. A lot of the ballets you guys dance are to his music, right?"

"Yeah," I say, impressed. "You know your stuff."

"Not really. But I know enough to know that what you do is totally amazing."

"Thanks," I say, giving a slightly embarrassed little shrug.

People always ask the same things when I tell them I'm a ballet dancer. They want to know whether the ballet masters weigh us and if we're on some special diet. They also wonder what percentage of the male dancers are gay. These are *totally* annoying questions, and it occurs to me that Jacob might be the first person to not ask a single one of them.

"You must love it," he says. His eyes hold mine until I have to look away.

I don't even have to think about the answer. "Yes," I say, gazing down at my pasta. "I do."

Trudy comes over to top off my glass. *Thank you*, I mouth. Then I turn back to Jacob. "But it's a lot of hard work. I mean, a *lot*." I think of the rehearsal schedule for the next day, and my chest tightens with anxiety.

He grins. "Well, as they say, 'One must imagine Sisyphus happy.'"

I raise my eyebrows at him. "Pardon?"

He scoots closer to the bar and leans his elbows on it. "You know the myth of Sisyphus, right?" he says eagerly. "He was condemned to roll a boulder uphill for all eternity. Every day he'd push it to the top, and every day it would roll back down. And basically this French philosopher, Camus, said you had to assume that Sisyphus was cool with it. That the struggle alone gave his life meaning."

I laugh and take a sip of wine. "There are parts of my day that are struggles, all right."

"But you get to be onstage at Avery Center. That must be incredible."

"It is," I acknowledge. "But you're no stranger to the stage yourself."

Jacob shrugs. "Avery Center this ain't," he says, grinning.

I sit up in mock indignation. "I hope you're not maligning my cousin's bar."

"Never!" he exclaims. "I love Gene's. It actually has a decent sound system, believe it or not. Plus, Trudy here is generous with the free beer." He winks at her.

"Are you a full-time musician?" I realize, of course, that it would be a miracle if he was: New York is full of actors/waiters and dog-walking painters.

"Nah, I wish. I would be if it paid the rent, but I haven't been able to convince the parents that it would." He smiles, and his blue eyes flash. "I'm at NYU, majoring in philosophy. Or else art history. Or maybe ecology." He laughs. "I'm having a hard time deciding. Basically, I declared four majors last year, and now I'm waiting for someone to notice and make me pick."

"Wow, that's a lot of different interests."

He nods his head and takes a gulp of beer. "Yeah, I go on these kicks. It's kind of geeky, maybe, but whatever. Right now I'm reading about the Meadowlands and saving up money so I can buy a kayak and explore the wetlands. They're amazing, but they've been used as a garbage dump for decades. When the old Penn Station was torn down, all the debris got tossed right there into the water."

"That's crazy," I say, thinking, *Shouldn't this guy be talking about beer pong and toga parties?* I'm glad he isn't, but still—I thought that was pretty much all your average college guy cared about.

"And I'm taking Italian lessons," he goes on. "From this old guy in Little Italy. About six months ago I got this idea that I wanted to watch all of Fellini's movies and not have to read the subtitles." He pauses and looks thoughtful. "Do I sound like a dilettante? A jack-of-all-trades, master of none? Probably I do. Oh well. So I have kind of a hard time figuring out just one thing to focus on. But I'm young—I don't need to know what I want to be when I grow up. Not everyone has his life figured out by age ten, right?"

I laugh. "I *was* ten. How'd you guess? But really, you've got a few years yet. When did you start playing the guitar? You're good."

"Thanks. I first tried when I was about three." Jacob smiles at the memory. "The guitar was bigger than I was and, needless to say, I wasn't that successful at strumming chords. But I started taking lessons in middle school, and I've been playing ever since."

"Did someone inspire you? I mean, I saw the Manhattan Ballet perform when I was, like, five years old, and I knew right then and there that I wanted to be up on that stage someday, too." I'm surprised at how comfortable I feel now. *I'm actually having a conversation with a nondancer*, I think.

"Well, I can play every Bob Dylan song ever written," Jacob offers. "But these days I'm into Will Oldham." He waves to Trudy, who sidles over with another beer for him. "I think he's kind of a genius."

"Cool," I say, making a mental note to find out who Will Oldham is. "So you're a student-slash-musician-slash-self-taught kayaker?"

"And after-school teacher," he adds. "It's my work-study job, and it's totally cool. My dad teaches high school history. He says teaching's a more socially responsible way to earn a living than being alone up on a stage, singing songs about lost love or what you ate for breakfast."

I laugh. "You have a song about what you ate for breakfast? What's it called?"

He grins at me, a lovely, lopsided grin. He is possibly the cutest guy I have ever seen. "'Waffles,'" he says. He picks up a spare fork and helps himself to a bite of my pasta. "Wow, that's delicious." His arm brushes lightly against mine.

My heart seems to flutter quickly in my chest, and my stomach feels funny, which is either a sign that my pesto isn't agreeing with me or that I'm developing a serious crush.

Jacob stabs another rigatoni. "But back to you. Ballet just sounds so intense. How do you do it? I mean, how did you get good enough?" He pauses. "Is that a weird question? Yeah, that's a weird question."

I shrug. "Really hard work. I mean, if you devote yourself to one pursuit, you can probably master pretty much anything, right?"

Jacob laughs. "Sure, if you can *choose* one thing."

"I was reading about this painter who lost his right arm in a car crash, and so he taught himself to paint all over again with his left hand. And now he's showing at this gallery in Chelsea, and his paintings go for, like, twenty grand at least."

"And don't forget those elephants who paint," Jacob adds. "They've gotten really good, too."

I look at him doubtfully. "Elephants?"

"Yep. Thailand's full of elephant abstractionists. Trainers hand them brushes, and the elephants go to town."

I laugh. "I can see the reviews now: 'Dumbo's paintings are lyrical and expressive, characterized by bold colors and interesting shapes,'" I say, affecting a snooty accent.

Jaocb laughs, too. "I like you," he says suddenly. "It's not just that you're pretty or you might know something about art, or because I think you have good taste in pasta. I just think you seem interesting — different from other girls I know."

I think Jacob seems very interesting, too. And he's definitely different from the boys I know at the company, but I don't have the courage to tell him that. So I just smile and push my plate of pesto pasta closer to him.

By the end of the evening, I've had three glasses of wine, Jacob's had two pints of Brooklyn Lager, and we've exchanged phone numbers and e-mail addresses.

Outside, he asks, "So I'll talk to you soon?" as he opens the door of a cab for me.

I nod, silent again.

Jacob leans close to me. I think he's aiming for my lips, and I have a rush of anxiety because I'm so inexperienced. I'm afraid I won't know what to do when his mouth meets mine. But then he kisses me ever so lightly on the cheek. I feel the brush of his collar against my neck, and I smell soap and pesto and beer. I'm both relieved and disappointed.

I duck into the waiting cab. My skin tingles where he touched it, and I keep my hand over my cheek as if to protect that faint fluttery feeling.

5

It's ten thirty in the morning and time for company class. Company class is our warm-up before rehearsals, as well as an opportunity to perfect our technique. It's optional in theory, but only principals ever consider skipping it.

The studio floor is littered with slouching and stretching bodies. Pointe shoes, Thera-Bands, and corn pads spill out of dance bags, and water bottles and coffee cups are tucked against the mirrored walls. Some of the dancers are chatting with friends while others prepare for class by listening to their iPods or just stretching in silence. Most still look exhausted from last night's performance.

By the door, Lottie Harlow twists her auburn hair up with a mouthful of long pins. Her oatmeal-colored sweater falls from her bony shoulders. The boys, who don't have to worry about their hairstyles, roll their calves out on tennis balls and do push-ups.

We start out by finding our places at the barre. Six barres are arranged in the center of the studio, plus the ones lining the walls. I squeeze in between Bea and Jonathan, who lives in my building and looks kind of like Bradley Cooper. He blows me a kiss and nudges his bag over with a pointed toe. If he liked girls, which he doesn't, I would have developed a crush on him long ago.

When Mr. Edmunds, the ballet master, enters, he motions to the pianist, who plays a slow, simple melody. We begin with a series of deep knee bends that engages our whole bodies. (You can always hear the pop and crack of people's hips and knees during pliés.)

Then, as Mr. Edmunds demonstrates the grand battement combination, I tap Bea's hand and she moves closer. "I met someone," I whisper. "His name is Jacob Cohen. He's a musician and he's really cute."

Bea's blue eyes open comically wide and she gets a big grin on her face, but then she has to get into position for the combination. After a moment she leans back over the barre. "No way! When was this?"

"Last night." I smile, feeling mischievous.

"*You* actually went *out*?" she whispers. "But you're such a goody-goody!"

"You should talk," I reply with a giggle. "But I know—it's totally unlike me." *And I feel guilty because I have a packed schedule today*, I think. *I just hope I don't pay for it in tonight's show.*

Then Mr. Edmunds passes by us, and we both stare straight ahead. He walks around the room, frowning or nodding, depending on the technique of the dancer he's watching.

His salt-and-pepper hair is feathered: It's a little too pouffed on top, and a little too long at the back. He was a principal dancer with the Manhattan Ballet twenty years ago, and he loves to poke us in the stomach or the bum to encourage us to tighten up. When he does this, we usually make puking faces behind his back.

"Oh, I wish you would have taken *me*," Bea moans. "I can't believe you met a real, live nondancer."

"Me either!"

In the second half of class, we move to the center, where we work without a barre. The floor is sprung and layered with linoleum, almost identical to the stage. Mr. Edmunds demonstrates another combination — something slow, an adagio — and we follow his lead. I try to talk to Bea again during petit allégro, but I swear Mr. Edmunds is keeping an especially close eye on us today.

So — silently — we balancé, we pirouette, we leap. My heart beats rapidly in my chest, and my leg muscles burn. The tempo of the music increases, and we begin to exaggerate our movements until we are jumping across the floor in grand allégro. Pretty soon my face flushes, and my breath comes in gasps. At this point I'm breathing so hard I wouldn't be able to talk to Bea even if I had the chance.

ço   ço   ço

After class I take a quick sip of water and then head back to the studio, where Otto is working with sinewy Lottie, choreographing his new ballet. Under the fluorescent lights of the studio, Otto's dark, deep-set eyes glitter. His dark hair has just a dusting of gray around the temples, and his olive complexion stands out against Lottie's porcelain skin as he clutches her tiny wrist to demonstrate a promenade. Even though he walks with a limp from a botched hip replacement, he's still considered the best partner around and regularly demonstrates choreography. If you saw Otto on the street, you'd think he was handsome but completely unapproachable.

Which he basically is.

"And développé," Otto tells Lottie.

As understudies, Zoe and I mirror her steps along the barre in the background. Otto has been changing the choreography as he goes, so one day he asks for piqué turns and the next day he wants grands jetés. It's hard to remember which version is which.

When we first started rehearsing, Zoe always tried to stand in front of me, but once she figured out Otto wasn't actually going to rehearse a second cast, she turned the level of competition down a notch.

"Of course we're understudying the one dancer in the company who, like, *never* goes out," she whispers as she marks the piqué turns.

"I know," I say. "She's, like, strong as an ox."

"And yet skinny as a carrot stick."

I stifle a giggle as Zoe leans in close to me. "I wish she'd eat a bad mussel or something," she says.

"But she hardly eats," I remind her. "Or so they say."

"Well then, we should spike her water with laxatives," Zoe says, leaning against the barre and grinning naughtily.

I sigh. "I'm so bored. Haven't we done this section fifty times already? Maybe I should pretend I have menstrual cramps just to get out of here."

"Oh my God, girl problems! Otto would be so uncomfortable that he'd just shoo you out of the room," she whispers with a giggle.

"It's worth a try," I say, but Zoe shakes her shiny blond head at me.

"This is just part of the job," she says.

"I know, I know. The crappy part," I mutter.

So I keep marking the steps and try not to think about the futility of my hopes to dance Lottie's part. As Otto moves on to the adagio section, I allow my mind to wander a little. I imagine what it would be like to kiss Jacob, the cutest singer-songwriter in all of Manhattan. Considering I pretty much melted from a single peck on the cheek, I'm worried that a real kiss would turn me into a quivering puddle of goo. But I'm willing to take the chance.

Of course, who knows when I'll get that chance again? Between rehearsals and the nightly performances, my schedule is beyond packed. After this rehearsal, I have one for *Vous* and another for *Prelude*, then a triple-header tonight. I'll be lucky to make it through without collapsing from exhaustion.

I sigh and look up at the vaulted ceiling. The fluorescent lights somehow create a disorienting effect, and after hours of rehearsal I always begin to feel a little dizzy. But as Bea once pointed out, the dizziness could also come from oxygen deprivation due to the lack of windows.

Suddenly Otto is standing in front of me, his dark eyes cool and appraising. "You'd better be picking this up, Ward." He looks down his nose at me, and I feel very small.

I nod my head vigorously and glance over to see Zoe snickering in the corner. All thoughts of Jacob are banished for the next two hours.

଼ ଼ ଼

Back in the dressing room, Daisy comes from the showers, drops her towel, and sticks out her taut brown stomach. Her wet black hair hangs almost to her waist. "I am a *hippo*."

"Oh Jesus," I mutter to Bea. I'm trying to find spare change for a soda. "She'd better not get a stress fracture from all that ridiculous dieting."

"No kidding," Bea whispers.

The apprentices and first-year corps girls are always getting injured because they don't know how to pace themselves in rehearsals and they diet like crazy. When they go out, we older girls end up dancing their crappy apprentice parts.

"You know she hasn't had a slice of bread for six weeks?" Bea whispers as she twists her hair into some new configuration. Unlike me — I pretty much always sport a basic bun or chignon — Bea likes to experiment with intricate twists and braids.

"Doesn't surprise me," I say.

"I don't get it," Daisy half whines as she flops down onto her chair. "I haven't eaten anything but cabbage and grapefruit for, like, nine days."

"We're doomed," I whisper to Bea, who rolls her eyes.

"I heard that gives you really bad..." Zoe snickers. She inspects her long, thin legs.

I try to stifle my laughter; Bea snorts.

"Oh my God, did you rip one last night during third movement?" I ask.

Daisy's cheeks turn bright red. "Shut up. Shut up! I can't help it!" She tries not to laugh, but she can't stop. "It's not like the audience heard anything. And anyway, not everyone is born looking like Zoe."

The mood in the room subtly changes. Bea fidgets in her seat. I find two quarters inside my makeup bag and keep pawing around for more. Zoe stands up and shifts her weight uncomfortably.

"Smoke time," she says. She pulls a Stella McCartney jacket over her leotard, then gets up and leaves, letting the door slam behind her.

"That *ain't* natural," I whisper to Bea. "Born like that? Please. And that whole vegan trip of hers? It's not because she cares about animal welfare! It's all about the calories. She'd dress head to toe in leather if *Vogue* told her to."

Bea nods. "And the smoking?" she says. "So gross." She wrinkles her freckled nose.

"I know! Talk about crazy dieting—I haven't seen her eat anything but carrot sticks in about six months. Would it kill her to eat a protein bar or something once in a while?"

Bea widens her big blue eyes. "God forbid! She doesn't want to fill out that concave ass of hers."

I laugh as I dig in my bag for a banana. But it's not really funny. Daisy thinks she's a hippo, and Zoe always complains about her big butt—and yet both of them are stick-thin. Their bodies hardly have a single curve.

I used to be like that, too: long, lean, and totally flat. I didn't get my period until six months ago, when I was eighteen, because the intense daily exercise delayed it. But now my body is just beginning to show puberty's effects. Surreptitiously, I eye myself in profile. I don't have hips, but my breasts are little mounds sticking out from the rest of my body. They ruin my line. I squish them down with my hands. *Much better*, I think.

"Speaking of protein bars, someone's been stealing my food," Bea says, her perfectly arched eyebrows knitting together. "I had a whole box in here, and now there are only two left." She stands and faces us. Her hip bones jut out of the front of her leotard. All of ours do.

"Not me," Daisy says, toweling off her dark hair. "They're, like, totally full of carbs." She knows the nutrition information of pretty much any food you can name.

"Whatever," Bea says, opening a Diet Coke.

"You really should drink water, you know," Daisy tells her. In addition to being a compulsive dieter, Daisy is water's number one spokesperson. She drinks about two gallons a day. "Diet Coke is terrible for you."

"Well, so is stress-eating your way through a bag of Oreos and two packages of Doritos the way you do every time Otto looks at you funny. That really messes up your metabolism, you know."

Daisy widens her eyes and then flounces over to the corner to sulk.

"She's starting to get on my nerves," Bea whispers.

"I am *not* dancing any of her stupid parts when she starts breaking bones," I say.

"What?" Daisy asks from the corner.

"Oh, nothing," I say, winking at Bea.

Then Bea quickly changes the subject. "Where is Leni? Doesn't she have rehearsal soon?"

Leni's the other dancer in our dressing room, but she's seldom here because she's more senior and doesn't perform as much. She used to dance in the corps of the Stuttgart Ballet, and she joined the Manhattan Ballet about ten years ago. She's thirty-four, which is pretty old for a ballet dancer. Lily used to share our dressing room, too, but she moved out a few months ago because she got pregnant. It hadn't been planned, and Zoe had cruelly stuck condoms to her mirror as soon as she was out the door.

"Leni's around," I say. "I think I saw her flirting with Caleb in the hall." I say this to tease Daisy, who has just started dating Caleb, another corps dancer. He's eighteen, and he has brown, slightly curly hair and a thing for V-necked cashmere sweaters.

Her little face crumples — until she realizes I'm joking.

"Very funny," she says, snapping her towel at me. "He took me to O'Neals' the other night, you know." She searches around in her theater case for another leotard. She's still half naked; her tiny breasts are encased in a training bra.

"I hope you didn't have the French onion soup," I say. "Jonathan told me that he found a rubber band in his bowl last week." The food at O'Neals' is mediocre, but the location is perfect. You could throw a dinner roll out the window and it'd land right at the theater's stage door.

Daisy wrinkles her nose. "Ew," she says. "I had a salad, no dressing."

"I hope you had a drink to loosen you up," Bea says, carefully placing a corn pad on her foot.

Daisy pulls out a leotard, rejects it, and then searches for another one. Goose bumps are rising on her skinny arms. "I hate the taste of alcohol."

"Well, good," I say, "because you're only old enough for Kool-Aid."

"Like I'd drink *that*," she says. "Way too much sugar." She finally finds a clean leotard and slips it on over her tights. "Caleb ordered me a club soda."

"Did you have a heart-to-heart about how to fix his sickled feet?" Zoe asks as she enters and flings her purse into her theater case. Having sickled feet, or poor foot turnout, breaks a dancer's line even worse than breasts do.

"Fast cigarette," I note.

"I changed my mind," she says breezily.

"No, Zoe," Daisy says, "we didn't—because he doesn't have sickled feet."

"Maybe not. But I think he might dig guys," Zoe mutters as she scoots past me.

Bea rises to Daisy's defense. "Did *your* boyfriend take you on

49

a date to the latest Manhattan Ballet board meeting?" she asks Zoe, her blue eyes flashing.

For the last month or so, Zoe has been dating Adam Kemp, whose dad is president of the ballet board. He's kind of a jerk, but Zoe likes the proximity to power that he offers.

"Yeah, does he send you romantic texts with the meeting minutes?" I add.

Zoe runs a brush through her glossy blond hair, which reaches almost to her waist. "For your information," she says coolly, "Adam is very romantic. So is his brother."

"His brother? Hello?" I say. "Two at a time?"

"Oh, you are the worst!" Bea exclaims. "Someone should call your mother."

"Considering my mother is having an affair with her grocery delivery guy," Zoe says nonchalantly, "I hardly think she's in a position to judge me."

All of our mouths drop open, and then we're shrieking for details.

When we've exhausted ourselves laughing over Dolly's latest fling, we head out to rehearsal. Before I shut off the lights, I look back at the dressing room. We each have our own little counter space and chair in front of a mirror, where we sit and fix our hair or take off and put on makeup. We stick photos on the edges of our mirrors and tape posters to the cinder-block walls, and around the holidays we string Christmas lights along the wire-caged bulbs.

There are towels draped over chairs, and sweatshirts spilling out of the closet organizers that are hung on a bar at the back. The tables in front of the mirrors are littered with hair spray, lotion, deodorant, eyelash glue, and pancake makeup. It's amazing to me that five people can make such a big mess.

Then I flip the switch — darkness.

In the hallway, Daisy turns to me and says, "Speaking of boys, what about this Jacob person Bea told me about?"

I take a gulp of water. "I don't know when I'll see him again," I say. Then I link arms with Bea. "But who needs boys when I have my girls?"

And everyone — even Zoe — smiles at this.

6

One chilly October evening, a rare night off, I decide to stick around after the matinee to watch Lottie perform the part I've been understudying. (Jacob invited me to a show he's playing in Bushwick, but that was just too far away for me to comprehend.) I want to see what Lottie looks like onstage, in all her costumed finery.

As I stand in the darkness of the wing, the black velvet curtain brushes softly against my skin. Onstage, corps dancers in eggplant unitards execute quick pointe work with complicated arm patterns while Lottie, in a pink chiffon knee-length dress, and her partner, tall, curly-haired Sam, are in front, moving as though the air were as thick as honey. He supports her in a sideways lift against his hip and then brings her down to face him, holding her carefully in his muscular arms. Lottie leans into him, and their lips almost touch. Then comes the moment when he lifts her in a press over his head, and she seems to float above him. But when she comes down, her face frozen in a smile, I can see that she lands wrong.

All of us watching backstage gasp as she stumbles.

"Oh my God," I hear someone whisper.

Lottie is no longer smiling, and pain flashes in her eyes. Sam reaches out and catches her arm, trying to support her. I can see her grit her teeth, and I know just what she's thinking: She wants to go on, but she can't. Even though her steps aren't even close to finished, she chassés offstage, her right foot gliding behind her as if it were part of the choreography.

Daisy skitters over to me. "What happened?" she hisses, her dark brows furrowed.

Lottie limps into the wings and bursts into tears.

"She came down wrong," I whisper. My heart is beating double time.

Sam improvises the next section alone. At center stage he adds a set of turns that seems out of place.

Annabelle Hayes, MB's ballet mistress, materializes out of the dark. "Hannah," she asks calmly, "how well do you know the ballet?" Her cool gray eyes meet mine.

A wave of nausea overwhelms me. My heart starts thumping, and my breaths come fast and shallow. "I—I know it."

I hear the words come out, and I hope they're true. Yes, I spent those days marking Lottie's steps, but I never actually *rehearsed* them. I never practiced the partnering, and I have only a basic idea of the counts.

But it doesn't matter what my answer is. Annabelle grips my arm and pulls me to where Lottie is weeping.

"Okay, you're going on," she says to me. "I'll stand in the wing and count the last section for you."

I look worriedly at Annabelle. She pats me on the shoulder and gives me a thin-lipped smile. "It's going to be fun."

I know that this is the most encouragement I will ever get.

Lottie moans as her costume is ripped off, and I'm stripped naked in the wing. My wool coat, hoodie sweatshirt, gold necklace, and jeans: They're all just dumped in a pile. Goose bumps rise on my arms and legs as the other dancers and the stagehands look on. A pair of frantic hands stuffs me into Lottie's costume — I'm taller and a little wider than she is, and the boning in the bodice digs into my skin — while another pair of hands knots my hair into a high bun. Bea appears with my pointe shoes. I can hear Lottie crying in the background and Christine telling her to be quiet. Then, onstage, Sam puts out his hand. I take a deep breath and leap from the dark wing into the light.

At first I'm startled by the spotlight. It blinds me; I can feel its concentrated heat. It seems as if time has stalled. I am standing in front of thousands of people without the slightest idea of what step comes next. I try to recall the steps from marking them in the back of the studio, but I'm disoriented from the lights. All I can think to do is count aloud to stay with the music and hope Sam talks me through it.

I prepare for the turning sequence, but my weight is too far back on my heels. I wobble a little trying to get back on my leg. I steal a glance at Annabelle, who's standing perfectly still in the second wing, looking glum as usual.

"The press lift is next," Sam says quietly.

I'm so relieved to hear his voice. I realize that I'm holding my breath, and force myself to exhale.

I'm buzzing with adrenaline. I run toward Sam and jump into his arms, and he lifts me high. My body arches over his. I see the rows of lights spinning overhead, and I feel like I'm flying. Suddenly I forget that I'm not wearing stage makeup and that I wasn't even warmed up. I lose myself in the music, even though my heart is pounding so loudly I swear the audience can hear it. The rush is incredible. *This is why I love my job!*

I concentrate on breathing and on keeping every limb extended to its greatest possible length. Almost imperceptibly, Sam smiles at me. I do a supported fouetté in the air and then dip down into the penchée promenade.

When the ballet is over, I walk to the edge of the stage and take my bow as Sam takes my hand and waist. I can see the faint outline of the eagle tattoo that he covers with makeup before each performance. I can't stop grinning. The audience claps loudly, and I can see smiles in the front row.

"Wow, Hannah, I always thought you had it in you," Sam whispers in my ear as we walk to the wings.

Backstage, Bea comes over and hugs me. "You were brilliant," she says.

I'm so winded I can barely thank her. *I can't believe I just did that!* I think as I bend over to catch my breath.

Daisy, too, comes bouncing toward me. "Wow, that was so intense! I'd *die* if I got thrown on. I mean, I'd love it, but I'd just be so nervous! All those people out there and what if I forgot the steps . . ."

She chatters happily, and I stop listening. This is exactly how Mai Morimoto, the stunning Japanese soloist who is one of Otto's favorite dancers, got noticed: She was thrown on as the Swan Queen when she was only seventeen, and she was promoted to soloist six months later.

And to think it could have been Zoe out there instead of me.

"Those manèges are a bitch, huh?" Bea says gently, handing me a tissue.

I'm soaked in sweat. I nod. "Was I really okay?" I ask. "Bea, I hardly knew what I was doing," I whisper. "I mean, tonight was supposed to be a night of lo mein and reality TV."

"Seriously," she says, "you were great."

I look around to see whether Otto is anywhere to be found. I want him to have seen the way I got thrown on and didn't screw up. I linger backstage for a while, waiting for him to appear. When he doesn't, I return to the dressing room, where Zoe is sulking in her chair. She narrows her eyes at me but keeps her mouth shut.

She doesn't ask me how the performance went, and I don't tell her. I just take off my pointe shoes and stick my legs up against the wall to drain them while I catch my breath. I'm beat, but I feel amazing. I would never say it aloud, but I'm pretty sure I must be on the path to promotion.

7

"So, Ballerina Bea, I have one final question: Do they weigh you?" Jacob asks, holding a wine bottle up to Bea's face as if it were a microphone.

It's a Monday night — our night off — and the two of them are sitting on my couch together like BFFs. Thanks to the bottles of wine Jacob brought, they've gotten tipsy enough to do a mock Larry King interview.

"Yes," Bea says, nodding vigorously. "Every morning at seven AM sharp, we report to the weigh-in room, where Otto has us step on the scales. If we've gained two ounces, food is withheld. If we've gained four, we have to run up and down the stairs for ten minutes. If we've gained six, we're forced to vomit, and we're forbidden to eat for the entire day."

"And what if you gain more than six?" Jacob presses. "Do they start chopping off limbs?"

Bea affects a very solemn look. "Honestly, Larry, I don't think you want to know." Then she giggles. She turns to me and mouths, *He's so funny.*

"I know!" I whisper as I open another bottle of Chianti. I invited Bea and Jacob over together because I wanted to see Jacob again, but I was too nervous to do it alone. I've never had a boyfriend—I've never had time for one. Bea hasn't had a boyfriend, either, though this is something we try not to tell everyone. But it's not like we're freaks of nature or anything. We're just a little underdeveloped socially, like nearly every other dancer in the company.

My plan was that we'd have a drink or two in my apartment and then we'd go out to eat. But Bea and Jacob swear that I promised to cook them dinner. The fact that I don't remember saying such a thing means nothing to them at all.

So here I am, in my kitchen, with an apron tied around my 7 For All Mankind jeans (I didn't even know I owned an apron). Believe me when I say I'm thrilled that Jacob and Bea are getting along so well. But I am not thrilled about the dinner business, because *I can't cook.*

I mean, I can make ice. And I am totally capable of making myself a bowl of cereal, a piece of toast, or a smoothie. Beyond that, though, my skills are nonexistent.

But somehow the two of them have shamed me into trying to feed them. "Grilled cheese and tomato soup," Bea said. "How hard is that?"

That's what she came up with after looking through my cupboards. Then Jacob came into the kitchen, and for a moment he stood behind me as I gazed dumbly at my empty refrigerator. I could feel the warmth of his body, even though he wasn't touching me. I didn't turn around — I was just frozen there, waiting to see what would happen. And then he put his hands on my shoulders. "How come you have about eight jars of mustard in your fridge?" he whispered into my hair.

"I don't know," I said softly. I felt almost dizzy.

Then he gave me a quick kiss on the cheek and disappeared into the living room.

So now I'm reaching for the new pan that my mother bought me for my birthday, perhaps in the hope that I would eventually learn how to do something with it. So far I've only used it as a holder for unopened junk mail.

"You okay in there?" Bea yells, though the distance from couch to kitchen is only about ten feet.

"Yes," I say, throwing the mail onto the counter. "Everything's just great."

I try to remember how my mom made grilled cheese. She buttered the bread, right? And then put it in the pan with more butter? How many slices of cheese did she use? Two? Three?

I decide on two. The thought of eating that much cheese and butter makes me feel a little queasy, but I remind myself that I was too busy to eat lunch and that it's nine o'clock, there's nothing else in the house, and all of us are starving.

I put a little pat of butter in the pan and watch as it melts.

"Smells good already," Jacob calls encouragingly.

When the butter is entirely melted, I fit the sandwiches into the pan and then stare at them. They look like they can stand to be alone for a little while, so I walk into the living room, where Jacob is now perusing my iTunes collection on my laptop. I feel a jolt of nervousness. *God, please don't let him see my Clay Aiken playlist*, I think.

"Clay Aiken, huh?" he asks, smiling.

"It was a gift," I blurt out. My cheeks are burning hot.

He nods. "Sure, whatever you say."

"I loved Clay Aiken so much when I was eleven," Bea says. She grabs the wine bottle and holds it as a mike. "*What are you doing tonight / I wish I could be a fly on your wall*," she sings at the top of her lungs.

I stare at her in shock. I've heard her sing in the shower, but never like this. I start clapping. "Awesome!"

"Wow — you dance, you sing," Jacob says. "You're doing a number on my self-esteem, Bea."

"*I'd make you mine tonight / If hearts were unbreakable*," she sings.

"Please don't come to Gene's," Jacob begs. "They'll fire me and hire you."

Bea blushes. Then she turns to me. "Hey, Hannah, do you think you should check on the sandwiches?"

I dash into the kitchen, convinced that they're burning. But they're not. The side that was down is now perfectly golden brown. I flip the sandwiches over, feeling very proud of myself, and turn up the heat under the soup.

Jacob puts Bob Dylan on the stereo, and Bea sings along to "Tangled Up in Blue" as Jacob accompanies her on air guitar. Looking at them, I realize that I hardly ever have people over to my apartment. I've been here two years, and I've never had a housewarming party; I never even invited Daisy, Zoe, and Bea over for takeout.

I remember the excitement of moving out of the MBA dorm and the thrill of finding my own apartment. It's a four-story walk-up the size of a closet, but I love that I have a space that's just mine. I ordered a sofa from Crate and Barrel and a table from IKEA; my parents brought my bookshelves from Weston. I even bought plants.

But I stopped there. I haven't had time to paint the bathroom, which was a violent shade of turquoise, and I haven't puttied the holes in the walls from the previous occupants' thumbtacks and nails. The plants have slowly withered and died from neglect.

I did, however, buy soft rugs and pillows, and I hung curtains from Urban Outfitters. It's cozy, and anyway, it's my own private space, a refuge from the world of the theater.

"How are those sandwiches coming?" Jacob calls.

"Shit!" I say. Once again I've forgotten all about them.

But they haven't burned—they are perfect, golden, and ready to eat. Cheese oozes out the sides, and my mouth waters.

Jacob joins me in the kitchen, and while I arrange the sandwiches on three mismatched plates, he ladles soup into three mismatched bowls. I stand close to him, and our arms sometimes touch.

"Dinner is served," I say, proudly carrying the plates into the living room.

We sit around my table, and I light the two candles in the centerpiece.

"How elegant," Bea says. "Ms. Ward, you set a lovely table."

"Looks great," Jacob agrees. His eyes meet mine across the table, and I blush.

"To Hannah!" Bea says. "Chef, hostess, and brilliant dancer, who got thrown on in a principal role and *killed it*."

"To the chef!" Jacob cries. Then he takes a big bite of his sandwich. As he chews, I watch the expression on his handsome face turn from contentment to confusion to distaste.

"What's wrong?" I ask. "I didn't burn them!"

Jacob is still chewing, and Bea takes a bite. Her freckled nose wrinkles, telling me that something is definitely not right with the sandwiches. Hesitantly, I try one. What should taste like bread and butter and gooey melted cheese tastes like . . . well, it tastes like a mouthful of *soap*.

"Oh my God, it's terrible," I say, spitting out the bite into my napkin.

"It's not that bad," Jacob says charitably.

Bea looks as though she's about to gag, and then she starts to giggle.

"I don't get it! What happened?" I ask, half-panicked, half-laughing.

"I bet it was the pan," Jacob says.

"But it was brand-new!" I wail.

"Maybe there was some kind of coating on it from the factory," Bea says helpfully. "Something that didn't get completely washed off."

I put my head in my hands. I hadn't even remembered to wash the pan — not that I would admit that to them. "I can't believe it," I say. "Am I completely incompetent? I can't even make a damn sandwich!" And I collapse into laughter. It's so pitiful that it's hilarious. "I'm only fit for the ballet," I gasp.

Bea's bright blue eyes flash with glee. "You and me both, babe," she says.

"I thought I was so Martha Stewart — I had on an apron and everything!" I cry, flinging my napkin over my head.

Jacob picks it up and hands it back to me. "Martha Schmartha. You're perfect the way you are, Han," he says. He touches my cheek with the back of his fingers.

And suddenly I wish Bea would leave. Even though she's my best friend in the whole world, I want to be alone with Jacob.

"Let's get takeout," Bea says brightly as she chews on the end of her braid.

"Pizza it is," Jacob declares as he whips out his cell phone.

I lean back in my chair and sigh. "Do you think we'll ever be normal?" I ask Bea.

"Nope," she says, taking the braid out of her mouth and reaching for the wine. "Definitely not. Here, have some more red."

8

By the end of the week, I don't even have enough pointe shoes to get me through the weekend, so before I head to the stage for my performance, I go down to the shoe room. Daisy trails behind me, chattering about her part in *Haiku*. We're both in full stage makeup and hair; I'm in the first ballet, and Daisy is in the second.

". . . and Adriana always makes this face when she does piqué turns," she says, but I'm hardly listening. At this point Daisy is kind of like white noise.

"Greetings, beautiful girls," Marco says, looking up from his newspaper as we approach. "Welcome to my humble domain."

Marco is in charge of the shoe room, a small, windowless chamber lined with cubbies that are stuffed, floor to ceiling, with pointe shoes. Each cubby is labeled with a dancer's name and kept stocked with shoes that have been custom-made for her feet.

We go through about eight pairs of pointe shoes a week, so it's a good thing they're free to company dancers. Pointe shoes, Band-Aids, and Advil: If we had to pay for these three things, we'd barely be able to afford our rent.

I reach into my cubby and pull out twelve satiny pairs. Even though they're handmade and customized for each dancer, we can't just slide them on and wear them. We have to break them in. I first stick the front of each shoe between the hinges of a door and then slam the door to smash the box — that's the toe part of the shoe. Then I step on the sole until I hear the pop of the shank (the stiff midsole) as it separates. Next, I peel back the fabric covering the shank and cut it down about half an inch, and then I put water on the outside edges of the box to soften it.

At this point I can wear the shoes, but I still have to break in the demi-pointe. When I hear the glue crunching, I know I'm getting close. And as the water dries on the satin, the shoes mold to my feet. The goal is to feel as if the shoe is just an extension of your foot.

"I've got a dozen pairs," I tell Marco, "and Daisy has . . ."

"Twenty," she says. To me she whispers, "I feel so greedy!"

Marco writes this information down in his ledger and smiles. "Good luck tonight," he says.

We thank him, and then I hurry upstairs to the Green Room to put on Lottie's costume. Helga, who is the meanest of the Green Room dressers, is practically seething as she grips Lottie's tutu in her hand.

"You should have come in earlier," she says in her thick Long Island accent. "You're on in two minutes."

This isn't even close to true. Helga always exaggerates— she seems to want to instill panic in us, as if we weren't already high-strung enough.

"Jesus, Hannah. I can barely close this!" she mutters as she struggles to fasten the hooks on the bodice. "Ech! How many more performances left? I think we'll have to take this out."

Lottie has a second-degree ankle sprain, so the part is mine for the last few performances of the season. "I asked Maria to take it out last week," I say, looking worriedly at myself in the mirror. My breasts are squashed inside the bodice.

Laura—another dresser and a friend of mine—puts a hand on my shoulder. "You look beautiful, Hannah," she says, smiling at me. "I can sew some elastic into it. I think that would make it more comfortable for you."

I smile back gratefully and then leave the room with Lottie's costume hugging my every curve. I know that a female dancer should have the body of an adolescent male: long, lean limbs; narrow hips; a flat chest. And I know that the way we look is considered a reflection of our work ethic and our devotion to our craft. But there's nothing I can do about it tonight.

I hurry backstage, where burly stagehands are carrying ladders, adjusting lighting equipment, and checking the rigging on the scrims while Christine goes over the spot sequence on her headset. There are dancers here and there—slouching on tall stools, leaning on steel ballet barres, or rolling out their muscles on Styrofoam cylinders or tennis balls on the floor. Like mine, their faces are caked with thick makeup, and their hair is pulled back tight and shellacked with hair spray.

I warm up at the barre until my muscles burn and sweat beads on my forehead. I pause to sew my ribbons and then step into the rosin box. I breathe deeply and concentrate on the choreography to come. I *love* dancing Lottie's part. I love having the chance to show Otto what I'm capable of, and not just as a part of a swirling mass of corps dancers.

I want to feel calm, but my heart flutters lightly and quickly in my chest. I'm not nervous, I tell myself; I'm just excited.

I relish the moment before the curtain rises, when the audience is waiting. In that moment, time seems to slow down, and it's as if the whole world is hushed. I stand alone in the wing and feel the soft velvet of the curtain against my skin. I imagine the conductor raising his baton on the other side, and as his arms come down, the bassoons begin to play, followed by the strings.

I wave at Sam from across the stage, and on my count, I dash out into the light. We meet at center stage, and he grabs me by the waist as we begin the pas de deux. I imagine that beams of light are coming out of my fingertips and my toes. I can't see Bea and Daisy and Zoe, but I know they are watching intently from the wings: Bea looking thrilled, Daisy half-awed and half-jealous, and Zoe sour, as if she just ate a lemon. And I'm pretty sure Otto and Annabelle are somewhere in the audience, too, watching intently. But I put that out of my mind and dance just for myself, as if Sam and I are alone in an empty theater.

There are moments onstage when everything else falls away, and I think of these as the magic times. In the magic times, I feel completely in control of my body; my limbs do everything that is asked of them, and I feel as if gravity has no hold on me. Tonight, dancing Lottie's part feels just like that.

During Sam's solo, I catch my breath in the wing before I reenter. I adjust my costume and try to slow my breath. I'm intensely focused on the performance, and I wait for my entrance like a cat with ears perked.

Then I run onstage to meet Sam for the finale. As I do the final turn sequence and run and leap into the wings, I nearly land on Harry, who's tucked in behind the curtain.

"I got you!" He laughs and grabs me so I don't fall.

"Sorry!" I say breathlessly. "Didn't see you there." My chest is heaving from the exertion, and my legs feel like jelly.

"Naw, it was my fault, hiding out here to watch you," he says, dropping his hands now that I'm stable. "You were magnificent."

By now Harry is usually up in the flies, which is the towering system of ropes, counterweights, pulleys, and scaffolding that allows the stagehands to part curtains, move lights, and rotate set pieces onstage. I wonder if he came down to the stage level to watch me. He normally doesn't even do that for the principals, so this would be a rare compliment. "Really? You think I was okay?" I ask.

He nods. "Absolutely."

My face flushes with pleasure. Unlike anyone else I can think of, Harry has no ulterior motive for praising me. And since he's been watching ballet for twenty-some years, he can be an exceptionally harsh critic. "Now get out there and take your bow," he says, and gives me a playful shove.

Then Matilda pokes her head out from behind one of Harry's massive legs. "You were beautiful," she gasps.

"Thanks!" I say. I reach out to ruffle her hair, and then I run onstage to receive my applause.

I'm back in the dressing room, peeling off my sweat-soaked tights, when Bea comes racing in with a copy of the *New York Times*. She's still in her stage makeup, and her face is dewy with sweat. "Han, look!" she says, jabbing her finger at the paper. "I stole this from the Green Room — the review mentions you!"

I rush over and snatch the newspaper from her. "Gimme," I say, "*please*." I begin reading, my heart in my throat. I skim past the mentions of the principals and soloists, of the ballets I wasn't in, searching for my name. And then I find it, in the fourth paragraph:

Hannah Ward, a late-season fill-in for Lottie Harlow, has marvelous focus in Division at Dusk, *Otto Klein's latest ballet. She dances with a pleasing mixture of innocence and impulsiveness, and her energy is contagious. While her phrasing is calculated, her dancing seems spontaneous and youthful; her legs and feet are brilliantly precise.*

I look up with tears in my eyes. I can't believe those words are about me. Quickly I read the sentences again.

Bea is beaming at me. "Isn't it amazing?" she whispers.

"What?" says Leni. She comes in from the bathroom with a towel wrapped around her head. Leni has long, sandy-blond hair and wide blue eyes; she looks a little like Brigitte Bardot, but her voice is low and mannish, with a thick German accent.

Bea turns to her and chirps, "Hannah got a write-up in the *Times*, and it's totally incredible."

Leni shifts her gaze to me as she dries her hair. "Wow, that's great, Hannah," she says. She bends over, rubs the towel vigorously over her head, and then stands up again. "Maybe now you'll be moving up in the world, little *Balletttänzerin*."

In my mind, I see Otto nodding in approval when I finish my performances; I see my name featured prominently on casting lists; I imagine learning solo roles and practicing them on a silent, empty stage. I imagine Otto telling me that I've been promoted. How I'd scream and cry and call my mom, and then she'd start crying, too.

Zoe and Daisy come in from their ballet. Daisy nearly trips over the old carpet that curls up at the edges of the room. "Ow!" she yells. "Do they want me to break an ankle or something?" Then she turns to me. "I heard about your write-up," she says. "That's so great! Maybe I should add you to my autograph collection."

"Very funny," I say. Daisy's been collecting the autographs of famous dancers since she was six years old. It was her mother's idea; it was supposed to motivate Daisy in her own dancing.

Sarcasm aside, I think Daisy's probably happy for me. And she's certainly being nicer than Zoe, who says nothing at all. She's been in a terrible mood ever since I got thrown on. She can't believe she missed out on an opportunity purely by chance; had she been in the wings, she could have danced Lottie's part instead.

If I were Zoe, I'd be jealous, too.

"And I bet this leads to other parts," Bea says confidently as she scrubs off her makeup.

At this, Zoe turns around so quickly she almost knocks over a chair. She storms out the door.

I look at Zoe's empty seat, and for a moment I indulge in the guilty feeling of triumph. The fact that she feels so threatened is a sign that my star is ascending. We've been neck and neck for years. And yes, it *was* sheer luck that I was in the wings, instead of Zoe — but it wasn't luck that I danced well and got written up in the *Times*.

Beside me Bea finishes removing her stage makeup and throws on her coat; Daisy crams a hat over her bun and waves.

"See you later," they call, and head out into the chilly November night.

Alone in the room, I look at myself in the mirror. My blond hair is in a messy ponytail. My cheeks are still pink from my performance, and my legs are aching. I stand up and inspect my body. So the *Times* reviewer thinks I was "brilliantly precise," which is amazing. But was Helga right? Am I just a little bit *softer* than I used to be?

With my hair pulled tightly away from my face, I look lean and determined. But is it *enough*? Will they ever tell me it's enough?

9

As I walk down the hallway after rehearsal, a little girl in a pale pink leotard runs by. She stops in front of the vending machine and stands on her tippy-toes to reach for the coin slot.

Thanks to *The Nutcracker*, which we've just begun to perform, the backstage hallways are filled with eight- and nine-year-old dancers. They stare at us and mimic our stretching; they bug us for signed pointe shoes and autographs. They think we're the greatest, which can be cute or annoying, depending on your mood.

The ballets we dance in our regular repertory seasons are contemporary and generally plotless, and we rotate through them as the weeks pass. But when Thanksgiving comes (which Bea and I celebrated this year with Korean takeout and a *Mad Men* marathon), it's time to perform *The Nutcracker*. Once *Nutcracker* starts, we dance the same parts and listen to the same

score night after night, for fifty consecutive performance
New Year's Eve. It's kind of like eating SPAM after a p...
filet mignon.

"Do you need a hand?" I ask the girl.

She freezes, and her eyes go wide. I can practically hear
what she's thinking: *Oh my God, it's a real ballerina!* The little girl
nods slowly, too awed, apparently, to smile.

I pick her up by the waist and align her with the coin slot.
She slips her quarters in, and a few seconds later a Diet Sprite
clunks down.

"Is that what you wanted?" I ask. I think she must have
pressed the wrong button. She's a kid—she should have Fanta
or something.

"Oh yes," she says. "Diet Coke's my favorite, but the machine
never has that." She retrieves the soda and grasps it tightly in her
little hands. "Thank you," she says, and offers me a little curtsy.

"No problem," I mutter.

I pick up the phone and dial Jacob's number. "They've got
eight-year-olds on diets," I say when he picks up the phone.
"They're, like, total baby bunheads."

"Huh?" he says. His voice sounds low and sleepy.

"Were you napping?"

He clears his throat. "Who, me? What? No."

I can tell he's lying, but I decide not to tease him about it.
"Well, I just called to tell you that I kind of hate *The Nutcracker*,"
I say.

He laughs. "Wait, I thought everyone loved *The Nutcracker*."

I groan. "Yeah, maybe if you're sitting in the audience,

and you're, like, ten years old." I grip the phone as I stride down the hall to the dressing room. "After about the fifteenth performance, it begins to feel completely soulless. We do it every season, so you'd think people would be bored of it by now. But we sell out every single show. And tickets are, like, eighty bucks."

"Sounds rough," Jacob says. I can hear him running water and then taking a sip. "But I bet you look nice in your Sugarplum costume."

"If only," I say. "Sugarplum is a principal role. I'm a lowly Flower and a Snowflake."

"Well, I'm sure you make a gorgeous Snowflake. But what does this have to do with eight-year-olds on diets?" he asks.

I push open the dressing room door and flop down onto my chair. "Oh, I don't know. One of the kids in the show—there are all these parts for little kids—had me get her a Diet Sprite just now. I mean, it's one thing if you're *hired* to be a graceful waif, but a little girl? That's sick."

"Better a Diet Coke than the sixty-four-ounce Slurpees my kids in the after-school program show up with," Jacob says. "They're rotting their teeth out of their heads."

"Oh yeah, I guess you have a point," I admit. I look at the clock. "Crap, I should go. I've got rehearsal."

"Wait. So there's this band playing at Rockwood Music Hall this Saturday, and some of my buddies and I are going," he says.

"Oh, cool."

"Yeah, so what do you say? I think Bea might really dig my friend Drew."

"I won't be done with the performance until eleven."

"Oh. Okay. So, all right, I've got my calendar right here. I'm free most nights after eleven, and I've got all my Mondays open. What do you say? How about dinner at Café Mozart? Or there's this great Indian place on Fifty-Eighth between Seventh and Eighth. . . ."

I want to see Jacob again, I do. But I think back to the experience of dancing *Division at Dusk*, and I also know that I want more parts like that. They won't come without extraordinary effort. If this is my year, I have to keep pushing myself every single day; besides rehearsals and performances, I need to take Pilates and yoga classes. Already Otto must be contemplating casting the winter season, and I want him to think of me. So I can't risk being distracted.

Focus, I tell myself. *Focus*.

I picture Jacob's face, the line of his jaw and the faint shadow of stubble on his cheek. I close my eyes. "You know, I just can't right now," I say. "I'm sorry."

There's a long, tense silence. I can hear Jacob breathing on the other end of the line. Pretty soon I can't stand it. "I'm really, really busy." I feel helpless, but it's true.

Jacob clears his throat. "Wow, I don't know too many nineteen-year-olds who can't make time to hang with friends. You sure are different, Ward." He pauses. "And I like that about you. And I think what you're doing is great. I just wonder if it leaves you any time for a life."

I bristle at this. "Dancing is my life," I say without thinking.

"Well, then—" Jacob starts to say.

I interrupt him. "But I want to see you."

"Well, call me when you've got a free moment," Jacob says. "Okay? I'll probably be here."

When I hang up the phone, I have a queasy feeling in my stomach. *Probably?*

10

The party invitations start coming in November, and the closer it gets to Christmas, the faster and thicker they come. *"Please join us for a celebratory dinner in honor of the dancers of the Manhattan Ballet"*; *"The pleasure of your company is requested at a cocktail reception hosted by Mr. and Mrs. So-and-So"*; *"Lights! Camera! Dance! Celebrate the season with the Whatever Foundation, proud sponsors of the Manhattan Ballet."*

The hosts are always people who give money to the ballet, and so we're strongly encouraged — and sometimes basically forced — to go. Otto doesn't consider patron parties a distraction. As far as he's concerned, attending them is a part of our job. And even though they're a little boring sometimes, they're also pretty glamorous.

Tonight's party is hosted by one of the ballet's biggest

patrons, which is why Bea, Daisy, Zoe, and I are on the Upper East Side in the middle of a December snowstorm.

"These heels were so not made for snow," Zoe whines, adjusting the strap on her patent leather Louboutins.

"I told you to wear leg warmers, like I did. You just take them off in the elevator and stuff them into your bag," Bea replies.

When the private elevator car opens onto the marble foyer of the penthouse, Bea, who is wearing her hair braided and pinned on the top of her head like Heidi of the Alps because she thinks it draws attention away from her slightly protruding ears, pokes me in the ribs. "Hey," she says. "Is this amazing? Or is it just gauche?"

Bea is from New England, where rich people drive ancient Volvos and let the wallpaper in their wainscoted dining rooms fade and peel. People with money let old things stay old. But in New York, there's no room for Yankee modesty. All the Manhattan Ballet's patrons seem to live in twenty-room apartments with views of Central Park. Every piece of furniture, every painting, and every pillow is selected by interior decorators, and every mote of dust is swept up by uniformed maids.

I give my vintage velvet-collared jacket to the coat girl and smooth the front of my black floral-print dress as I take Bea's arm. I look at the huge gilded mirror that hangs in the foyer and then up at the trompe l'oeil ceiling, which features fat little cherubs floating around in a blue sky. "I think it's sort of gauche," I say in a low voice.

Bea nods as she eyes the giant bouquets of snow-white lilies and roses that dot the room. "Yeah, that's what I was sort of leaning toward."

As we step into the parlor, a waiter dressed head to toe in black sidles over to us. "Sugarplum-tini?" he asks smoothly, holding out a tray of lavender drinks with snowflake stirrers in them.

"Oh my God, they're *purple*," Bea mumbles. I nudge her.

"No, thank you," I say to the waiter. "I'm going to find the champagne."

He nods deferentially. "Allow me to procure you some," he says, and glides away.

Bea fiddles with the hem of her sequined BCBG mini. "I never know what to do at these things," she says.

"Drink," I say. "Eat French cheese." I point to a table piled high with cheeses, olives, and fruit. "Or desserts," I say, gesturing to the table of petits fours, tartlets, and delicate little cookies. Waiters circle the room with plates of delectable-looking appetizers: mini lobster rolls, stuffed figs, and tiny quiches.

I walk over to the cheese table and pop a bit of chevre into my mouth. "I wonder who they think is going to eat all this stuff," I say. "Not the ballet dancers. Zoe's vegan, Daisy's back on her fruit diet, Adriana is doing her raw-food thing, and Lottie hasn't had carbs in thirty years."

"The boys will eat it." Bea points across the room. "Look at Jonathan. It looks like he's trying to murder that salami."

I giggle, and Jonathan, who's wearing a fitted gray suit and a navy bow tie and is sawing into a salami like a starving man, looks up and waves his knife at us. "Hi, ladies," he calls. "You know I love me a charcuterie table. And if you see the cute guy with the shrimp skewers, send him my way."

I look down and see hot-pink socks peeking out from his shoes.

The waiter returns with our champagne, and then Daisy comes bouncing over in a polka-dot dress that she probably bought in the children's section at Macy's. "Oh, hey, you guys," she says. "Did you see Julie as the Sugarplum? She totally blew my mind tonight."

"Yeah, she was great," I say. Julie is a principal dancer, and she's tall and strong and has eyes so dark they're almost black. But the truth is I didn't watch her; I was busy composing witty texts to Jacob and then deleting them before sending them.

The waiter returns with a glass of ginger ale for Daisy, since she's so obviously underage. "Can't," she says, beaming at him. "The calories!" Then she turns to me. "Did you hear that Emma pulled her calf? She's going to be out for a while."

"I heard," I say grimly. "She was my alternate, remember?"

"Oh, right—I forgot you were supposed to have nights off."

"Yeah," I say exasperatedly. "And now unless Emma miraculously recovers, which is highly unlikely, I'll be dancing every single performance we have left."

And it's always like this. For the corps de ballet, dancing *The Nutcracker* becomes like a tag team as dancers get injured: The uninjured girls have to double up their parts until they, too, become injured, and then those girls are replaced by others who have to double up, until everyone is doing two or three times the number of parts they were meant to do. If you're not injured, you're exhausted, sick, or plain burned out. Jonathan and Luke call it *The Nutfucker*, which I think is totally appropriate.

A sweet-looking old woman wearing a royal-blue sequined evening gown walks over to us, the jewels at her throat flashing like Christmas lights. "Hello, my dears," she says, smiling benevolently at Bea and me. (Zoe and Daisy are at the bartender's table, probably because the guy looks like a young George Clooney.) "Are you making yourselves at home?"

We nod and smile.

"I think this year's corps de ballet looks the best it has since 1976," she goes on. "And that Christmas tree seemed larger than I remembered. I love the way it rises up from the stage."

Inwardly, I sigh: I don't have time to go to a party with Jacob and cute NYU guys, but I do have time to talk about *The Nutcracker*?

Bea, who is the politest of all of us, says, "Did you know that the tree weighs a whole ton?"

"Really!" the woman exclaims. "That is incredible. But you know, the Snow dance was always my favorite."

Everyone loves Snow. Or I should say, everyone who's never danced Snow loves Snow. The Snowflakes get showered with fifty pounds of white paper precipitation. This "snow" is swept up for reuse after each performance, so all the dust and dirt and lost earrings that are gathered up with the snow pour down on us in the next performance. The snow slips down into our costumes and gets into our hair and our mouths. It's flame-retardant, and it tastes like permanent marker.

81

"Oh, of course," I hear Bea say obligingly. "Snow is very popular."

While Bea is occupied with the bejeweled woman, I snack on olives and start drinking a second glass of champagne. I'm contemplating finding a corner to sit in, when a tall, well-dressed guy appears in front of me. He leans against the wall and crosses one ankle casually over the other. "You look less than thrilled to be here," he says, gesturing to the room at large. His voice is a deep baritone. "And you're doing a terrible job of mingling." His dark eyes sparkle when he smiles.

I give him a quick up-down, the way I would if he were another dancer. With tanned skin and dark bangs that he has to push out of his eyes, he's better looking than anyone else in the room. He's wearing an expensive-looking charcoal-gray suit but no tie. His smile is dazzling, and I can't help smiling back.

"I'm Matt," he says. "Matt Fitzgerald."

"I'm Hannah," I say. I hold out my hand, but instead of shaking it, he brings it to his lips and kisses it.

"Pleased to meet you," he murmurs.

Matt is probably about Jacob's age, but that's where the similarity ends. Jacob looks like a college student: He wears vintage T-shirts and corduroys, and he waits a few days between shaves. Matt, however, looks likes a Hollywood actor—or at the very least, like the kind of person who shops at Jeffrey and vacations in all the fabulous parts of Europe.

"I'm a huge fan of the Manhattan Ballet," Matt says. "I've been watching you since you performed in the student workshop at the academy. You're a fantastic dancer. You look like Grace Kelly onstage."

"Wow," I say, blushing. "Um, thanks—that's really nice." I look down at my champagne. I like compliments as much as the next girl, but it's a little strange to meet someone who already seems to know me. Matt goes on to say that he never misses a performance unless he's in Paris. In other words, he's a balletomane, which is what we call a rabid fan. (The *mane* comes from *mania*.)

"I'm in the front row every night," he adds.

"Wow," I say. It's one thing to dedicate your body to ballet every single night. But to just watch, to merely dedicate your eyeballs and your sitting butt—that's a bit obsessive. I try to push aside these thoughts, though, because I'm pleased he seems to be interested in me; there are soloists and principals he could be talking to. "That's really dedicated."

"I take my extracurricular interests very seriously," he says, smiling.

"Lucky for you that you have time for them," I say, taking a sip of my drink. "I don't even have time to do my laundry."

He takes my elbow and leads me to a pale blue sofa, where we both sit. "You need an assistant," he says.

I brighten at the thought. "An intern!" I say. "Aren't high school and college kids always trying to gain work experience? Maybe I could get myself a straight-A student from Nightingale-Bamford. She could dust my shelves and take my laundry to the cleaner."

"Excellent idea," Matt says. "She'll be gaining real-world

experience in multitasking and proactivity. She could do your grocery shopping, too."

"Yeah, and if she's really good, she can be promoted to writing letters to my grandmother in Florida."

Matt laughs. "Allowing her to opt out of English 101. See? We've solved your problems."

I grin ruefully. "If only."

Matt leans back against the cushions and crosses his long legs. "Hey, I interned for a lawyer in college, and all he ever had me do was manage his golf outings."

"Sounds rewarding," I say. I settle back on the sofa. This is definitely more fun than talking to old ladies about *The Nutcracker*.

He shakes his head. "Nope, but I did get college credit for it." A waiter passes by with a tray of drinks. "Are you sure you don't want a sugarplum-tini?" he asks.

I shake my head. "I have to work tomorrow. Also, I try not to drink things that look like melted Jolly Ranchers."

"I admire your conscientiousness." Matt waves the waiter away. He gets a faraway look in his eye, and he clears his throat before he speaks. "Sometimes you dance as if you're all alone out there, like we're all there to see only you. It's an amazing energy you have." He leans in closer. "And you're even more beautiful up close," he says.

Although this remark is a little forward, it also seems simply *nice*.

"You were better than Lottie in *Division at Dusk*," Matt goes on. "She used to be amazing, but if you ask me, she's past her prime. You'll get bigger parts in winter season, I'm sure of it."

"Hey, I've got an idea," I say. "Why don't you do the casting instead of Otto?"

He laughs. "I would if I could," he says. He clinks his glass against mine.

Then Daisy and Zoe come rushing over. "Willem Dafoe is in the other room," Daisy cries. "And Sarah Jessica Parker, who is wearing, like, this totally insane silver dress. It makes her look like an icicle." Daisy is practically bouncing with excitement.

"It's a Carolina Herrera," Zoe says knowingly. She has on a formfitting red satin cap-sleeve dress with a low cowl neck (designer, I'm sure). "My mom took me to her Fashion Week show." Then she notices Matt, and I see a sudden gleam in her green eyes. She pouts her lips ever so slightly. "I'm Zoe," she says, holding out her hand and tossing her shiny hair.

But Matt doesn't kiss Zoe's hand—he only shakes it politely. And then he turns to me. "Well, if you'll excuse me," he says, meeting my eyes and touching my shoulder. "I should go make small talk with some of the members of the ballet board."

"Who was that?" Daisy asks, watching him glide through the crowd.

"Matt," I say.

"Matt who?" Zoe asks.

I shrug.

Zoe watches his broad, retreating shoulders. "Did you see his Patek Philippe?" she says.

"His what?" I ask.

"His watch," Zoe says. "It's worth, like, at least three hundred thousand dollars." She pauses. "Did you get his number?"

"No," I say, elbowing her.

"Well, you should," she says, narrowing her eyes, "because if you don't, I will."

Daisy waves her hand at us. "Hello? Can we get over the hot guy for a second? There are movie stars to talk to. Willem Dafoe is totally short, and Sarah Jessica Parker has, like, the most incredible highlights in her hair." She touches her black waves. "Do you think blond highlights would look too weird on me?"

"Yes," Zoe says definitively.

A few feet away, the woman in the sparkling blue dress continues to monopolize poor Bea. I hear about her love of opera and ballet, as well as her recent health problems.

"Ever since Mr. Fitzgerald made a fortune in finance, he's been such a loyal patron of the company," she says. "He and his boys come nearly every night! He is such a generous man, and isn't his apartment beautiful?"

I nearly choke on my caviar blini. This is the apartment Matt grew up in? I assumed he was rich, but not *this* rich.

If I thought the way Zoe thinks, I'd fling myself at him. But I don't really know what to think of Matt. All I know is that I'm tired and my brain is beginning to feel fuzzy from the champagne. I wonder if I should just go home.

Then Bea wraps her pale, freckled arm around my neck. *"Deck the halls with boughs of holly,"* she sings into my ear. Giggling, I push her away.

"Let's go find the guy with the lobster rolls," she says.

"Have you ever noticed that lobsters look like giant red bugs?" I ask.

"Does that mean you won't eat one?" she demands.

"Of course not. But what about that fruit diet Daisy was trying to talk you into?" I ask.

"Screw it," she says. "It's the holiday season!"

๑ ๑ ๑

Later, as I'm leaving, Matt tries to persuade me to go with him to the Boom Boom Room, a bar at the top of the Standard Hotel.

"It's after midnight," I point out. "Remember how you admired my conscientiousness?" My coat is on, my scarf is wrapped around my neck, and I'm ready to be home.

"Yes, but there's a party for Chloë Sevigny there," he says. "You should meet her — she's totally cool."

But I am exhausted, and tomorrow is another long day. Also, Matt — despite his charms — is not Jacob, who five minutes ago texted me a *Still thinking about you* message.

"Thanks so much, but I have to work tomorrow. Plus, I don't know if I'm really Boom Boom Room material," I reply.

Matt smiles good-naturedly, but I see a look of slight surprise in his eyes. He's probably the kind of guy few people turn down.

"Give me your number," he says, touching my arm.

"Fine, hand me your phone," I say, surprising myself. I don't normally give out my number to guys (not that many are asking). But there's something about Matt that I can't ignore. He's exotic to me: He's debonair and confident, and his wealth seems to cling to him like an invisible but perfectly tailored suit.

And I can't pretend that his appreciation of me and my dancing isn't gratifying. He *gets* it—all of it. He knows the art and all the hard work and dedication it takes.

Matt puts me in a cab and hands the driver twenty dollars. "Take good care of her"—he cranes his head into the backseat to read the cabbie's name on his badge—"and I mean *really* good care of her, Qusay Adnan."

"Whatever," I hear Qusay mumble, but he nods dutifully.

Then Matt opens my door and gives me a quick, light kiss on the mouth. It lasts less than a second, and yet I seem to feel it in my whole body. It's like a tiny electric shock—not entirely pleasant, but not unpleasant, either. I'm taken aback, and I guess this shows on my face.

Matt smiles. "Sorry," he says. "Couldn't resist."

Then he closes the door, and Qusay Adnan puts the car into drive. Closing my eyes as we head west to my apartment, I feel tipsy and happy and more than a little confused.

The next morning the lobby of my building is full of red balloons. There are dozens of them, gathered in clusters like rosebuds on steroids. Taped to my mailbox is a note in a neat hand: *I think you're great. —M.*

I smile and bite my lip. This is sweet; this is totally embarrassing; this is like nothing anyone's ever done for me.

11

Daisy turns to me. "Balloons!" she exclaims. "Two dozen red balloons?"

I blush. Daisy has some inexplicable superpower when it comes to unearthing gossip. I think it's because she can literally read lips — or else she's just so little and unobtrusive that people don't notice her eavesdropping. She was the one who first spread the news that Lily was pregnant. She was also the one who claimed to have seen Otto driving off with Julie in his Mercedes, his arm around her shoulder and her head buried in his neck, their destination unknown but obviously illicit. Or so she says. So of course Daisy has heard about the balloons, even though I told only Bea.

"Just so you know," she says to me as she stitches a ribbon to her pointe shoe, "I did some recon work, and Matt sent balloons to Serena last summer and to Joanna last year."

She's probably right, and I should not take his extravagant gesture too seriously. But I don't want to give her the satisfaction of admitting to that, perhaps because, thanks to Caleb, she's more experienced than I am — even though she's only sixteen. "Really," I say blithely. "Thanks for the info."

Bea wanders in from the hall, sipping from a giant bottle of water. "And anyway," she says, joining the conversation as if she'd been in the dressing room all along, "what about Jacob? I *love* him."

"I don't know," I answer. "He lives on the Lower East Side. He wants me to come to his shows, but they're always in, like, Brooklyn. He's so cute — some other girl is just going to snap him up while I'm stuck here dancing Snow again."

Daisy leans close to the mirror and inspects her teeth. "Zoe says Matt's your man. He's friends with Chloë Sevigny." She points to the wall of the dressing room where she's taped up *Us Weekly* pictures of badly dressed celebrities. There's an unflattering snapshot of the actress in a lacy teal cocktail dress that looks like a costume from *Alice in Wonderland*.

"Interesting criterion for a boyfriend," Bea mutters.

"Well, ladies, thanks for your input in the romance department. But let's get ready for the show, okay, and drop the subject?"

The other girls smirk at each other, but I ignore them.

It's time to put on my stage makeup, which I've always loved. I can go from a blond girl-next-door type to a dramatic, dark-lashed vixen so quickly my own mother would hardly recognize me.

"All right, whatever you say," Daisy says, shooting one last longing glance at Chloë. "Still. You could at least get me her autograph."

I ignore her as I apply pancake foundation with a moist sponge, then wait for it to seep into my pores. I use a big powder puff to press in a thick layer of pale powder so that my face is completely matte white.

"But you know what Zoe says about dating," Daisy goes on. "You're a dancer, and you've got social currency. Why waste it on a college guy? *Pedestrians* go to college."

In the world of ballet, *pedestrian* is the word for a normal person. It's somewhat derogatory, especially when Zoe says it. I face Daisy, my blush brush in my hand. "One, I thought we were going to drop the subject, and two, why are you parroting Zoe?"

Bea snickers. "Yeah, she's not exactly a role model."

"Well, she has a terrific work ethic," Daisy says. "She's learning *Lasting Imprint*— which Julie, like, always dances— just because she wants to."

"You don't say," I respond, trying to sound as if I don't care. I don't want to think about Zoe right now. I hold my blush brush firmly and create contour with the pink powder, accentuating my bone structure. Next I apply brown and shimmery purple shadow in the outer creases of my eyes and along my lower lash line.

Beside me, Bea reaches for her own brushes and powders. "Why don't you go ask *her* for her autograph?"

I snicker as I swipe dark liquid eyeliner along my top lashes, followed by dark pencil on the lower outer edges of my lashes. I reach for my mascara and apply a thick layer on the upper and lower lashes.

"Very funny," Daisy says, and Bea giggles.

I secure my false eyelashes with glue. This last part can be tricky—the first time I did it, back when I was a brand-new apprentice, I almost glued my eyes shut—but now it's practically second nature. Finally, I apply a berry-red lipstick, blot, and then last, but certainly not least, I dab on lip gloss. I can't go onstage without shine on my lips.

Done. I look in the mirror and sit up a little straighter; a ballerina stares back at me.

After Bea, too, has put on her stage makeup, we go down to put on our Snow costumes, then hurry to watch from the wings. The Christmas party is over, the grown-ups are fast asleep, and Marie has shrunk down to the size of a mouse. She must defend her beloved Nutcracker against the evil Mouse King, and so she hits him with her shoe, distracting him long enough for the Nutcracker to kill him.

"Just another day in the life of a Victorian girl," Bea whispers.

Then Marie's house splits open and snow falls in through the ceiling. The snow is steady and thick, and it falls all around Marie, who's in her nightgown and wearing only one shoe. Hand in hand with her Nutcracker Prince, she wanders through the woods in silence as the snow lands in their hair and on their warm faces. The blue lights make it feel like night; the snow seems to cool the air. If you can forget what that snow tastes like, it's absolute magic to see.

I'm on in moments. I stand in the darkness of the front wing, waiting for my first entrance. I smooth the bunched-up tulle of my skirt, adjust my jewel-encrusted crown, and slide my fingers into the wiry webbing of the fanlike contraptions I carry in both hands. On the ends of the wire are small white pompoms that seem to float through the air, following the movements of my arms.

I run into the snow, with my feet pointed in front of me, and tour jeté in unison with the girls alongside me. I imagine that I'm a snowflake falling from the sky: I am brushed by the wind, and swoop this way and that. I cross paths with other snowflakes; sometimes I go faster, depending on the velocity of the wind. We move in unison, inverting our formation — sauté, chassé turn, sauté, pas de chat — and then I run back into the wing. A moment later we chaîné back onto the stage as if the wind is pushing us.

When we huddle together in the back corner, I hear all the girls panting around me. Though we might look like snowflakes, we are flesh-and-blood humans struggling to get enough oxygen. I smile at Bea, and she smiles back. Even though we've performed this part over a hundred times, there's always something magical about the snow and the music, and about dancing with your friends.

12

It's Christmas Eve, and instead of being home in Weston and eating take-out Chinese with my parents, I'm waiting for Bea to get out of the shower so we can go to Zoe's apartment, where her mother will either be fashionably tipsy or be absent because she's at some A-list party.

We only have tomorrow off, so most of us are staying in the city. At first I thought it would make me feel grown up and independent, but the more I think about it, the worse it makes me feel. I'd rather be eating wonton soup with my parents and then driving around the neighborhood to see all the crazy Christmas light displays. (There's a guy up the block who puts a life-size Santa and all nine reindeer on his roof.) I want to eat the red-and-green pancakes my dad makes on Christmas morning, which are, he is always careful to point out, made in the spirit of irony.

To make myself feel a little less lonely, I send Jacob a text: *Merry almost-Xmas from a hardworking Snowflake.*

A minute later he replies: *Bah! Humbug. I'm Jewish, remember?*

I laugh. The fact that he wrote me back so quickly has to be a good sign. *Me too. Well, half. And I love Xmas.*

So do I. I have Santas on my boxers.

Really?

Want to come check?

Ha-ha.

Figured out when we can hang out yet?

I think about this for a while. Maybe a date (and *not* more Pilates) is exactly what I need after the drudgery of *The Nutcracker.* I type: *Next week?*

Ha! I get to turn YOU down. I'll be in PR.

PR?

Puerto Rico, baby!

JEALOUS.

Then Bea comes out of the shower, wrapped in a towel that says *Acapulco* in big, bright letters. Her red hair drips, forming little pools of water on the floor.

"Nice towel," I say. "Is that one of those 'My nana went to Mexico and all I got was this lousy beach towel' kind of things?"

She grins ruefully. "How'd you guess?"

My iPhone beeps. *You *should* be jealous*, Jacob writes.

I am, I type. *But I gotta go. Have a good trip.*

Bea pulls a sweater out of her theater case. "How'd you get ready so fast?" she asks.

I shrug. I'm wearing tight jeans, a mohair sweater, and a pair of high-heeled boots I found at a West Village thrift shop. "I'm just efficient. Now hurry up, it's late."

"Sheesh! I'm coming, I'm coming," she says, bending over to towel dry her hair.

"Sometimes I feel like we spend most of our time getting either dressed or undressed," I observe. "I wish there were more hours in the day. Like, maybe twenty-eight of them."

Bea makes an upside-down face at me. "Are you kidding me?" she asks. "I'm so pooped by the end of the day, I can't *wait* to fall into bed."

"I know. But I'd still like to have a little more time — to be a normal person, you know? To explore other things . . ."

Bea stands up straight, tosses her towel onto the floor, and then quickly buttons her blouse and pulls on a skirt. "Yeah, well, if you shatter your ankle, you could be a normal person by tomorrow."

"Fair enough," I say. I touch my ankle protectively.

It's snowing when we leave the theater, and Bea and I have to maneuver over a gray snowbank to hail a cab.

"Are you kidding me?" I hear Bea wail, and I look over to see her knee-high boot partially submerged in an icy puddle. The wind snaps against our cheeks.

"Come on," I say, and I grab her hand and pull her into the waiting cab, which feels as hot and steamy as an oven. We head east to Fifth Avenue as Christmas music plays on the cabbie's radio.

Zoe lives in the kind of building where the doorman wears matching gloves and cap and stands outside even though the temperature is below freezing. He greets us politely and wishes us happy holidays.

"I don't blame Zoe for not getting her own place," Bea says, marveling again at the grand, sparkling foyer.

"Me either," I say. Her mother is never around, and the apartment has about a million rooms.

Bea is cursing her wet sock when the elevator door opens. Her freckled cheeks are pink from the cold.

"Hey, guys, come on in." Zoe smiles sweetly. She's wearing a simple red wool dress with tights, and her hair is still up in a bun from the show.

"You have snow in your hair," Bea says as she removes a piece of paper snow from Zoe's head.

Zoe sighs. "I found some in the silverware drawer yesterday. That stuff gets *everywhere*."

Bea kicks off her boots and damp socks while I hand my parka to Gladys, the housekeeper. By the fireplace is an enormous Christmas tree dripping with iridescent crystals and white Christmas lights.

"You like our tree?" Zoe asks, following my gaze. "It got featured in *New York* magazine. Mom hired, like, an entire team of people to design and decorate it." She plucks another piece of paper snow from her tights. "Seriously," she says, sighing, "am I going to be picking this stuff off me for the rest of my life?"

"Or until you get promoted," Bea says. The Pekingese — Dolly's third in four years — nips at Bea's feet.

"Down, Gucci!" a voice cries out, and Dolly appears in a black column dress with a large flute of champagne in her hand.

"Girls! Don't you look cute! Bea, I don't know why the boys aren't throwing themselves at you. And Hannah, I had a pair of boots exactly like that once! I gave them to charity a few years ago. But really, welcome, all of you. Eggnog and cookies are by the tree." She shoos us along with her thin, graceful fingers, which are dripping with diamond rings. I wonder idly if that's how many proposals she's received, or if she's bought all those jewels for herself.

Gucci the Pekingese is now trying to lick Bea's bare feet. The entire apartment is covered in cotton snow and dripping with crystals.

"It's like they robbed the North Pole," I whisper.

Bea giggles. "Or a window at Macy's," she agrees. "Zero sense of irony."

Leni comes in from the dining room, scoops up Gucci, and waves the little dog's paw. "Merry Christmas, girls!" she says in a German doggy voice. Her gold hair falls in waves well past her shoulders.

Daisy comes out of the kitchen holding a tray of cookies and a wonky gingerbread house that looks as if it might collapse at any minute. "Look what Leni and I made with Gladys!" she says with mock pride.

They both had the night off thanks to their alternates, and it seems that they've already gotten a little tipsy. Because of Emma's pulled calf, I've been dancing every performance. And I've found paper snow in pretty much every item of clothing I own.

I ooh and aah over the gingerbread house as if it were some

rare artifact. "That's very Frank Gehry," I say, fingering the lopsided roof. "My dad would love it. He's an architect."

"I think it has Whitney Biennial potential," Leni says, laughing.

"Totally," I agree.

As we wander into the palatial living room, I notice Dolly tiptoeing past us and slipping out the front door in a pink chinchilla coat. She doesn't even wave good-bye to her daughter. I don't know why she still disappoints me after all these years—you'd think I'd be used to it. Zoe certainly is.

Zoe, Daisy, Leni, Bea, and I all huddle around the fireplace and sip eggnog. Gladys brings out silver platters with peanut brittle and sugar cookies shaped like the baby Jesus.

"Are *these* ironic?" Bea whispers as she bites into one of his feet.

We sink into the huge, plush sofas and watch *Miracle on 34th Street* on the wall-mounted flat-screen TV, which, when it's not on, hides behind a screen that looks like a Jackson Pollock painting.

Before the movie is over, though, Zoe becomes impatient. "Let's do presents!" she says, and so we all scoot down and sit on pillows in a circle on the floor.

The gift exchange was Leni's idea; since she's older, every once in a while she likes to get maternal on us. Bea gives everyone little bottles of bath salts, which are perfect for our aching bodies, especially during *Nutcracker* season. Leni gives us tins with German toffees, Daisy hands out mini lip gloss kits from Sephora, and Zoe—who could afford to go over the ten-dollar limit—passes out Marc Jacobs key chains. I had made everyone an animal ornament out of Styrofoam balls and pipe cleaners and placed them inside little wooden boxes that I bought at the Columbus Circle crafts fair.

"What is mine?" Bea asks, holding it up.

I eye it. Honestly, it's not easy to tell. "It's a reindeer," I say brightly.

"Oh," she says. "Awesome."

We're busy examining our presents—Bea is trying on lip gloss while Daisy dangles her new key chain in front of Gucci's nose—when Gladys comes in with a platter of chow mein and moo shu chicken. Suddenly I remember that I haven't eaten any dinner, and I am so delighted I leap up and give her a big hug.

She pats me on the cheek. "I would have preferred a nice glazed ham, but Zoe insisted because this is your favorite," she says.

I'm so touched that I dash back over to Zoe's pillow, plop down on it, and give her a kiss on the cheek.

"Merry Christmas," she says, laughing and shoving me away playfully.

And she's right—it is.

WINTER SEASON

13

"Here we go again," Bea says as she throws her clean laundry into her theater case.

"Back to the salt mines," I say cheerfully, which is something my dad used to say when he went to his office at the architecture firm on Monday mornings.

Today is the first day of winter season. On New Year's Eve, we had our last performance of *The Nutcracker*, thank God. Then we had two days' break—not nearly long enough to recuperate.

But at least it was long enough for the dressing room to get a thorough cleaning. Now it smells clean and piney, and our mirrors are no longer marred by fingerprints and smudges of makeup. The room looks as nice as it's ever looked, and I wonder how long it'll take us to destroy it again. Considering Bea's leotards and tights are already spewing out of her theater case and piling up on the floor, I'm guessing about fifteen more minutes. She might be the politest of us, but she's also the sloppiest.

Daisy holds up her water bottle in a toast. "Finally some real repertory!" she cries.

"Amen," says Bea as she wads a pair of leg warmers into a ball.

I hear my phone vibrate with a text, and I dig for it in my bag. I'm hoping it's Jacob, but it's not—it's Matt.

Merde on your first day of winter season!

Merde, which is French for "shit," is the dancer's equivalent of "break a leg." I smile to myself and toss my phone onto the countertop.

"So what are your New Year's resolutions?" Daisy wants to know. "I want to wear my size twenty-four jeans by March."

Bea says, in all seriousness, "I'm going to read *War and Peace*."

"Good luck with that." I laugh.

She shoots me a look. "Why, just because you can't finish *Frankenstein*, which I'm pretty sure you've been trying to read since last summer?" she teases. "Anyway, I'm also going to get a boyfriend, or at least go on a date."

"Now, *that* I can get behind," I tell her. "And for your information, I'm three-quarters of the way through the book."

"Zoe?" Daisy asks. "What about you?"

Zoe is busy lining up all the new makeup she bought at Bergdorf's. She looks up. "I don't believe in New Year's resolutions," she says, grinning slyly. "Because, really, what could I possibly change? I'm perfect as I am."

"You could drink more water and less Diet Coke," Daisy

says, "as I'm always telling you. That would be a good resolution. And you could also quit smoking."

Zoe scoffs as she experimentally swipes blue eye shadow over her lids. "Whatever," she says, sounding bored.

Daisy turns to me. "Han?"

"Um," I say, stalling for time. My sole New Year's resolution is to get promoted, but I'm not going to announce *that* to the room. "Eat more kale?" I offer.

Daisy rolls her eyes. "Clearly only Bea and I take this sort of new beginning seriously," she says. "Dr. Shapiro says that voicing your intentions is an important part of manifesting your dreams."

Dr. Shapiro is Daisy's therapist, whom she's been seeing since she started at the MBA. I don't know many sixteen-year-olds with a personal shrink on call, but if I had a crazy stage mother like Daisy's, I'd want a therapist, too.

Blah-blah-blah, Zoe mouths, and I can't help but giggle.

"Oh, hey, you guys," Daisy says. "Did I tell you what Caleb got me for Christmas?" She's practically clapping her hands in glee.

Zoe leans over to me. "Seriously? They're still together? I thought she was just a layover on his way to Gaytown."

I stifle a snort while Daisy tells us about the clothes Caleb picked out for her at Barneys. My phone buzzes again: *Trattoria Dell'Arte lunch by stage door. Enjoy!*

Wow—Matt left me lunch, which means I get to eat something besides yogurt and a banana today. I'm flattered and pleased, but it also makes me feel a little strange—like I can't tell if he's trying to hit on me or be my mother. Instead of responding to Matt, I text Jacob, who's still in Puerto Rico for his brother's bachelor party.

So how much fun are you having?

I stare at the screen, waiting for a reply. But apparently he's having too much fun to write back.

งวะ 　 งวะ 　 งวะ

That afternoon Zoe and I enter the studio along with Adriana, Olivia, and a handful of understudies, who linger in the back of the room. We've been called to learn a new piece by a guest choreographer named Jason Pite. I've heard of him, but I've never seen any of his ballets; supposedly, he's some kind of choreographic genius.

Zoe pinches my arm when Jason walks in. He's a former dancer, as most choreographers are, and he's tall, with sandy hair and chiseled features. He's barefoot and wearing green cut-off sweatpants and a threadbare T-shirt with the neck stretched out and the arms cut off. Jason looks me right in the eye and smiles. I'm caught off guard and have an embarrassing coughing fit. Zoe giggles prettily and then swoons as he introduces himself in his charming Australian accent.

"I watched one of your performances this past fall," Jason says, "and it got me really excited to work with you guys. What a strong group of dancers. I thought I'd play the music for you first and then teach you some phrases I've been working on."

Zoe's tongue is practically hanging out of her mouth as Jason walks to the stereo and puts on a CD. The music is a scherzo from one of Beethoven's piano sonatas; it's bright and fast.

He nods along with the beat, and after a few moments he asks us to spread out in the studio. The movements he begins to teach us feel more like modern dance than classical ballet. "Can you move your weight down?" he asks Zoe, who bats her eyelashes at him. "I want you to feel connected to the floor."

Some of the movements he teaches us resemble African dance: We isolate our ribs, quake our pelvises, and buckle our knees. Some movements are sharp and quick, while others are languid. At first I feel pretty stupid and self-conscious trying to mimic him, but after a while the dance begins to feel liberating. I've never moved like this before, and I like it. We're not pulling up and turning out as if trying to defy gravity, the way we do in ballet. We even get down on the ground!

Above us, Jason is smiling and nodding his head. "Yes, you," Jason calls out, pointing to me. "You're feeling it, I can tell."

When rehearsal is over, Zoe comes to my side, panting. A stray piece of blond hair is stuck to her cheek with sweat. "I thought I liked him, but maybe I don't," she whispers. "Those last five minutes with the weird hand gestures? What was that all about?"

"Oh, you're just jealous because he said I was feeling it," I tease.

Zoe sniffs. "All I can say is I would never date a modern dancer. I just wouldn't be able to respect a person who devoted his life to rolling around on the floor."

"Hey, at least it's not *The Nutcracker*." We head down to the

Green Room, where we change into costumes for our dress rehearsal.

Onstage, Otto perches atop a stool and motions us into our places for *Violin Concerto in D*, which we will perform tonight. The corps in this ballet — there are sixteen of us, in belted leotards — pose in horizontal rows while Mai Morimoto throws herself into high jump after incredibly high jump on center stage. Almost imperceptibly, Otto nods his approval as Mai does a crazy layout. Her jet-black hair slips out of its bun and seems to almost float in the air.

Zoe and I are doing a series of poses in the back, and we happen to be next to each other at this point in this ballet. We've danced *Violin* so many times that we can carry on a conversation between steps, though we try to keep our lips still, like ventriloquists, so we don't get yelled at.

"Whoa, did you see that? Mai is fearless," I murmur through my clenched teeth.

"Shut up, I'm concentrating," Zoe teases. "Han, wouldn't it be awesome if we were cast in the duet in *Temperaments*? I'm mad for that part," she whispers.

We lunge away from each other and then piqué back together again.

"You know that Emma understudied the duet last year," she whispers, "but she's still out, and Leah's gained so much weight that I doubt they'd ask her to learn it."

Since *Temperaments* is coming up in a few weeks, we'll start rehearsing it soon. We switch our weight, then piqué into an attitude and pose in B-plus.

"I mean, I would so much rather do classical than Jason's weird modern stuff," Zoe says, posing with her arms jutting forward.

"Oh, loosen up," I whisper. On the count of six, we kneel with our heads down, and Zoe and I are practically touching. (Conveniently, this makes it easier to talk.)

"Listen to you," she says. "Ms. Goody Two-shoes, you're one to talk. Unless that musician of yours is becoming a bad influence?" We stand and thrust our hips forward and then shift our weight again.

"Hardly," I snort. "Considering I haven't seen him since, like, November."

"Are you thinking about Matt, then?"

"No!"

"Well, you should keep your options open," Zoe says. "I'm sure Jacob's keeping his open, if you know what I mean."

I shoot Otto a look, but his attention is on Mai, whose pale skin now glistens with sweat. "What?" I ask Zoe.

"If he's as cute as you say he is, there must be another girl out there."

It's not as if I haven't wondered about other girls before, but hearing Zoe say it makes me feel terrible. "Oh yeah? Thanks for the vote of confidence."

"All right!" Otto calls, his voice echoing in the empty theater.

Zoe and I freeze, ready to be reprimanded for chatting. But instead Otto is simply offering that half smile of his — the most we ever see — and motioning us off the stage.

"Okay, thank you," he says. He touches Mai's arm protectively. "Save a little for tonight."

Back in our dressing room, Leni is doing some insane yoga pose in the corner. She's balanced on her hands, with her feet tucked behind her neck.

"God, how do you *do* that?" Zoe mutters, flinging herself into her chair. "You look like a pretzel."

"It opens up the hips," Leni says calmly.

I collapse onto the floor and then sit up so I can stretch my hip flexors. I tell myself to stop worrying about Jacob, to focus on the upcoming performance and the rehearsals tomorrow and the next day. But then I call him anyway, and this time I reach him.

14

It's bitterly cold, and the sidewalks have hillocks of old ice. As I walk to meet Jacob, the wind whips around the buildings so fiercely it seems to get under my clothes. I blow my nose, and I swear I can feel it getting bright red and swollen. (All of us in the dressing room have colds now; the debris on the floor includes tissues and nasal-spray bottles and cough drop wrappers, in addition to the normal piles of clothing and corn pads.)

Jacob said he'd be waiting on the steps outside the Metropolitan Museum of Art, and I find him leaning against the massive face of the building, thumbing through a book. He's bundled up in a navy blue peacoat and a scarf that looks like something my grandma might have made. My heart does a tiny leap in my chest, then settles. He leans in and kisses me on the cheek.

"Long time, no see," he says with a grin.

I smile up at him. "So how was your trip?"

Jacob chuckles as we turn to walk inside. "If I never see another bottle of rum in my life, I'll be happy. And I'd like to never hear another karaoke version of 'Cheeseburger in Paradise.'"

I nod understandingly. My dad plays Jimmy Buffett once in a while, and his music always makes me want to bury my head under a pillow. "I promise not to burst out in song," I say. But I hum a few bars anyway, and Jacob ducks away, covering his ears.

"Please stop," he moans, and I can't help but laugh.

Inside, the great hall is thronged with people. The sound of their collective voices echoes in the marble space, a murmur amplified into a wordless roar.

"I love the Met," I sigh.

"Me too," Jacob says. "It's one of my favorite places in Manhattan."

"I came here in August," I say. "Before fall season. I stood for, like, an hour in front of *Madame X*. You know, that John Singer Sargent painting?"

Jacob nods. "I do. I love Sargent."

"I read that Madame X — I don't remember her real name — was so spoiled that she almost couldn't even stay still for her portrait. Sargent called her a woman of 'unpaintable beauty and hopeless laziness.'"

Jacob laughs. "Laziness! You wouldn't know a thing about that, would you?"

I shrug. "Hey, I sleep in on Mondays. Like today — I got up at nine thirty!"

"If that's your definition of laziness, the world could use more lazy people like you."

I put my hand in the crook of Jacob's elbow as we wait in line to pay admission. "So where do you want to go?" I ask him. "I bet you're the modern-art type."

"I like my Picassos and my Duchamps," Jacob says, handing the cashier a twenty. "But I have another place to take you first."

"I hope it's not Arms and Armor or the American furniture wing," I say. He hands me a little purple button, which I affix to my coat. "Because I don't really care about axes or Tiffany side tables." I glance at the museum map on the wall. "And I hope you're not thinking of taking me to the Degas ballerinas, because, believe me, I'm familiar with those. Degas and his dancers are practically the only art a bunhead knows."

"Nope. Hang on." He pulls out his phone and sends a quick text to someone. There's the beep of a reply, and then Jacob nods and takes my hand again. "Okay, we have to hurry."

"Hurry where?" I ask as he pulls me toward the elevator.

But Jacob doesn't answer; he only smiles as we enter the car. When the elevator stops, we're on the top floor of the museum, which, compared to the crowded hall below, seems almost deserted. Our footsteps echo as we walk down a corridor lined with black-and-white photographs of exotic birds.

A guard is standing by the doorway to the roof garden. "Hey, Frank," Jacob calls, and Frank, a young but balding guy wearing thick hipster glasses, raises his hand in a salute.

"Don't know why you want to go out there on a day like today," Frank says, "but whatever, dude." Then he opens the door with a key from a ring of them and motions us through.

Jacob steps into the chilly, pale sunlight, and I follow. The roof is empty and bare, and I turn to him, wondering why he's brought me here. If he wanted fresh air, we could have just stayed on the steps outside the museum.

He reaches down for my hand as we walk to the edge and look down over Central Park. Far below us the ground is brown and strewn with rocks. The trees, with their bare gray branches, look like skeletons of their summer selves.

"Ever been up here?" he asks.

I shake my head, my teeth chattering a little.

Jacob clucks his tongue at me and pulls me closer; he opens his coat and tucks me inside it to protect me from the wind. "And you've lived here for five years?" he asks. "I figured you hadn't been up when it's closed, but never? They have exhibits when the weather's nicer: Frank Stella, the sculptor, and Claes Oldenburg, the pop artist. There's even a café."

Maybe I should be embarrassed by my failure to frequent the Met and its apparently fabulous roof, but all I can think about is how warm I am standing near him. I wish I could live in the folds of his coat forever. It reminds me of the soft velvet of the wings. "I don't have a lot of time. . . ." I murmur.

Jacob turns and gazes out over the trees, and then he looks back at me. Our faces are so close, we could almost kiss. "You're standing on the rooftop of the greatest museum in the world, looking out over the greatest city in the world—that's something to *make* time for." His voice is soft but earnest.

I shiver, but whether it's because I'm cold or because I'm close to Jacob, I can't tell. "Are you lecturing me? If you are, you can quit, because I'm making time for it now."

Jacob laughs. "I'm going to take all the credit for it, then," he says. "Since it was my idea to meet here." With his arm still around me, he leads me around the rooftop. "I like it up here because in the winter you can see everything. In the summer the park is just a sea of impenetrable green." His fingers tighten around my shoulder, then loosen again. "I guess it's just a matter of perspective. Things are prettier in June, but they're clearer in January."

"That sounds like a metaphor for something," I say.

He laughs again. "Yeah, it does. But for what I'm not entirely sure." He runs his hand through his dark hair. "I also wanted to impress you with my ability to sneak you into a closed roof garden."

"I'm impressed," I assure him.

He points out various buildings across the park — the Majestic, the Dakota, the Langham, and the San Remo, all on Central Park West. I half expect an architecture lesson (certainly, I'd get one if my dad were here), but thankfully Jacob doesn't say anything about neo-Italian Renaissance facades or art deco motifs.

"You know, John Lennon was shot right outside the Dakota," he says, pointing across the park.

I have my own trivia about the Dakota, which I know because of a documentary I got for Christmas/Hanukkah one year. "And Rudolf Nureyev lived in the Dakota," I say. I think about watching him leap across my TV screen. I wish I could have seen him dance live, but I was only a toddler when he died. "He was one of the greatest dancers who ever lived."

We're quiet for a minute. I look up to see Jacob's blue eyes searching my face. "This may seem like a weird thing to ask, but I've been wondering . . . what's it like to dedicate your entire life to one single thing? You've got to be so devoted."

I shrug. "The only way to really succeed is to give yourself completely to it. It's kind of like the Olympics, but it's every day of our lives."

"That singularity of purpose." He thinks for a moment. "You're like Captain Ahab in *Moby-Dick*, but without the whole psychotic, evil thing."

"Wow, thanks," I say. And I make a mental note to add it to my reading list.

"His one goal — to kill the white whale — drives him mad and ultimately kills him and almost the entire crew," Jacob explains.

"Oh, great. That sounds like just the kind of person I want to be."

He laughs and pulls me closer to him.

"But you know I do more than just dance," I say. "I mean, I . . ."

But then I'm at a loss. What else do I do regularly? I can't think of anything besides write in my journal. I pick up a stray dead leaf from the ledge and rip it into shreds. "Never mind. Maybe I am Ahab."

Jacob rubs his hand across my back in little circular patterns. After a few moments he turns to me, smiling. "I think you're probably a lot more attractive than Ahab."

I laugh and punch him in the arm. Lightly, but not too lightly.

"Are you hungry?" he asks, smiling.

"Starving," I tell him.

I tuck my arm through his again as we take the elevator down and pass through the halls filled with Old Master paintings. I point out a Goya I like; Jacob says he loves El Greco.

As we make our way to the lobby, he says thoughtfully, "Don't take this the wrong way, but the ballet world seems almost cultish."

I turn to him. "What do you mean?"

Jacob smiles uncertainly. "I mean, think about it. . . ." he says.

"What? Just because we're expected to behave a certain way, and we follow strict schedules and rules? I mean, we're just *disciplined*." I stare at my shoes as I stride toward the door. But then I stop and look up. "But then again, Otto does kind of reign over us. Like, his word pretty much determines the course of our lives. And we can never question him — I hardly know anyone who's even *talked* to him. So maybe you have a point."

"I didn't mean it in a bad way," Jacob says.

"Oh, you meant it in a good way?" I laugh. "Because cults have such a great reputation. Well, whatever. If we're a cult, we're a very artistic and high-minded cult."

Jacob laughs, too. "You're an *amazing* cult," he says, leading me down the Met steps.

We walk east to Lexington Avenue to catch the number 6 train downtown. The subway car is crowded, and we get separated in the crush of people. I'm wedged between a stroller and an overstuffed backpack, while Jacob is opposite me, pressed up against the door. For a minute, I wish he were more like Matt, who would never take anything but a cab — or maybe a limo. But then Jacob smiles at me from across the car, and a wave of excitement washes over me. As the train screeches along the tracks, taking us to the East Village, I feel as though Otto and the Manhattan Ballet are miles away. I feel free and light — if a little squashed.

We get out at Bleecker Street and walk to a cozy Italian restaurant on Second Street.

"This place is one of my favorites," Jacob says. "Il Posto Accanto. The name means 'the next place.'"

The room is small and dimly lit by flickering candles. A huge bouquet of flowers sits on a bar next to colorful platters of antipasti. Against the far wall, a long mirror reflects us back to ourselves, and I notice that my nose is red from the cold.

"So, I played at Gene's again last week," he says as he pulls out my chair.

"Did you sing about waffles?" I ask teasingly.

He fakes a look of indignation. "As a matter of fact, I have a new song cycle that has nothing to do with breakfast. It's all about . . ." and here he pauses, as if trying to decide whether to tell me. "It's all about dreams, actually. It sounds kind of corny, but it's not, I promise." Then he looks at me hopefully, expectantly, as if my opinion matters. It's not a look I'm used to.

"I think it sounds great," I tell him. "I can't wait to hear them." Thankfully, he says nothing about the Pete's Candy Store show that I missed, or the fact that he has sent me invitations to a dozen other shows I've failed to go see.

A pretty waitress with a tattoo of a snake on her wrist comes over to give us our menus, and I scan my options. Zoe had instructed me on the proper date ordering technique. "Pick the thing that won't make you look like you were raised by wolves," she'd said. "For instance, forget spaghetti." It seemed like good advice at the time, but I realize that with Jacob, I don't really have to worry. I bravely order salmon fettuccini.

Jacob asks for the porcini risotto and then turns to me. "And actually I wrote a song for you, too," he says.

Immediately I can feel myself flushing, and I look down. I've always wanted someone to write a song for me. (Find me a girl who hasn't!) "Really?" I almost whisper. There's a part of me that doesn't believe he means it. "What's it called?"

And now it's Jacob's turn to blush. "'Girl in a Tutu,'" he says. He looks out the window and twists his hands together nervously.

I'm *dying* to hear the song. I want to reach across the table and hold his hand, but I'm overcome with shyness. Eventually I find my voice. "I love it," I tell him.

He turns to look at me. "But you haven't heard it yet," he says, smiling.

"Well, of course I want to." My throat feels dry, so I take a sip of wine. "But so far, so good."

"I'm glad you approve," Jacob says.

"You could sing a little of it for me now," I say. Because I really have to know: What does it say about me?

"Only if you *dance* a little for me now," he responds, grinning.

I shake my head vehemently. "Never. Only if you're in the

Avery Center audience." I say this because, for one thing, ballet—unlike singing—is not something one can quietly do at one's dinner table. And for another thing, I prefer it when my audience is invisible.

"Only if you're in a tutu, you mean?" Jacob asks.

I smile. "Something like that."

His attention is momentarily diverted by the delivery of a plate of spaghetti to our neighbors. "Did I tell you about Paulo?" Jacob asks suddenly. "The spaghetti reminded me."

I shake my head.

And then Jacob begins to tell me more about the after-school program he works at in Spanish Harlem, and about a boy named Paulo who follows him around like a puppy. Paulo is always getting into trouble for one thing or another, and he seems to take great pleasure in being a source of chaos. "Once," Jacob says, "he took a piece of spaghetti he'd saved from lunch, and stuffed the entire thing up his nose."

"Ew!" I say.

Jacob holds up his hand. "Wait—it gets better. Somehow he had the one end coming out of his nose, and he got the other end coming out of his mouth, and he basically flossed the back of his throat with the noodle."

Hearing this, I let out a little snort of laughter. Embarrassed, I look around as if trying to spot the person who made that sound.

"What was that?" Jacob smiles. "I didn't take you for the snorting type." And then he reaches over to tickle me.

"I have no idea what you're talking about," I say indignantly. "It was that guy behind me!" Pretty soon I'm desperately trying to stifle my giggles and wriggling away, trying to dodge his hands. Eventually he gives up, and I catch my breath and relax in my chair. Our eyes meet. Suddenly he reaches across the table, takes my face in his hands, and leans toward me.

Oh my God, he's going to kiss me, I think. I feel a physical, almost magnetic pull toward him; I close my eyes. There is one delicious millisecond of anticipation, and then our lips touch. I feel the surprising softness of his mouth. A surge of energy rushes through my body, and I'm hot and cold at the same time. It's as if I have a fever, but the feeling is one of indescribable sweetness.

After a moment Jacob pulls away and sits back, his blue eyes glowing.

I want him to kiss me more, but now the waitress is beside our table. Her face betrays no reaction to our PDA. I suppose she's seen a lot worse in her day.

"Bread," she says. She slips a basket of steaming rosemary-studded focaccia between us and then turns and glides away.

I glance down at the bread. Suddenly I'm no longer hungry. I just want Jacob to kiss me again.

15

"Do you think Zoe's leotard is bright enough?" Bea whispers as she tries to smooth down a few red flyaways. "She looks like a highlighter."

"That's because you-know-who is teaching class this morning," I whisper back.

When Otto teaches company class, everyone—all one hundred of us—shows up. There's a mad scramble for the best positions: Who can place herself directly in Otto's line of sight? Who will be stuck in the back, a half-visible form waving her arms to be seen? Daisy stands next to the piano, where the teacher usually demonstrates, and Zoe positions herself by Lottie, whose ankle has healed. Everyone strips down to leotards and tights when Otto's around. He calls layers "garbage."

By ten thirty, we're all in our places along the barre. I'm

somewhere in the middle, next to Bea, who has wrapped her hair around her ears like Princess Leia (the look is somehow cute on her).

Even with a limp, Otto has a certain feline grace and a subtle malevolence. He is wearing tight jeans and a billowy button-down shirt, as usual. He is also carrying, as usual, a bottle of Evian. I have never seen him without one; he must drink even more water than Daisy does.

Within fifteen minutes of the start of class, I have rivulets of sweat running down my chest and soaking my pale pink leotard. My back muscles are burning, and my legs are beginning to throb. Bea's freckled brow is furrowed as she concentrates on the combination.

"Don't think, just do," Otto barks.

He doesn't want us to overintellectualize the choreography, because sometimes it's better to just take the plunge. But today my muscles ache, and I'm hyperaware of him gliding through the room, inspecting our line, our devotion. Could he be casting a new ballet? Or looking for expendable dancers? Who is getting his attention? Who's meeting his approval?

I decide to do everything I can to stand out from the horde of bodies moving in sync. During center, I position myself in front, where Daisy and Zoe usually stand. I can feel them giving me looks, but I ignore them. In the adagio, I create resistance between my limbs and control every muscle fiber as I développé into arabesque. During the promenade, I look out over my fingertips, past the colored blur of dancers staring back. In the grand allégro across the floor, I expand my movements and try to outjump not only the women but also the men.

I can only hope that Otto notices.

৶   ৶   ৶

I have five minutes to eat a banana and change my shoes before *Pas de Trois* rehearsal. I'm still breathing heavily from class when I enter the studio. Zoe's already marking through the choreography (she's been early to everything lately), and Daisy is nursing her water bottle and rolling her calf on a tennis ball. I strip off my warm-ups just as Annabelle Hayes walks in and sets her coffee on the piano. The three of us hurry to our formation. In the previous rehearsal for this ballet, I was placed in the center of the formation, with Zoe and Daisy on either side. They didn't say anything, but I could tell that Daisy and Zoe took this to mean that I was the preferred dancer.

"Let's begin from the top," Annabelle says, glancing at the pianist as she walks to the front of the studio.

Daisy and Zoe arabesque tombé away from me while I arabesque toward the front of the room. A moment later Annabelle claps her hands to halt the pianist.

"Terrible, girls! You're not watching each other," Annabelle says, frowning. She motions to the pianist and then to us. "Again."

"Terrible" means nothing — it's only an adjective. I've heard it before, and I'll hear it many more times before the season is over. But "again" is a command: It demands a response, which is complete obedience.

We step into our poses, and the pianist begins. This time I try to connect more with the other dancers.

Annabelle nods, though a frown still creases her brow. She was a corps dancer for many years, so she knows how tough it is. She tries to prepare us as best she can (despite limited rehearsal time) by making sure we know the choreography and counts, and also by drilling the ballets over and over so that we have enough stamina for the performance.

"Okay, better," Annabelle says when we're through. "I'd like to run it again from the top, but this time we'll face away from the mirror."

I think I hear Daisy sigh.

As we begin to dance, I realize how tired I am. My legs feel weighted, and I can't seem to get enough air into my lungs.

"Okay, girls, take five for water," Annabelle says, and we all sigh in relief. I go out into the hallway to catch my breath; my legs feel like they're made of jelly. Jonathan wanders by and waves at me; I lift two fingers in response, which is all I can manage. I wipe the sweat from my neck with a hand towel and lean briefly against the cool cinder-block wall.

Zoe pops her head out the studio door. "You okay out there? Annabelle says we have to run the finale."

I smile grimly at her. "I'm great," I say. "I'm ready." And somehow I make it through.

When rehearsal is over and we're gathering our things to

leave, Annabelle motions to me. "Hannah," she says, "could I please speak to you for a minute?"

But it's not really a question. And it's rarely a good thing to be called over by a ballet master or mistress, so I approach warily as I use my sweatshirt to mop my damp neck and chest. A tiny part of me hopes that she's noticed how hard I've been working. Maybe she's about to offer up a rare compliment?

Annabelle, who is tiny and birdlike and wears her hair in a short, severe bob, places her hand on the white keys of the piano and hits three high, atonal notes, *plink plink plink*. She points her thin, sharp nose at me; she's as wispy and dry as a thistle. "Hannah," she says, "you've gained weight. Something must be done about it." *Plink*. The piano sounds one more time, like a punctuation mark at the end of a sentence.

Then the room is silent. I stand there, dumbfounded and horrified. I glance over Annabelle's head to find myself in the mirror. I have to stop myself from putting my hands on my hips or covering my chest.

"Before Otto says anything," Annabelle goes on, "you must lose weight in your breasts."

"What?" I whisper.

"I don't want him to pull you from *Momentum*," she says. She purses her lips and waits for me to reply.

Momentum is a notoriously and ruthlessly exposing ballet danced in white leotards and pink tights. We are already rehearsing it.

I am speechless, so Annabelle goes on. "And if I were you, I would consider wearing an undergarment."

"An undergarment," I repeat. My cheeks are hot with embarrassment. In the wall of mirrors, my body is reflected back to me, and suddenly I can see only curves and softness.

Annabelle nods curtly as she pushes the bangs of her fine brown bob away from her forehead. She means a bra, of course, something no dancer should ever be big enough to need.

"Yes, an *undergarment*," she says. "Something to bind..." And she motions to her own nonexistent breasts. "You understand." Then she picks up her purse, nods at me once more, turns, and exits the room.

After she's gone, I can still smell the faint hint of her perfume; it smells like the lavender sachets my mother keeps in the linen closet, and the familiar scent makes my knees weak with longing. I feel like I've just been punched in the stomach.

Eventually I leave the studio, my head spinning. If anyone asks me what's wrong, I'll cry, so instead of going to the dressing room, I take the elevator down to the basement, where the costume shop is. An ugly piece of fabric serves as a door to the shop — it looks like someone shot a 1970s couch and then skinned it and hung its hide up to dry. I hurriedly brush it aside. Peering in, I see Bernadette, one of the three costume makers, and I feel like I can breathe again. She's always been so sweet to me — the opposite of Helga, the dresser. *She'll know what to do*, I tell myself.

"Hey, lady, I need your help," I say. My voice wavers as it comes out.

Bernadette, who has a kind, round face and an orangish wig that's slightly askew, looks up from the bodice of a costume.

She's sewing black piping onto maroon satin. A pile of tulle lies at her feet. "Anything, my dear." Her voice is warm and maternal.

I put my mouth right up to her ear and whisper, "Do you have anything that will make me look flatter?" I point to my chest, and my cheeks flush again.

Bernadette smiles gently. "Oh, my dear, I can do better than that. I will make something just for you. A special . . ."

She, too, seems to have a hard time saying the word *bra*. Once again, I feel like crying. But instead I just smile and touch her round shoulder. "Really? That's such a relief. I'll pay you for it, you know."

Bernadette waves away my offer. "It would be my pleasure," she says.

֍ ֍ ֍

In the privacy of my apartment that night, I inspect my body in the full-length mirror that hangs on my bedroom door. With the exception of my breasts, my body is firm and taut, even hard to the touch.

To anyone on the outside — to a *pedestrian* — I look thin and willowy, without an ounce of extraneous fat. But in the world of the Manhattan Ballet, my figure is apparently unacceptable. It's so repugnant, in fact, that Otto would keep me from performing in order to shield the audience from seeing me in a white leotard.

Bitterly, I flop down onto my bed.

After a few minutes of stewing, I pick up the phone and call Bea, but she doesn't answer.

"Bea, where are you?" I whine into the phone. "Call me." I pause. "Or don't, it's late, whatever. I'll see you tomorrow."

I flop over on the bed and bury my face in my pillow. I knew that the Manhattan Ballet body standards were strict, but I never thought I'd be pulled aside for getting breasts. I mean, I *had* to go through puberty eventually; it's a biological necessity!

But the *reason* for weight gain doesn't matter to Otto; only the fact of it does.

Am I supposed to diet now? It's not like I eat bonbons all day: I eat small meals of protein-packed, high-energy foods, and I drink gallons of water. What is there to cut out?

I don't know, but I have to figure out something, because *Momentum* goes on in only a week and a half.

16

"It's just the same old crap," Bea says, hurling her leg warmers into her theater case.

"Tell me about it," I say. It's February, and Sammy Gordon, the Manhattan Ballet office manager, has just posted another winter season casting, and we're all dancing the same corps roles we've done for three years now, along with the apprentices and first-year corps members.

My stomach rumbles, and I take a giant bite of my apple. I skipped breakfast, but then in rehearsal for *La Mer* I started shaking.

"What do I need to do to get them to pay attention to me? Should I wear neon lights around my wrists and ankles?" Bea asks, her freckled face nearly white with anger.

"Well, there are always other parts later in the season," I say. I'm trying to be philosophical about it, even though I feel demoralized. "I mean, they'll post another casting in a week or two."

Bea scowls as she twists her hair into Pippi Longstocking braids. "You're right. But still. Why am I dancing with Daisy? No offense, Daze."

Daisy thinks about this for a moment. "I know I'm young," she says. "But I want better parts, too, you know." She reaches into her backpack and pulls out a bag of Doritos and holds them tightly in her tiny fist. She glares at the nutritional information on the package and then looks up at us. "I'm going to go call Dr. Shapiro," she says.

She leaves, letting the door slam behind her.

Abruptly, I stand up and face Bea. "Do I look like I've gained weight?" I ask.

"What, are you insane? You're gorgeous, Hannah," Bea says, fastening a braid with an elastic.

I poke her knee with my toe. "You're not even looking at me."

She lifts her head and smiles. "Okay, now I am."

"Listen," I say. "Annabelle said Otto might pull me from *Momentum* if I don't lose weight in my breasts." I feel like I'm going to cry just saying the words aloud. "That's why I called last night."

"That's absurd!" Bea yells, and I shush her, even though no one else is in the room. "But come on," she says, her voice quieter now. "It's not like you're a Scores dancer or whatever."

Bea is right, of course: I'm hardly huge. But all my friends are small enough to wear halter tops or training bras, and suddenly I need a special contraption to mash my boobs against my rib cage.

131

I rip out my ponytail holder in frustration and toss it onto the counter. "She told me to lose weight in my breasts! How is that physically possible? Oh, I'll just direct the calories like a traffic cop toward my extremities and shoo them away from my chest?" Tears start rolling down my cheeks.

"Well, you do look curvier than you used to," Zoe says as she appears in the doorway. She clasps a pack of cigarettes in one hand and a Diet Coke in the other.

"Wow, thanks, Zoe," I say. "Your support is really meaningful to me." I hate that she overheard this conversation.

"You should try cutting out wheat," she says. "Or you can take up smoking. I'm heading up to the roof. Want to come? Or you, Bea?"

Both Bea and I shake our heads. "No way," Bea says.

When Zoe's gone, I turn to Bea. "Seriously, do I look fatter to you?"

She shakes her head vehemently. "Don't be ridiculous. You have a beautiful figure," she says. After a moment she picks up *Life & Style Weekly*, which Daisy left on her chair. "Oh deary. Britney has made another tragic fashion mistake."

I want to hug her and kick her at the same time, for trying to make me feel better and for lying to me.

လ လ လ

A few days later, I find a little, unmarked brown-paper bag at my dressing room spot. Inside is a nude bra constructed of a tightly woven, thick mesh fabric. I take it into the bathroom stall with me because I don't want the girls to know that I need such a thing.

The door in front of me is Daisy's Bad Plastic Surgery Wall, and taped to it are dozens of pictures of Hollywood celebrities, each of them — with the help of expensive plastic surgeons — trying to be bustier than the next. The irony of my own position vis-à-vis big breasts is not lost on me. I glare at Heidi Montag as I shrug into the bra and then pull up my leotard.

Back in the dressing room, I stand in front of the mirror. The bra is perfect. Virtually invisible underneath my workout clothes, it holds my breasts close to my body. I don't look *flat*, but I look *flatter*. I'll be able to wear it during class and rehearsals, and under costumes as long as it doesn't show. I sigh with relief and sink down into my chair.

Just then my phone rings.

"So, you ready to see that Fellini movie tomorrow?" Jacob asks. "I've been working on my Italian verbs."

My heart does a little leap when I hear his voice — but then it sinks when I realize what I have to tell him.

"Jacob, I actually can't make it anymore," I say. "I'm so sorry. It got crazy around here again." *Because I have to lose weight in my breasts*, I think. And then I get this crazy image of a pair of boobs on a treadmill, which almost makes me laugh but then makes me depressed all over again.

"You know, you're making me feel like a reject," Jacob says. There's a humorous note in his voice, but I can tell he's confused.

I clutch the phone to my cheek as I search for my water

bottle in the bowels of my dance bag. "I have to prepare for this upcoming ballet. It's kind of a big deal," I say.

I can't explain to him the sudden importance of taking Pilates and Bikram yoga during my break and then spending an hour on the elliptical at the gym before the performance tonight, because it makes me sound pathological. Especially to a guy whose only real commitments are four college classes a week and a part-time work-study job.

"Okay, I can take a hint," he says.

"It's really not about you," I say earnestly. "There's no hint to be taken."

I locate my water bottle and take a swig. With my other hand I'm clutching the phone, as if squeezing the life out of it will somehow make Jacob understand why I'm saying what I'm saying. And I don't want to have this thought, but I do: *If I were dating another dancer, none of this would be an issue. Or* — and this is Zoe's voice I hear — *if you were dating Matt.*

"I thought we had a nice time the other week. What's with the mixed messages?"

"You think I *want* to bail on you? Because it's actually hard for me."

Jacob scoffs. "Yeah, I can tell you're really broken up about it."

"I am. Give me a break, okay?" I plead.

"My friends have been telling me that I should give up on you, and I'm starting to think they might be right. Maybe I should just try hanging out with someone from NYU. Someone with more time . . ."

"Jacob, listen, in another week or two, things will slow down a little," I tell him. "Then we'll see each other. We'll totally watch *8½*, or any Fellini movie you want."

"Okay, okay," he says. He still sounds irritated, though, and I understand why.

I'd be irritated, too, if I were him.

17

During my afternoon break, I take the elevator down to the darkened stage to find the sweatshirt I left there after a rehearsal. I'm in a hurry, and I almost don't see Mai standing at the front of the stage, wearing a white spaghetti-strap leotard and a pale gray chiffon skirt, moving her arms in a graceful arc.

Mai is the rock star of the Manhattan Ballet. Not the *star* star, but the rock star: She has that wildness, that edge. She also has the longest, blackest hair I've ever seen, and if you passed her on the street, you might think she was a twelve-year-old girl whose mother had something against hair salons. But she's absolutely stunning onstage. Luminescent. Her pale skin almost seems to glow in the spotlight.

Mai is incredibly thin, and Otto uses her as the model for the ideal ballerina body. I've heard that she eats only once a day, and then only white foods. As I look at her, I can believe the rumors, even though I don't want to.

I watch her begin to dance. She must think she's alone. She lifts her arms and then falls out of a turn. She does that a lot, actually. She's sloppy but totally fearless, and I admire that bravery. After all, sometimes I feel scared of just about everything; that's probably why I've always been scared to break any rule. For me, it's always been easier just to do as I'm told.

I hear a noise behind me and turn to see Zoe approaching with two big steaming cups of coffee.

She smiles and hands one to me. "Jonathan ran out to Starbucks, so I had him get us some."

"Thanks," I say, taking a grateful sip. I don't know how any of us would function without caffeine.

"What's Mai doing out there?" Zoe asks, wrinkling her upturned nose.

Mai does a complicated fouetté sequence. "The solo from *Tschaikovsky Pas de Deux*, looks like."

"She's like an overcooked noodle, all floppy."

I smile. "She's better than that and you know it."

Zoe sighs. "I know. I'm just jealous she gets to dance that part."

It's rare for Zoe to admit any sort of vulnerability, so it's sort of comforting to hear that. We watch for a while in companionable silence until my stomach growls loudly and I remember that I still haven't eaten.

"Oh crap, I forgot to eat," I say, the near panic apparent in my voice. Matt's out of town, so I can't hope for one of his surprise gourmet lunches.

Zoe puts a hand on my shoulder. "Chill, lady. I've got an extra yogurt and a banana upstairs that Gladys packed."

This sparks a tiny flare of suspicion—why is Zoe being so extra nice? Does she want something from me? Is it because she feels sorry for me for having breasts? But I'm too hungry to pay much attention to my suspicion, and so we leave Mai to her solitary dancing and go up to the dressing room, where Zoe feeds me lunch prepared by her housekeeper.

"Do you think Mai ever wishes she had a life outside the theater?" I ask. "I mean, it's her break right now, and she's not even taking it."

"What, you think she should take this opportunity to read *Frankenstein*? Or go on some environmental reading kick like your crush? She's a dancer, Hannah. She *dances*."

I swirl the spoon around in the yogurt. "Yeah, but sometimes I just wish there was time for other things."

Zoe pulls a pair of black knit shorts over her tights and shiny purple leotard. "Remember what Annabelle said." Then she does her best Annabelle impression: She somehow manages to fold into herself so that she seems much smaller, and she squints her eyes. The expression on her face suggests she's just smelled something very unpleasant. Her voice comes out high and clipped. "'A dancer's job is not to live, stupid girl. A dancer's job is to do tendus until she drops!'"

I laugh, but the impression's so uncanny that it gives me goose bumps.

℘   ℘   ℘

As part of my new fitness regime, I talk Bea into coming to Bikram yoga with me, even though she thinks the practice is gross because of all the sweating. In Bikram, the room is heated to over one hundred degrees, and classes take place in front of a wall of mirrors. It's one of the most intense forms of exercise I know, and I hope that it will help me get back the body I used to have.

As we enter the studio and unfurl our mats, I point to the front of the room where Taylor, the instructor, is waiting for everyone to get settled. Taylor has black hair, deep blue eyes, and the kind of strong, masculine jawline you see in cologne advertisements. He also likes to wear tiny shorts that show off his muscular legs. Bea winks at me and lifts an eyebrow. I point at her and mouth, *He's all yours!* Bea then blushes and drops into lotus position. She refuses to look at me or at Taylor until class begins.

After ten minutes of bending and balancing in seemingly impossible ways, I feel sweat running down the back of my neck and my legs and onto my mat. Taylor wanders through the room, offering friendly encouragement ("Breathe through the pain; it will make you stronger") and indecipherable yoga philosophy ("Remember that the tourniquet effect encourages blood flow and opens up new pathways of thought and consciousness"). By the time class is over, I'm nearly nauseated with exhaustion.

"I feel wrung out," I tell Bea as we rinse off in the showers. "Like an old towel."

"You certainly smell like an old towel," she says, laughing.

She's beet red from the exertion, while I've turned pale and splotchy. But I know this is good for me. Another few weeks of this is all I need.

That night I fall asleep on my couch and dream that Otto comes at me with a knife. He tells me in cool, reasonable tones that he is going to cut off my breasts. "You will dance so much better without them," he whispers. He flicks off the light, but I can still see the knife glinting as he walks toward me. I wake in a pool of sweat.

The next day, before company class, I go to the gym again and work out twice as hard. The gym scale tells me I weigh two pounds less.

18

"Can I take a picture?" Matilda, Harry's daughter, asks. She holds up a pink digital camera covered in stickers and points it at me hopefully.

I still have a few minutes before I have to go on for *Rhyme, Not Reason*, so I pause on my way to the wings. "Sure. How about one of me and your dad?" I ask.

Harry appears out of the shadows and reaches for the camera. "Better yet, how about one of Mattie and Hannah?"

Matilda nods wordlessly and steps delicately over a pile of cords to stand by me. Then her little warm hand snakes its way into mine, and we stand side by side as her dad takes our picture. Mattie is wearing her ratty tutu and sneakers again; I'm in a blue-gray leotard with a chiffon skirt.

"Great," Harry says. "Just great. My two ballerinas."

"Thank you," Matilda whispers to me.

"No problem," I whisper back.

And then I hear the intro to my music, so I wave as I hurry to the wings. There, Adriana is tapping her bony fingers against the wall, counting out her entrance. She marches out, and then four counts later I follow her into the white lights of the stage.

Rhyme is set to Chopin, with choreography inspired by the interplay between shadow and light. The corps wears shades of gray, and the principals wear stark white, so they appear to glow against the black backdrop. The shadowy lighting accentuates our muscles; the piano's tune is lilting and melancholy. I imagine that it's dusk, when the shadows are soft and long. Those of us in the corps are the shadows, and the principals are the lingering sunshine that bounces off the buildings in bright, fleeting bursts.

I love ballets like *Rhyme*, ones with simple costumes and almost no scenery. I like to feel as though my body is unrestricted and free, and to imagine that I'm performing outside under the sky.

When the ballet is over, I linger for a moment in the wings, breathless.

"Lovely," Harry says, passing by with Matilda in his arms. "Just lovely."

I smile because I had a great time out there. Maybe it's the Bikram, and maybe it's the bra, but who cares? I feel confident and strong, and that's what matters.

Harry stops and turns back. "I'd love to see you in some solos soon, okay?"

There's another casting coming up, and I've been killing myself to be noticed.

"Me too," I tell him. "Me too."

෯ ෯ ෯

Matt calls me the next morning as I'm getting ready to leave for the theater.

"I'm back!" he says. "I was in France. Paris, then Normandy."

"Don't you ever work?" I ask, trying to get my coat and scarf on without dropping the phone.

Matt laughs, but it has sort of a hollow ring to it. "For your information, I was scoping out companies for my dad's investment sideline. So, yes, I work."

"Well, welcome home. I hope it was fun." The other line beeps—it's Zoe, no doubt reminding me to bring her the leotard I borrowed—but I let it go to voice mail. "I missed your lunch deliveries."

"Have you read Proust?" Matt asks.

I laugh as I slip on my boots. Proust is on my reading list, but I don't exactly have time for a 650-page novel these days. "No," I tell him. "I haven't even had time to buy groceries."

"Well, don't consider it a character flaw; very few people have. *Remembrance of Things Past* is a masterpiece, though, and it basically killed Proust to write it. But that's not my point. My point is that, in *Swann's Way*, which is the first volume, the narrator falls in love with a woman simply because one night he can't find her and doesn't know where she is. It's the oldest trick in the book."

"Oh, really?" I say. I'm not sure where Matt is going with this, so as I fumble for my keys, I wait for him to continue.

"I figured that if I made myself scarce, my charms would only come to seem more charming." His tone is slightly self-deprecating, but not *that* self-deprecating.

"Interesting strategy," I say, laughing a little. It hadn't exactly worked, but I'd heard worse theories about romance. For instance, Jonathan's belief that he could win over cute, blond Tommy Hatfield by feigning complete indifference to him. (I kept telling him he had to at *least* say hi to Tommy, but he wouldn't do it, and now Tommy's dating Jude Forrester, who, if you ask me, dances as though he's constipated.)

"And did I tell you about dinner?" Matt asks.

I give myself one last glance in the mirror before I step into the hall. I have a bad case of bedhead, but since I'll be putting my hair in a bun the moment I get to the theater, I suppose it doesn't matter much. "What about dinner?" I ask.

"I'm taking you," he says. "Tomorrow night."

"Really?" I say, taken aback. "Did you want to check with me about that first?"

He laughs. "I know what you need, and that's a break. I'll meet you outside the theater at eleven."

"I don't think I can —"

"If you try to tell me that you can't, I'll simply kidnap you."

I can hear that dazzling smile of his in his voice. He's just so certain I'll say yes.

And I surprise myself when I do. My reasons for accepting aren't entirely clear to me, and honestly I don't feel like figuring them out. Sometimes you just want to say yes. As Otto always says, "Don't think, just do."

So that's how I've ended up at Per Se, which is one of the most expensive restaurants in Manhattan, decked out in my black vintage Marni dress with my patent-leather wedge Mary Janes. Across the table from me, Matt is pouring wine into my glass and telling me that I would love this couple he's friends with in France because I am a free spirit like them. He says he can see me racing down the highway in a Jaguar with a scarf trailing behind me, the ocean on one side and the French hills on the other.

While I don't want to be rude, I'm forced to point out that this is a ridiculous cliché. "I've seen that in about six movies," I tell him, taking a sip of the wine. It tastes like pears and honey, and I decide to drain my glass as quickly as possible. Maybe it'll make me feel less jittery.

He laughs. "All right, so you're saying I need to try a little harder to impress you."

I nod, hoping to project the confidence I don't entirely feel. "Probably. Although this salad is impressing me." Which it had better, I think, considering it cost *forty dollars*. According to the menu, it has ramp top "subric," Oregon morel mushrooms, and "émincée" of green almonds and roquette. I don't know what most of that means, but it's delicious.

"I like that you're one of the dancers who isn't afraid of food," Matt says as he spreads a slice of thick-crusted bread with

French butter. The white button-down he's wearing accentuates his tan, which he probably acquired on some gorgeous Ibiza beach.

I give him a stern look. "Do you take a lot of dancers out to dinner?"

He clears his throat and for a moment looks slightly uncomfortable. "Well, I do go to a lot of holiday parties," he says. "You know, for the ballet."

"I'm only kidding you," I say. "You should take as many dancers out to dinner as possible. We poor girls live on Bugles and tuna fish."

He laughs. "Oh, but I only want to take *you*," he says.

He watches me consume my salad as he plays the part of the gracious host: pouring me wine as fast as I can drink it, asking me if I want more bread or another bottle of San Pellegrino. And it feels nice to have someone taking care of me for a little while. Matt makes lighthearted conversation as he slices into his entrée, which is squab or game hen or some other small, helpless bird. I try not to look at its sad little carcass on his sparkling china plate.

"You'd also love this little town down in the south of France," he says. "It has the most incredible view of . . ."

In a way, what he's saying hardly matters, and he knows it. It's as if he can tell that I'm exhausted from the performance and that I don't have much juice left for conversation. I'd like to give him points for being perceptive, but if he's really dated as many dancers as Daisy says he has, then he'd have to know how we feel at the end of a night.

He's funnier than I thought, though, and he likes books, too. He's on an Ernest Hemingway kick, he tells me. He read *The Sun Also Rises* last week and *For Whom the Bell Tolls* the week before. On weekends he reads P. G. Wodehouse, whom he swears is a comedic genius. I write this down in my notebook so I can remember the name the next time I'm at a bookstore, which probably won't be until summer break.

"What's the last good book you read?" he asks.

I poke at a piece of brightly colored radicchio. "Well, I've been working on *Frankenstein* since, like, August. Does *People* magazine count?" I say wryly. (I don't mention that I just ordered *Moby-Dick* from Amazon.)

"Well, it's not like you're some illiterate. You like to scribble in that notebook," Matt says, eyeing it. "What do you write? I'll bet there are lots of juicy secrets in there." He makes a move as if to take it from me, and I snatch it away.

"Over my dead body," I say. I'd stab him with my butter knife before I'd let him touch it.

He laughs. "But I just want to get to know you better." His dark eyes flash with amusement.

I shrug. "I'm sure you'll come up with other ways."

He's still chuckling as he shakes his head. "Yeah, I suppose I could. Maybe next week we could check out Marea. I heard it's awesome."

As I eat my ridiculously expensive salad, I wonder if it makes sense for me to be with someone like Matt. There'd be no need for awkward explanations about why I have to cancel plans. I'd be able to complain about Jason Pite's obsession with pelvic release or Otto's epic adagio combinations without having to explain the dance terms. And I'd get a lot of nice dinners, lots of very elegant salads, out of it.

But maybe I shouldn't worry about Matt *or* Jacob. Being alone might be easiest. Annabelle Hayes would certainly say so.

I picture her narrow, pinched face, her small, unforgiving mouth. *Your job is not to live. Your job is to dance.*

19

Two weeks pass in a blur of rehearsals, performances, and extra yoga classes. I push myself all day long, and then at night I lie in bed and visualize myself dancing solos. And I know I'm getting stronger: I used to be nearly dead after the third movement of *Prelude*, and now I can dance the whole thing and barely break a sweat.

But then in early March, when I go to check the new casting sheet, I hardly see my name at all. My breath catches in my throat. I'm not called to learn any of the solos in *Sleeping Beauty* or *The Fawn*, Otto's new ballet. In fact, my parts are even worse than last year.

But Zoe got a solo in *The Fawn*.

I walk the hallways in a fog of disillusionment, my legs still wobbly from the morning's rehearsal. "Earth to Hannah," Jonathan says, waving his hand in front of my face. I notice that he's painted his nails a barely perceptible pink. "Hannah, I said do you want to go to the deli with us?" But I duck my head and keep walking.

"Wonder what her problem is," I hear Luke say.

"God knows," Adriana leans into Luke and gives him a little kiss with her thin red lips.

I guess that means they're dating now.

Jonathan giggles as he wraps a cashmere scarf around his neck. "She's got PMS. We're on the same cycle, you know."

And I can't even smile.

For a while I sit by the laundry machines, listening to the sound of the dryers. A few people come up to get Cokes, but no one says anything to me. No one even seems to look my way.

When I first became a corps member, Otto regularly had me demonstrate during company class, and once he told me that he admired my work ethic. He never *promised* me anything, but I always thought that he saw potential in me. And I've tried so hard to impress him — always, but these last months especially. Night after night, after a full day of rehearsal and then performances at night, I'd collapse into bed, exhausted but incredibly happy, because I knew that I had lived that day.

But today the very same routine makes me feel invisible and expendable.

"I wish they'd just put me out of my misery," I mutter as I walk into the empty dressing room.

Leni pops up from her mat on the floor, blinking as if startled. She's wearing navy sweatpants and a delicate cream camisole, and her blond hair is mussed and sticking up on one side.

"You shouldn't say things like that, Hannah," she says, brushing the tangled strands out of her eyes.

"Where did you come from?" I ask dully.

"I fell asleep doing my spinal series on the floor. They're so relaxing." Her cheek has the imprint of her rubber mat on it.

I put my head in my hands.

"What?" she asks.

"Casting," I say dully.

She sighs. "Right."

"It all just feels utterly *pointless*. Why do we work so hard to get strong, to improve, if no one cares or notices?" *I even lost weight*, I think, *just as Annabelle wanted!*

Leni comes over to put her hand on my shoulder. She rubs the hard, tight muscles there for a while before she speaks. "I know it's tough, I know. But you have to enjoy the moment. You must embrace the process of dance. How do you think I kept with this for fifteen years?"

The process of dance. She sounds like my hippie-dippie mother, with her whole "journey of creativity" trip. I push my fists into my eyeballs because I think it might help me not cry. "I thought that I loved all of it — the grueling rehearsals, the intensity, and the long hours and everything. But if I'm still doing the same parts that I did as an apprentice . . ." I trail off. I can feel my eyes fill with tears despite the knuckles I've wedged into them.

"I know how it feels. I did the Garland Dance in *Sleeping Beauty* for five years," Leni says.

I look up at her. "Are you serious?"

She nods as she digs her thumb into a sore spot near my neck. "And I did Snow and Flowers in *The Nutcracker* for eight."

"You're a better person than I am," I say.

She pats my shoulder and moves back toward her mat. "I don't know what else I would do if I didn't dance."

"I don't either," I cry, "but there are other possibilities out there! I mean, this theater is *not* the entire world, contrary to what most people around here seem to think. There are museums and restaurants . . . and rock shows, or so I hear."

Leni sits down, stretches her legs out in front of her, and reaches down to cup the balls of her feet in her hands. "The point is to love dancing. And once you stop loving it, it's time to do something else. It's just too hard otherwise."

"I love being onstage. But it's so painful feeling invisible," I tell her.

"I see you, *Balletttänzerin*," she says softly. "You are not invisible."

But I must be—how else can I explain the way I was overlooked?

20

"It's just too much," Zoe says, twisting her pale gold hair around her fingers. She's barefoot, wearing pink cutoff tights and a soft blue T-shirt, and she's sitting in my chair with her feet up against my mirror, talking to Daisy, who looks both awed and jealous. "After the pas de deux, my calves feel like they are going to rip. Then I go straight into the solo with no break. I mean, the solo itself is nearly impossible. It's like Otto's testing me or something."

Daisy shoves a handful of Doritos into her mouth. The tips of her fingers are bright orange. Since the last casting was posted, Daisy's consumption of junk food has been in overdrive.

"Do you mind?" I say.

Zoe looks up and lethargically removes her feet one by one, then returns to her spot on the other side of the dressing room. She goes on, undeterred by her displacement. "I mean, it's all jumps for what feels like forever. You go pas de chat, then grand jeté, pas de chat, then you open out into high kicks, then these chaîné turns, then all these coupé-jeté things. . . ."

"Blah-blah-blah," I mouth, and Daisy stifles a giggle. Zoe is oblivious; she goes on blabbing. She reminds me of my junior high history teacher, Mr. Schmidt. He never noticed that no one, and I mean *no one*, was listening to him.

I take out my notebook and start doodling in the margins. At least Mr. Schmidt had *facts* to impart — Zoe is just bragging but disguising it as a list of complaints.

"Has anyone seen Bea lately?" I ask, interrupting Zoe's catalog of dance steps. "She has my leggings." I'm wearing green sweatpants that I want to change; my shirt is green, too, and together they're making me feel like Oscar the Grouch.

"Not me," Daisy says. "She might be in the Green Room already. She's in the first ballet."

To get away from hearing Zoe brag about her great new part, I decide to watch the beginning of *The Thorn*, the first ballet, from the flies. The scaffolding of the flies forms a U above the stage; it allows the stagehands to pull the appropriate ropes and direct the spotlights from above.

In my opinion, it's the best seat in the house. Because it's basically a bird's-eye view, you can see the kaleidoscopic formations of the dancers and the way they call and respond to one another. You can see how their movements have a logic as well as beauty; it's like a secret language of lines and angles and shapes.

Harry has a small wooden desk on the right side of the flies. A green-shaded banker's lamp arches over his lighting charts, his scrim schedules, and whatever paperback novel he happens to be reading.

When he sees me, he looks up, and his bifocals slide down his nose.

"Hannah!" he whispers. "Let me get you a chair."

"Oh, it's fine, I'll stand. I've got to go soon; I have to finish my makeup."

Harry waves down to the dancers on the stage. "This piece is a total bore. Lottie gets carried around like luggage the entire time. The Bach is terrific, though."

I look over the railing and see the way the corps, wearing pristine white tutus, move in unison as Sam drags Lottie downstage. "Yeah," I say with a sigh.

"You okay?" he asks.

I shrug and bite my lip.

"Mattie's been asking about you."

"Really? Tell her I said hi."

"She wants you to come to her performance, but I told her you're too busy. She's going to be an elf princess or something. Seems like every week the wife's got to sew a new costume."

"She'll be so cute," I say, watching Bea's buoyant hops on pointe below me.

"So, how's company life?" Harry asks.

I gaze down at my pointe shoes. "Do you want the real answer or the polite one?"

"I'm a tough guy. Do I look like I care about polite?" he responds. Teasingly, he makes a fist and flexes his forearm. It's the size of a Christmas ham.

"Yeah, I'm not doing that great," I say, digging my fingernail into my thigh. I should be warming up, not talking. I'm on after intermission, and I need to give myself a barre and stretch my hips.

"Didn't get the roles you wanted." This isn't a question; Harry knows what's going on.

"No." I pull at a string on my sleeve. "It's just so frustrating. I don't know why I work so hard if nothing seems to happen."

Harry exhales and pushes his glasses up on his forehead. "I don't get it either, Hannah. I've seen a lot of girls come and go in this place, and there's no question in my mind that your talents are being overlooked."

I shake my head and kick my foot against the railing.

"What is it that you want, Hannah?" Harry asks gently.

I sigh. "I don't know, some indication that it's all worth it?"

I glance down over the railing at the ballet unfolding beneath us. The pizzicato pluck of the violins is joined by the drone of the cello as Sam lifts Lottie in an overhead press. The excitement builds, and the tempo picks up as the dance nears its finale.

Harry nods. "A little validation."

"Imagine if I asked Otto for some validation," I say. "Man, would he look at me funny!"

Harry shrugs. "My whole *life* people have been looking at me funny. I look funny at them right back." And then he furrows his brow, widens his eyes, puffs out his cheeks, and pushes his ears forward.

"Oh my God!" I exclaim, laughing. "You look like a *chimpanzee*."

Harry's face returns to normal. "Exactly." He slaps his hand on the top of his desk. "The point is, don't let the bastards get you down. You know what you need to do."

I glance down one more time at the ballet unfolding beneath us. It's time for me to get ready. "Thanks, Harry," I say. "I feel a little better."

"Anytime, sugar," he says. "Now go get 'em."

21

The next day Zoe comes over to me after the run-through of *Stormy Melody*. She steps right in my way as I'm heading to the vending machine.

"You've been ignoring me ever since casting was posted," she says. Her green eyes stare right into mine, and her nose is just inches away.

I sigh and look up at the ceiling. "That's because you've been insufferable," I tell her. I try to get past her, but she reaches for my arm and gives it a little squeeze.

"I know, and I'm sorry," she says. "I really am."

For once she sounds like she actually means her apology. "Really?" I say. I still have my doubts.

Her brow furrows prettily, and she makes a pouty face. "I've just had a lot going on lately. I can tell you're upset with me."

"It's actually not about you, believe it or not," I tell her.

"Oh, Han," she says. "I know I can be a total ass. But you mean so much to me. We're still friends, right?" She leans her head on my shoulder. I can smell her expensive, lily-scented shampoo.

And the truth is I do care about her. We've been friends for five years. We got our apprenticeships together, we bought tampons together for the first time, we had our first underage drinks together. And even if we stopped speaking tomorrow, I'll always be grateful for the way Zoe befriended me in those first weeks at the MBA. I might have died of loneliness without her.

But she doesn't wait for my answer. "Anyway," she goes on, "I should be a tiny bit mad at *you*." She squeezes my arm and grins.

"Oh really? What for?"

"It's March tenth — my birthday," Zoe says, "and you and everyone else totally forgot."

"Oh!" I pull her to me so I can guiltily hug her; Zoe always remembers my birthday, even though it happens during our summer break. "Happy birthday!"

"Twenty years old," Zoe says into my shoulder. "Can you believe it?"

I step back and look at her. "You don't look a day over sixteen," I say. "What are we doing to celebrate?"

"I don't know. Drinks? Do you have any good ideas?"

I thought about the text I'd gotten from Jacob: *Prove you're not chained to that theater. NYU party in Wmsburg, 675 Bedford Ave.*

I could go and surprise him. I just hope he won't die from

the shock. "We'll go to Brooklyn after the performance," I say. "There's a party that sounds pretty cool."

I figure there's no use moping around. Maybe a little distraction will do me good. Of course, I can imagine Otto's displeasure if he found out that two of his dancers were planning such a field trip. But at this particular moment, I don't feel that I owe him anything.

ھ ھ ھ

A strung-out-looking teenager asks us for spare change as we climb the gum-covered stairs from the L train platform. I cling to Zoe with one arm; the other I shove into the pocket of my leopard coat to keep warm as we teeter along the cracked pavement in our heels. Zoe is close to six feet tall in her Manolos, and she giggles as she stumbles and rolls over her ankle.

"Oh my God, be careful," I cry, picturing a torn Achilles or a shattered metatarsal.

"I'm fine," Zoe says. "In fact, I'm great!"

"You're drunk is what you are," I say.

Zoe holds up her thumb and forefinger half an inch apart. "Just a *little tiny bit*," she says, purposely slurring her words. (She drank most of a bottle of wine at my apartment.)

As we approach the address Jacob gave me, I can feel the sidewalk vibrating from the bass.

"This is going to be good," Zoe howls at a streetlight.

The building looks like an old factory — a place where tires or refrigerators were once made. A large garage door opens and slides along the ceiling, and a woman ducks out to greet us. She's got a cup of some fluorescent green cocktail in her hand. "Hey, guys! Grab some paint," she yells over the music.

Zoe and I look at each other in confusion. "Did she say grab some paint?" I ask. "And who is that, anyway?"

Zoe shrugs as we enter. The room looks sort of like an old loading dock, with a cement floor and dingy cinder-block walls covered with graffiti. Inside, the music is even more deafening.

I stop a guy passing by with a foamy beer. "Hey, have you seen Jacob Cohen?"

"Who?" he yells back.

"Jacob Cohen!"

"Ah, I don't know. But look, we got Girl Talk," he yells. "Right over there!" He points to a slightly scruffy but good-looking guy who's sporting a faded T-shirt and designer jeans and spinning records on a mounted plywood bridge overlooking the party.

I scan the space for Jacob. Posters for old rock shows hang on the walls, and empty bottles of beer litter the floor. The bathroom—for which there's already a huge line—is partitioned off by a sheet and a large piece of plywood. There's a couple making out near a recycling bin, and a guy in a Nirvana T-shirt blowing smoke rings up to the ceiling.

"Where do I put my coat? Doesn't this place have a housekeeper?" Zoe yells to me. Then she nudges me in the ribs to make sure I know she's joking.

We walk toward the center of the loft, where there's a

pulsating mob of people dancing. They look strange and other-worldly, and for a second I can't figure out why.

"What are they wearing?" Zoe screams in my ear.

I look more closely and realize that they're covered in fluo-rescent paint. They're holding buckets and cups of it, and they're pouring it all over one another. Paint drips down their arms, turning them brilliant yellow and lime green. I see one girl wearing nothing but her underwear and splashes of chartreuse paint.

"What the hell?" Zoe hollers.

"I guess it's creative expression," I yell. "Like, if Jackson Pol-lock did a lot of acid and then had, like, a birthday party in a fix-it shop . . ."

Zoe points to the drinks table, which is stocked with giant plastic bottles of vodka and gin. "That's all fine and good," she says, "but where's the Ketel One?"

"Try not to be a snob, just for a little bit," I cry. I pour us drinks of slightly flat club soda and cheap vodka. "Look, they have lemons for garnish, at least."

We toss our coats onto a pile in the corner and clutch our vodka sodas. They don't taste very good, so I drink mine quickly. A little voice in my head warns me that I'm going to pay for this tomorrow, but I don't care.

"No way am I going in there," Zoe yells, pointing at the seething mass of paint-splattered dancers. "My dress is from Barneys."

As Girl Talk mixes Beyoncé's "Single Ladies (Put a Ring on It)" with the Brazilian Girls' "Don't Stop," the crowd whoops and jumps in a rhythmic, pulsing cluster. The music is so loud I swear I can feel it in my bones, and almost involuntarily I start to bounce a little to the beat. The funny thing is that I'm embarrassed to dance in a situation like this; I don't know how to do it like a normal person. I'm used to having everything choreographed for me, not all improvisational and loose. Some dancers I know are really good at party-dancing, but I fall at the self-conscious and awkward end of things.

Zoe still looks haughty and slightly on edge, and she shakes her head as I tug on her hand. I pause for a second, and then grab a bottle of bright pink paint and squirt out streams over the dancers. They rub it all over one another with their open palms, and the paint oozes through their fingers and drips down their arms.

As I watch them writhe and leap, it occurs to me that I have the entire East River between myself and the Manhattan Ballet. The feeling is thrilling.

For a moment I think of all my classmates back in Weston, Massachusetts, kids who spent the last four years going to parties and hooking up and laughing while I was sweating and rehearsing and dedicating myself, body and soul, to dance. I don't suppose I can really make up for lost time tonight, but I can at least join in the fun.

I kick off my ankle boots and squeeze my way into the center of the mob. The closer I get to the center, the more paint I accumulate: orange, green, blue, violet. My James jeans will never be the same, and thank goodness I'm only wearing a wife-beater for a shirt. I have streaks on my arms, splotches on my stomach — I look like a rainbow on drugs. I beckon to Zoe, who shakes her head as she nurses her vodka against the wall. *No way,* she mouths.

"Oh, relax," I yell. "It's your birthday!" Then I run over and take her by the hand and pull her toward the mob of painted dancers. I grin slyly. "It's not like you can't afford another dress like that!"

"Oh, fine, you win!" she yells, smiling back. She grabs a bottle of yellow paint and squirts it onto my chest. I respond by pouring a cup of hot pink onto her. And we dance wildly, crazily, covered in paint. There's nothing graceful about the way we move at all. People step on my feet and crash into me; a girl stumbles and falls into a puddle of green. I'm not counting the beats or worrying about what steps come next — I'm just flinging myself into the dance. My heart pounds, and my rib cage rattles from the bass.

From out of the crowd, a striking, dark-skinned guy with dreads almost down to his waist materializes. Wearing only boxers and a paint-splattered gray T-shirt, he bounces over to Zoe. He touches her arm, and she whirls around.

"Oh, hi! Where did you come from?" she yells, looking longingly at his muscular chest. He responds by pulling her to him.

"Um, excuse me?" I tap him on his enormous shoulder. I don't want to shout at him, but there's no other way to be heard. "Hi, uh, do you know Jacob Cohen?"

Dreadlocks Guy nods. "Yeah, you missed him," he says, voice booming. "He ducked out, like, twenty minutes ago." Then he turns back to Zoe, who has an expression on her face like she's just opened a truly fantastic present.

"Happy birthday to me!" she screams, grinning wildly. "Happy fucking birthday to *me!*" Then she lifts up her arms and yells, "Bombs away," and the paint comes pouring down on us, coloring us, making us indistinguishable from everyone else.

"That's what I'm talkin' about," hollers Dreadlocks Guy.

"*Vive les* pedestrians!" Zoe shrieks.

ℒ   ℒ   ℒ

The following morning I awake with the worst headache of my life. I consider skipping company class to spend another hour sleeping, but I know I shouldn't, so I drag myself out of bed. I put on dark sunglasses and have the deli guy fix me a coffee the size of my head just to get myself to the theater. My ears are still ringing and I feel dizzy, not to mention a little nauseated. During barre I think I'm going to be sick, so I run into the hallway to get a sip of water. On my way back into the studio, I see Mr. Edmunds gazing straight at me. It's the first time he's noticed me in weeks.

"You will show now," he says, making a flicking gesture with his fingers. "You."

My heart sinks. He knows perfectly well that I don't know the combination, because I've just stepped in from the hallway. He raises an eyebrow and coolly motions to the pianist. The music begins, a simple Chopin étude. I just stand there with my eyes cast down, trying to make myself as small as possible. I can feel every single person in the room staring at me. After a moment the music fades out awkwardly.

"What's wrong?" Mr. Edmunds demands.

"I don't know the combination," I whisper.

Behind me a person coughs, and someone giggles. I wish I could turn into a puff of smoke and disappear.

"*I* know it."

The voice is, of course, completely familiar. I turn to see Zoe stepping up, a deferential smile on her face.

"Excellent," Mr. Edmunds says, and turns his attention to her.

I go back to my place, humiliated.

And angry. I wish Zoe was able to keep herself, just once, from being a total suck-up. And how she seems to feel so good after all that vodka, I don't know. I only know that my first impulse of the morning was the right one: I should have stayed in bed.

Because the day goes on, and it gets even worse.

That afternoon in the final run-through for *Stormy Melody*, Otto claps his hands and brings the rehearsal to a halt. The music stops, and everyone steps out of position as he marches over to me.

"What is this?" he demands. He flings his arms around as he marks the brisé volé.

I can feel everyone looking at me, and my cheeks burn. I show him the step again; it's one of the most difficult petit allégro steps.

He does not look pleased. "What is the matter with you? Cross them!"

I jump again, crossing my ankles in the air as much as I can.

"Again!" Otto says.

I do what he says, but he only frowns.

"Again."

This time my legs are becoming fatigued, and I stumble.

"Again!" he shouts.

By now he isn't even looking at me anymore; he has turned his back and is walking away. I can't get enough air, and I feel the tears coming, although I will them not to.

"Again."

A dozen other corps members are watching me struggle. I can feel their eyes on me. Otto finally turns around as I gasp for air.

"From the top!"

This is a command to all of us. The other dancers groan in unison and return to their original formation. We'd been three-quarters of the way through the run, and now, thanks to me, we have to do it all again.

"Jesus Christ," I hear someone say.

My chest is heaving, and my calves feel like they're about to rip. But my body is not nearly as depleted as my ego. In the privacy of the wing, I bite my lip to keep the tears at bay. One escapes, though, and I dab at it with my sleeve before anyone can see it.

22

"Otto wasn't even looking at me," I moan to Bea. "He kept saying 'again,' but his back was turned."

"He's a sadist," she says, tilting her black beret just so. "There's just no getting around it."

I nod. "It's like he feels the need to break people so they're more obedient."

Bea laughs. "Totally. He can't have free spirits running rampant around the theater. Too hard to control. You know that last year he told Mai she was fat? *Mai!* That girl is a stick!"

"That's sick," I say. But then I shake my head. "I didn't mean to bring this up. Let's pretend we're regular people. What do regular people talk about?"

Bea glances around the NYU auditorium I've brought her to, which is slowly filling up with college students. "I don't know — movies? Homework? All the dates they went on?"

"Yeah, maybe they just talk about how fun their lives are." I smile. "But we're having fun, right?"

In an attempt to redeem myself from the debauchery of the paint party—and to further investigate the mysterious life of a pedestrian, as well as to engage in yet another thing Otto wouldn't approve of—I persuaded Bea to come with me to a poetry reading on our night off. I even put on a dress for it: a navy short-sleeve mini that I paired with tights and my second-favorite pair of ankle boots. (My favorite ones now look like a Jackson Pollock painting, even though I kicked them off before joining the paint-splattered dance mob.)

Okay, I also wanted to see what Jacob's college life might be like. And maybe I had this tiny idea that I might even run into him.

"Fun? I don't know yet," Bea says, prompting me to poke her in the arm. "All right, yes," she says, "this is fun. You just have to promise to leave if any of the poems involve car crashes or bodily fluids."

"Okay, I know you're squeamish."

Bea shifts in her seat and wraps her flowered scarf tighter around her neck; like me, she probably feels out of place and slightly nervous. I look around at the NYU students, studying them as I would a foreign species.

"She gave me a C," I hear someone say. "She said I hadn't effectively articulated Derrida's theory of logocentrism and its relationship to Lacan's theory of consciousness as a semiotic system."

"Bummer," her friend says. "But that whole structuralism/

deconstruction/post-structuralism thing is really hard. I mean, I can hardly remember what's the signifier and what's the signified."

I don't have *any* idea what they're talking about. But still, I could be one of these girls, couldn't I? Maybe even here: NYU is my dad's alma mater.

"Do you ever imagine what it would be like to be in college?" I ask Bea.

"Huh?" She furrows her freckled brow.

"Like, you know, back in school——"

Just as Bea's about to answer, a professorial-looking woman in a flowing red caftan steps up to the podium and clears her throat. "Welcome to the tenth annual student showcase of the NYU MFA program," she says.

Immediately Bea turns to me, without waiting for her to finish. "You brought me to a *student* reading?" she whispers. "I thought we'd see a famous poet or something."

"Sorry," I whisper as the first reader sets herself up at the front of the room. "Slim pickings on a Monday night. It was this or amateur comedy night at the Dew Drop Inn." Truthfully, I hadn't looked very far in the listings section of the *Village Voice*—I just saw that there was an event at NYU and decided that's where we should go. Because maybe, just maybe, we'd run into Jacob.

I write down *Signifier? Signified? Derrida?*

"Are you taking notes?" Bea demands. "Because I don't think there's going to be a quiz."

"No. But I like to be prepared. Maybe poetic inspiration will strike."

In my notebook is a line from Rimbaud (we read his work during my senior year at School of the Arts): "*I have stretched ropes from steeple to steeple; garlands from window to window; golden chains from star to star, and I dance.*" I don't know what it means, exactly, but I've always liked the image. It makes dance sound like something that exists in the larger world and not just in a dark theater.

Also in my journal — for contrast — is a line from the ballet movie *The Red Shoes*. "*Sorrow will pass, believe me,*" says the ruthless director to his most gifted dancer, whose heart has just been broken. "*Life is so unimportant. And from now onwards, you will dance like nobody ever before.*"

Which is the more accurate take on dance, Rimbaud or *The Red Shoes*? It's hard to say.

Once the readings are over, I look at Bea and see that she has nodded off.

Before I wake her up, I sit and think about Jacob, who is very possibly studying in the library five hundred yards away from me. When I get home, I send him an e-mail.

Hey Jacob. How's life? I called you a while back, but I didn't leave a message because Otto was force-feeding me some cayenne-and-lemon drink he said would increase my metabolism. Winter season is almost over and I've been totally frustrated with my parts. Anyway, I wonder if you want to hang out sometime. I'm still off on Mondays. Oh, and Sunday nights. I used to go to the gym after the matinee, but I don't do that so much anymore.

I debate for a long time how to sign it: *xo, Hannah? xH? Later, HW?* In the end, I don't sign it at all. I just send off the e-mail with my fingers crossed.

23

Jacob calls me a day later. His voice is friendly but slightly cool. "So you're coming up for air," he says.

"I'm cutting back a little," I allow.

"I hope Otto doesn't know about this," he says.

Involuntarily, I shudder a little. What would Otto or Annabelle say to me? *You look like cooked asparagus in class, and you want to cut back on your workouts?* "I hope not, too. But it's not like I'm skipping class or rehearsal. I'm just bailing on Pilates and the gym." *Because why kill myself if no one notices?* "I tried to find you at that party, you know," I go on. *And I was hoping to somehow catch sight of you the other night when I was at NYU*, I think. I pause while I work up the nerve to say what I already said in the e-mail. "So, do you want to hang out sometime?"

It takes Jacob a little while to reply, and in those moments

I imagine a parade of pretty NYU girls, each one of them more than willing to make time for him.

Eventually he says, "Yeah, but under one condition."

"What?"

"I want to see what it is that keeps you so busy," Jacob says. "I want to see you dance."

My stomach does a somersault of nervousness, but what can I say? I dance for strangers every night — I ought to be able to do it for a guy I've got a crush on. "Um — all right," I say.

"Great," he says firmly. "When?"

"I'll get you a comp ticket," I say. Then I picture him alone in the audience, too far back in the vast, ornate theater to even see which one of the corps girls is me. "Or no, never mind that," I say. "Come on Saturday night. Are you free?"

There's another pause. In my imagination, a lovely brunette slips Jacob her number in the library. "Uh, yeah," Jacob finally says. "I am free, actually."

"Great," I say, erasing the brunette from my mind. "You can stand backstage."

"That sounds awesome," Jacob says. "I can't wait."

Half an hour before the Saturday evening performance, I have all my makeup on. My hair is up in a high bun, with a silk flower pinned to it. But I'm still wearing my sweats and a loose-fitting T-shirt.

I take the elevator down to the stage door at street level.

Arden, the security guard on duty tonight, gives me a smile. Thank goodness it's not Frank working tonight. He won't even let delivery guys come into the building, much less allow guests backstage.

"Hey, Arden." I smile sweetly at her.

Arden looks up from her sudoku book and tosses her braids off her shoulder. "Hi, Hannah-girl."

"Hey, is it cool if my friend comes back for a sec?" I point to Jacob, who's sitting on a bench by her desk, waiting to get buzzed in. He looks up and waves.

Arden inspects him, a slight smile on her face. "He looks trustworthy," she says after a moment. "No problem."

I motion to Jacob, who rises. As he comes closer, he looks at me carefully, sort of like he's not really sure who I am.

"Hey, bunhead." He turns his head slowly from side to side. "Wow, you really shellac that stuff on." He reaches up and touches my eyelashes gently with his finger.

"They're fake," I say, fluttering them at him.

Jacob laughs. "Yeah, I thought they looked a little longer than usual."

As we walk up the stairs to the stage level, Jacob reaches out and takes my hand. "I'm kind of nervous," he whispers.

I smile at him. "*You're* nervous? You're not the one who has to go onstage!"

"True," he acknowledges. "But you gotta admit, I stick out a little." He points to his sneakers and jeans. "I would have worn my leotard, but it's at the cleaner's."

I wrap my fingers tighter around his. I'm so glad to see him, even if I'm too shy to show it. And having him here makes me feel better about everything — even the terrible rehearsals I've had. "So, I'm not really supposed to do this, but you're going to watch from the wing."

His brow furrows with concern. "I don't want to get you in trouble."

"You won't. Just stay out of people's way. And don't make a sound." I realize that sounds a little harsh, so I smile and squeeze his hand again. "You'll be fine. If anyone gives you a problem, just say you're my brother."

He shoots me a doubtful look. "Maybe we should stop holding hands if we're related," he teases.

"No one's going to notice you. Just make sure to turn your phone off," I tell him, and watch as he slips his phone from his pocket and switches it to vibrate.

We take the back hallway to stage right in order to avoid Christine, who's jabbering into her headset as she tries to deal with a loose scrim.

Backstage, Adriana is stretching her near-skeletal limbs at the barre, Julie is running her solo, her dark eyes fierce with concentration, and Daisy is putting on her shoes by the rosin box. Jacob's eyes grow wider as he takes it all in. I want to stay with him, but I'm anxious to get my shoes and costume on, so I place him in the front wing, nestled between the black velvet curtain and the scaffolding that holds up the lights.

I slip on my shoes and sew in, and then I hurry to the Green Room to put on my costume. I'm jittery as Laura helps me into my flesh-tone chiffon dress.

"What's with you tonight?" she asks. "Days of moping around, and now you're bouncing like a Mexican jumping bean."

"I had a big coffee," I lie.

I hurry backstage again to find Jacob watching intently as Julie marks through her pas de deux with Sam. I sneak up behind him and tap his shoulder. He whirls around, a look of near panic on his face. Then, when he sees it's me, he smiles.

"Wow, I thought I was busted," he says.

"Nope, just me," I say, poking him.

"You look..." He pauses as he steps back to get the full ballerina effect. "Well, Hannah Ward, you look amazing." Then he leans close to me again and whispers, "I'd give you a kiss, but I don't think your lip gloss would look that great on me."

Beneath my pancake makeup I can feel myself blushing.

"Places!" Christine calls, clapping her hands together.

"Whoa — gotta go." I flash Jacob a smile and then dash off to find my opening position onstage next to Daisy and Adriana.

"*Merde*," I say to Daisy, and I give her butt a little pat.

The lights go down as the orchestra tune their instruments. Then the strings begin the overture. I smooth my costume and wait for the curtain to rise.

"That's him, isn't it?" Daisy whispers, grinning.

I glance over toward the first wing. It's almost pitch-black, but as the lights illuminate the stage, I can make out Jacob's profile from behind the boom.

"Yes," I hiss.

"*Merde*," she says, winking at me.

Then the curtain rises, and the cool air from the house is

released like a billow of wind over the stage. I'm aware that Jacob's watching, but instead of being distracted, I'm fueled by his presence. I piqué arabesque, tombé toward the wing, and soutenu opposite Daisy. I look over to the front wing to see Jacob smiling broadly.

When the violins begin the adagio section, we bourrée and pose in a semicircle around Julie as she executes her first solo. We sauté, chassé, tour jeté, and kneel as Sam enters for the pas de deux, and then we turn and bourrée into the wing.

I catch my breath and take a quick sip from my water bottle. I have a few moments before my next entrance, so I walk over to Jacob. The expression on his face is one of amazement.

I touch his shoulder lightly. "So, what do you think?"

"This is the coolest thing ever," he whispers. "I love being back here — it feels like I'm right onstage with you guys."

I smile as I dab the beads of sweat from my brow. "I should have gotten you up in the flies. The view's even better from up there."

"The what?"

I point up to where Harry is sitting at his desk. "Way up there," I say. "Well, maybe you can try that next time. I've got to go. See you in a few!"

I jog to the last wing, feeling his eyes on me. I like knowing he's there, and I want to impress him.

I reenter for the coda with Emma and Daisy, and I push myself as the music reaches a crescendo and we near the finale. My lungs feel like they're going to explode, but I make it to the final pose without a single misstep.

Moments later, during the bows, I glance over to see Jacob clapping with such enthusiasm that I'm afraid Christine's going to yell at him. As the curtain comes down, I go over to him, breathless but energized. He holds his arms out as if I should step right into them, but I don't, because I'm dripping with sweat.

"You're incredible, Hannah," he says.

"All in a day's work," I say. I'm so glad he saw a good performance — the way I've been feeling lately, I wasn't sure I had it in me.

"Don't be so modest."

"It's a fun ballet," I say. "Some of them I don't like as much." I bend over. "Ooph, I have got to get these shoes off."

"Do they hurt?"

I stand up and look him in the eye. "*Everything* hurts."

He takes my arm as I walk back to the Green Room. "Let me buy you a drink. I need to toast your amazingness."

"Stop flattering me, will you?" I say, laughing.

"Flattery implies insincerity, and I'm completely sincere when I tell you that you blew my mind," he says.

"Enough! If I agree to one drink, will you stop talking about it? You're embarrassing me."

"Fine," he says. "It's a deal."

Jacob waits outside the theater while I shower and change. He gives me grief for coming outside with wet hair, and he wraps his arm around my shoulder protectively as we walk up Broadway in the chilly night.

We head toward Kelly's Pub, which is sort of a dive, but it's close and they don't card. Once inside, we seat ourselves on stools at the bar. I'm relieved that no other dancers are here. It's not that I want to keep Jacob a secret, but I don't want to be interrogated in company class tomorrow, which I would be if, say, Jonathan were somewhere in the room. I order a glass of merlot, and Jacob orders a beer. We swivel on our stools, and our knees keep touching.

"It was so cool to see you in your element," Jacob says. "I mean, I pictured what you did, but this is really on a whole other level. You're a total pro."

I elbow him. "You said you'd stop talking about it."

"You're blushing." Jacob grins. "Fine. What should we talk about instead?"

I search my mind for an appropriate topic. The thing is, I'm so tired by now that my brain hardly works. "I have absolutely no idea," I say.

"Well, I played at this new place last week," Jacob offers. "It's called Satyricon; have you heard of it? No? What a shock! Well, this drunk guy kept trying to sing along with my set. At first I tried to harmonize with him, but I had to give up because he was terrible. After a while he just passed out, and the bouncers carried him out to a cab." Then Jacob spins around on his stool. "Voilà," he says. "There's a little anecdote from my life. Now it's your turn."

I try to spin around, too, and I almost knock over my wine. "That makes me think of last year when a guy climbed onstage during intermission," I say. "He was trying to find the split in the curtain so he could get backstage. They had to delay the show, and Christine called the cops and everything. I was stretching back there when they brought him through in handcuffs."

Jacob peers at me over his beer. "You guys must have all sorts of crazed fans, right?"

I think about Matt and how he sent me all those balloons and gourmet lunches. *Not all crazed fans are bad*, I want to say. "I read about this ballerina in the eighteen hundreds, and supposedly her fans would cook her slippers and eat them with, like, pasta sauce."

"You're joking."

I hold up my hand. "Scout's honor."

"I must say, that is truly disgusting."

"I know!" I say, laughing. "Not even pesto could make that taste good."

Jacob laughs, too, and then he motions for me to lean close. "You were really beautiful out there," he whispers.

I can feel his breath on my cheek, and it sends a shiver down my spine. "Thanks," I whisper back.

Then Jacob sits up straight again and takes my hand in his. "And since you introduced me to something new," he says, "I think that the day after tomorrow I should do the same for you. It's only fair. And since the day after tomorrow is a Monday, you can't possibly tell me that you have rehearsal."

Two weeks ago I would have had back-to-back Pilates and yoga classes, and I would have turned him down. But tonight is different.

"Where are you going to take me?" I ask.

"A place you've never really seen before," he answers. And then he raises his glass and clinks it against mine.

24

"What in the world are we doing?" I ask, hunching my shoulders inside my wool coat as the wind kicks up around us.

Jacob and I are in the middle of Times Square—a place I normally avoid at all costs—standing in a line of tourists: dads in Green Bay Packers jackets, moms in lumpy down coats, kids of various ages who are sporting hats and carrying bags full of cheap souvenirs. "Everyone here looks like they're from Kansas." (Everyone, that is, but me and Jacob, who looks sloppily gorgeous in an old navy peacoat, a pair of cords, and a brown knit hat.)

"Well, the Green Bay Packers are from Wisconsin," Jacob says. "And maybe you missed the girls from France behind us, and that Japanese family."

I don't bother to turn around. "Still. We *live* here. What are we doing hanging out with a bunch of tourists?"

"I thought I'd take you on a tour of the city." He smiles and puts his arm around my shoulder. "You know, since *you* actually seem to live in the theater."

Just then a red double-decker bus pulls up to the curb. Its doors hiss open, and the line of tourists starts moving forward.

"Wait, so you're taking me on a tour?" I ask, incredulous. "*This* is what I've supposedly never seen before — New York from a Red Apple tour bus?"

Jacob shrugs. "What better way to see your city than from the top deck of a carbon monoxide–spouting behemoth? There's an announcer who tells you all sorts of New York trivia." And he guides me forward, onto the bus and up the steps to the roof.

Feeling somewhat less than thrilled, I flop down in a seat near the railing. Jacob squeezes in beside me.

"We could get off and on again, but I figure since time is precious, we'll just want to ride this one the whole time. I brought snacks." He reaches into his bag and pulls out two bottles of San Pellegrino, two clementines, and a giant bar of dark chocolate.

"Well, in that case . . ." I say, my mood brightening. I help myself to a square of chocolate.

Our guide clears his throat, taps his mike, and fixes us with an oversize grin. "Welcome, everybody, welcome! So glad to see you! Here we are in the red-hot center of the city that never sleeps! Times Square! Times Square was known as Longacre Square until 1904, when the *New York Times* moved its headquarters here! Before that it was a neighborhood of Broadway theaters and *brothels*!" he says.

"Why is he so excited about everything?" I ask, grimacing.

"I think that's in his job description," Jacob says. He peels a clementine and hands me a slice.

"By the First World War, Times Square had become the premier theater district in the nation, but fifty years later it had sunk back to the district of streetwalkers and sex shops again!" the man calls out. "A dirty business!"

I give Jacob a dubious look as the bus lurches forward into the sea of cabs and delivery trucks and cars heading south on Seventh Avenue. "Do you really want me to listen to him?"

"Actually I was thinking of giving you my own personal and private tour as we go. What do you think?" he asks, cocking his head sweetly.

Intrigued, I nod. "Just try not to sound as excited as that guy."

"All right, then, no exclamation points. So, here we are at the corner of Seventh and Thirty-Eighth, which is where I once nearly passed out after consuming too many Singhas at one of the karaoke clubs in Koreatown following a truly incredible rendition of 'Sweet Child of Mine.' One block east and a little north is Bryant Park, where I saw a summer showing of *The Graduate* with a girl I thought I was in love with."

We idle at a light, and I turn to Jacob. "What happened to her?" I ask, imagining once again a pretty brunette with sultry dark eyes.

"I bought her pottery classes for her birthday—and she cheated on me with the instructor. I think his name was Sven."

"Ooh, that's harsh."

He nods ruefully. "Yeah. But don't worry—this trip isn't entirely about me and my minor life disasters. Did you know that Broadway is one of the longest streets in the world? It starts in lower Manhattan, and it doesn't stop until Albany, which is a hundred and fifty miles north."

"Really?"

"Yeah. And the Empire State Building is one thousand two hundred and fifty feet tall, not including its lightning rod and antenna." He points vaguely in the direction of the landmark.

I try to look very serious and studious. "Fascinating."

We've left the flashing neon signs of Times Square and we're in the no-man's-land of lower midtown: tall, windowed office buildings, bodegas, crowded sidewalks. Jacob rests his arm along the back of my seat. "And here we're passing the lovely Penn Station, which is the busiest train station in all of North America, serving up to a thousand people every minute and a half."

"I'm starting to feel like one of your first graders," I tell him. "Like maybe I should be taking notes for a pop quiz."

He grins. "Back to the personal tour, then. I once got hit on in a Penn Station bathroom by a six-foot-tall transvestite. He—or she, I guess—was actually very pretty, though I did turn her down. And I think I can tell you in fairly good confidence that the Sbarro by track seven serves the worst pizza in the world."

The wind rips around the buildings, and I lean in close to Jacob as the bus rumbles downtown. The tour guide starts to say something about the Chelsea Hotel a block and a half west of us while Jacob points out bars that he's played in the neighborhood.

"Hey, look," I say, nudging his arm. "There's Loehmann's, where I once bought a Marc Jacobs sheath for eighty percent off, and where Bea knocked over an entire rack of sunglasses when she was overcome by the urge to demonstrate the running man."

Jacob smiles. "See? You could be a tour guide, too."

As Jacob goes on, I learn that his friend Damian organized a flash mob at the corner of Twelfth Street. I find out that Greenwich Village was once marshland, and that the area beneath Washington Square Park was a potter's field.

"So, there are something like twenty thousand dead bodies under you as you drink your latte and watch the dogs in the dog run," Jacob says. "Pleasant, isn't it?"

"Yeah, really," I say. I shiver and pull my scarf tighter around my neck. "I'm freezing. When is it going to be spring?"

Jacob puts his arm around me. "We're actually within walking distance of my apartment. Should we get off?"

I nod. My nose is beginning to run. Jacob offers me his sleeve to wipe it on, which is kind of gross, but it also might be the sweetest thing a guy has ever done for me. (I don't take him up on it; I wipe my nose on my own sleeve.)

We get off at Christopher Street just as the tour guide is describing for all the people of Kansas and Wisconsin the history of the Stonewall Inn and the three-day riot that was the beginning of the gay rights movement.

"Thanks," Jacob says to the tour guide, tipping him five dollars. The guide doffs his hat and continues his monologue.

Jacob takes my hand as we walk east, threading our way through the crowds of shoppers.

How strange and nice it is to walk down the street with my hand in someone else's. I can't believe I've lived almost two decades on this earth and I've never done it before. People passing us will think we're a couple. And, I don't know, maybe all of a sudden we are.

On Fifth Street between Avenues A and B, we come up to a narrow, slightly shabby-looking brick building with graffiti tags on the concrete steps leading up to the front door.

"Home, sweet home," Jacob says. "I'm on the fourth floor."

I follow him up the narrow stairway, favoring my left ankle, which has been bothering me ever since the killer bourrée section in *Recluse*. The hallway smells like Chinese food and feet.

"It's not that fancy," Jacob says as he opens the door into a railroad apartment, "but the price is right. It's actually my uncle's place, but he never comes into the city anymore. He just paints out at his cottage on the North Shore."

Although the apartment is small, it's also inviting. Unlike my place, his shows real signs of being inhabited: Posters and pictures hang on the walls. There are end tables bearing stacks of books and papers and mugs with cold coffee resting on CD cases. Two guitars lean against the wall in the corner. It's not messy, exactly — just lived in.

"Okay, so the next order of business is lunch. I know how to make about ten different things," Jacob says, taking my coat and hanging it in an overstuffed closet. "They're pretty much all pasta, because that's pretty much all I eat. I can do penne arrabiata, spaghetti aglio e olio, puttanesca—ramen, if that counts as pasta."

"Pesto," I interrupt. "You like it so much—you must make pesto, right?"

"I usually make that by opening a jar," Jacob confesses. "But my arrabiata is from scratch. Can I interest you? It's really spicy."

"Sounds great," I say.

I follow him into the tiny kitchen, where he peers at me over the counter, holding up a large cast-iron skillet in one hand and a dishrag in the other. He mimes the act of washing. "Note how I make sure my pans are free from any petrochemical coatings."

I lean over on the counter, resting my elbows on a stack of *Rolling Stone* magazines. "I hear petrochemicals are the new oregano."

He grins. "You're so ahead of your time."

I watch him knocking around in the kitchen for a while, and then I get up and peruse his music collection and his book-shelves. I'm not snooping; I'm just getting acquainted with his taste. Jacob seems to like a Japanese novelist named Oé, and he has about twenty different Neil Young albums.

I sink into the couch and pick up an old issue of the *New Yorker*. But I don't read it—I just close my eyes.

"Bud Light for your thoughts," Jacob asks, coming around the counter and handing me a beer bottle. He's wearing an apron that says *Kiss the Chef*. "I know you're more of a wine girl, but I forgot to go to the store earlier."

I take a tentative sip and wince just a little; I'm not a big fan of beer. Also, it's still only two in the afternoon. I stare at my discolored and blistered feet and wiggle my toes. My toes that I dance on every single day.

Jacob sits beside me on the couch, and I tuck my feet up underneath me. He has sauce on his cheek. "So . . . your thoughts?"

"Well, despite my skepticism, the bus tour was pretty cool," I admit. "It's good to know that there's more to the city than the Manhattan Ballet." I point to his cheek — "You've got a little something there," I say — and he uses a corner of his apron to wipe the sauce off.

"Thanks," he says. "And now brace yourself because this might just blow your mind. . . . There's more to the world than just *New York City*." His eyes widen, and he mimes an explosion with his hands.

"Wait, what?" I feign shock. "You mean, we won't fall off the planet if we walk below the financial district?"

Jacob shakes his head slowly, with an expression of utter seriousness. "Crazy, right? That reminds me — I found this place that rents kayaks by the hour. I thought it would be fun to see the city from the Hudson," he says.

"*È fantastico*," I say hesitantly.

He looks surprised. "I'm impressed! Have you been practicing?"

"Yeah, a little," I admit, smiling. "I bought an Italian app for my iPhone last week. I want to be able to hold my own when we finally get to watch a Fellini film."

"I — wow — that's so cool," he says.

I look earnestly into his eyes. "I'm envious that you have the time to explore so many different things." Then I giggle. "Oh, and I also know how to say *He has a large hat* and *Where is the beach?*"

His blue eyes light up, and he gives me the biggest grin I've ever seen.

And then his expression turns more serious, and he's looking at me in a way that he never has before. He leans toward me, and in another second his lips are on mine, soft but insistent. Almost as if it belongs to someone else, my hand reaches up his back, and my fingers find their way to the warm skin of his neck, into the shaggy ends of his hair. His arms tighten around me, and I feel like I'm melting into him.

Eventually he pulls away from me, and he reaches out and tucks a piece of hair behind my ear. "Have I mentioned that I like you?" he asks.

I nod. Outside a car alarm goes off, and then another. Jacob's radiator hisses and knocks as the heat comes on.

"I think it would be nice if you liked me, too," he says. "Do you?"

And I just nod again. It's like the first night I met him, when I couldn't say anything at all. Jacob leans in and kisses me again. In the kitchen I smell something burning, but I don't say a word. I lean back on the couch and he bends over me. I feel his weight. We keep our eyes closed. We sink into each other.

"You know, I——" Jacob begins to say. His mouth is on my neck.

"Stop talking," I whisper. And I pull him to me and kiss him deeply.

25

The next morning, Bea comes over with two cups of coffee and a plastic tub of fruit salad from the corner deli. I rub my eyes as I let her in; it's not even nine o'clock yet.

"I hung out with Max Gruner yesterday," she says, dumping the fruit into two bowls and fetching forks from the kitchen. Her bright red hair falls in waves from under her black beret.

I give a little yelp of excitement. Max Gruner is another corps member. He's cute, despite having a minor acne problem in the chin area, and he's an incredible dancer. I once overheard Otto say that Max had promise, which, for Otto, is very high praise. "Tell me everything," I demand. But then I have to sink down into a chair. I didn't get home until after two in the morning, and then I couldn't fall asleep.

Bea sighs. "I was really nervous, and he was, too. The whole time I couldn't stop thinking about how awkward and embarrassing everything was. Like, there would be these long silences—and then we'd both start talking at the same time."

"Wait, start over. Who asked who?"

"I asked him to a movie."

I applaud. "Good for you!"

"So I thought. I asked him on Sunday after the matinee. I was still in my stage makeup, and so I pretended I was someone else. Someone braver."

"Like Zoe?" I ask.

Bea laughs. "I said braver, not sluttier."

"Well, I don't care what you say. I'm proud of you. That took guts."

She pokes at a piece of pineapple with her fork. "I don't want to be the last person on earth who's never had a boyfriend."

"First of all, who cares, and second, you're not. Think of the corps: Jordan has never had a girlfriend."

"He's totally bizarre—he rides a Segway, for one thing—so please don't compare me to him."

I grin. "Right, sorry."

Bea puts some pineapple in her mouth, chews, and then sighs. "I guess I wonder what the point of it is."

"The point of what?"

She looks at me as if I'm a little on the dumb side. "Trying to be with another person when it's so much simpler to be alone," she says.

"Bea, you don't *have* to have a boyfriend," I say. "You can do whatever you want." I blow on the coffee and then take a sip. It's strong, but not nearly strong enough.

"Yeah, I know." She sighs. "How are you and Jacob?"

"Great. Or it *would* be great if not for this." I wave my arm around.

"Your apartment?"

Now it's my turn to shoot her that *are you stupid?* look. "No, my life. The company. The ballet world. Like you said — it complicates things."

Bea stands up and goes into the kitchen. "Don't you have any clean glasses?" she calls. "Oh, here they are." I hear the faucet running as she fills a water glass. "Yeah, it's hard for all of us. But we knew what we signed up for, when we were, like, nine."

"I know, Bea, but people change in a decade," I say. "I'm different now than I was even a few years ago."

"Eh, thank God. We were such dorks," she says, laughing.

"Remember how we were dying to be *shrubbery*, just to be onstage with the company?"

She cringes. "So we grew up, and now we have a better understanding and appreciation for what we do."

"Yeah, of course, but —"

"You're just a little burned out," she says confidently. "Give it a week and you'll feel better again. Feelings come in waves."

I really hope she's right.

Bea looks at me closely with her pretty blue eyes. I can't read her expression. Finally she says, "Are you going to eat your pineapple?"

I push the bowl toward her. "All yours."

"Thanks," she says. "Now go get ready. Class starts in an hour."

∾   ∾   ∾

It's not an easy morning. Lack of sleep, combined with fatigue from weeks and weeks of dancing without a break, means that by the second rehearsal of the day, I'm beginning to feel spent, even though I still have three more hours of rehearsal and then *A Night Piece, Concerto in C,* and *Foresight* to dance tonight before I can eat a proper meal and take a bath.

"Pull up, Hannah," Annabelle Hayes barks. "It looks like you're sweeping the floor!"

Obediently, I pull up my abdominals and try to stay alert, but my back aches and my thighs are blown out, so it's nearly impossible to engage my legs. Blown-out muscles feel like someone punched you in the leg as hard as they possibly could; even a light touch is excruciating.

Annabelle claps her hands to pause the rehearsal. "Is everything all right?" she asks me. "Are you ill?"

I shake my head. We're taught from a young age never to speak in class or rehearsals unless absolutely necessary, and not to *ever* complain. So I'd never tell her that I'm utterly exhausted, my shoes are completely dead, and my thigh is blown again.

"From the top, then," Annabelle says, frowning. The girls all groan, and Zoe looks at me with blatant annoyance.

The pianist begins again, and there's nothing to do but try to pull myself together and ignore my discomfort.

I remember that when I was a younger dancer, there were days it hurt to roll over in bed, or to breathe, or to do anything but lie motionless on the floor. Back then I found something satisfying in the soreness, because I knew that I was *alive* and that my discomfort was the product of something great.

I wish I could capture that feeling again.

৵   ৵   ৵

That night, before the performance, I shellac my face with pancake makeup and follow it with layers of powder. My entire face is white, and I look like a ghost of myself.

I decide to get a Diet Coke from the vending machine, and then a little bit of air, so I leave the eye shadows, liners, lashes, and lipstick for later. I run up the stairs and plop my quarters into the slot. While I'm waiting for the soda can to fall, I spot Otto and Mai at the other end of the corridor. Mai's normally pale cheeks are flushed pink, and her tiny chest rises and falls visibly; she must have just been rehearsing. Otto moves his hands animatedly and appears to be almost smiling as he speaks. Mai listens, nodding, and then responds. I can't hear what they're saying, but I hardly need to — it's enough to see that they are having an actual conversation. I wasn't aware anyone did that with Otto. In my experience, he barks something out, a command or a complaint, and everyone just keeps quiet and does what he or she is told.

My Diet Coke clunks down the chute and crashes into the open mouth of the soda machine. I flinch at the noise, and Otto turns his head toward me. His face is blank at first, and then a look steals over it — disdain, I'd say, or maybe even disgust.

A tiny shiver travels up my spine, and I wonder if he's looking at me like that because my makeup is only half done or because he hasn't forgotten the rehearsal in which I couldn't do the brisé volé. I flash a weak smile, but he continues to gaze at me as if I am wholly unwelcome in this hallway, or in this theater, or on this planet.

In the next excruciating moments, every dark, disloyal thought I have ever had swirls into my mind. Wishing that they'd just put me out of my misery. Dreaming that Otto wanted to cut off my breasts. I feel my heart thudding in my chest. I clutch the soda against me as if it were some kind of shield.

After what feels like an eternity, Otto looks away. I duck my head and coax my legs to move. Then I flee to the safety of the dressing room.

૭ ૭ ૭

Later that night, I'm almost late for my entrance in Jason Pite's ballet. But when I step onstage, I feel strangely relaxed — almost detached. I leap high into the air and kick my legs up for a rond de jambe. As I move across the stage, my mind is clear and calm. Even my breath seems to come easier, lighter, and I hear the music as if it is coming from far, far away.

I just dance as if in a dream until the final notes of the orchestra swell and then fade.

I guess this is what it feels like not to care.

Annabelle Hayes stands beneath the exit sign, its red light reflecting on the crown of her head. Her tiny arms are folded across her chest; she looks like a sparrow. She motions to me. Then she opens her mouth and says something, but she's too far away for me to hear her.

"Sorry?" I say, inching closer. Unconsciously I touch my bun and adjust my costume.

Annabelle blinks at me. "That was much better, Hannah," she says.

I stammer out a weak "thanks," and Annabelle nods in acknowledgment. I can't remember the last time she said anything nice to me. How strange: Today she was riding my butt in rehearsal, and now she's actually giving me a compliment.

I walk back to the Green Room, where everyone is in various stages of readiness for the final ballet. It's a big corps ballet, and all of us are in it.

"How did the Pite go?" Bea asks.

"Apparently, good," I say, reaching for my bottle of water. I drink half of it in what seems like two gulps. "I got a compliment from Annabelle, God knows why."

Daisy's dark head pops up over Bea's shoulder. "No way," she says.

Zoe has just come in, still a little out of breath from the performance. "A compliment? I wonder what got into her," she says.

I finish the rest of my water and then check my makeup in the mirror. I need to retouch my lipstick and change my bun to a low chignon. "I mean, I totally relaxed for once. It was kind of freeing."

Zoe lifts an eyebrow. "Whatever works for you," she says, sounding unconvinced. "But his ballet is hardly a real ballet, you know—I mean, all that rolling around on the floor stuff! Ugh."

"I'm sure you looked great, Hannah," Bea says.

Zoe snorts under her breath and turns away. And I can't help smiling to myself.

ஒ ஒ ஒ

But back at home in my apartment, my mood shifts again. The bath has filled—Epsom salts, a little lavender essential oil—and I've sunk into it. I lean back and close my eyes so I don't have to look at the hideous turquoise paint on the walls. In the warm water, I can feel my spine lengthening, my quads releasing some of their tension. I hum to myself, some melody my mother used to sing to me.

The Epsom salts hiss as they dissolve, and I sink deeper into the water.

The phone rings, but I don't answer it.

I've placed one of my oldest pairs of ballet slippers on the bathroom shelf so I can stare at them. The leather is cracked and faded, and what used to be a lovely pink is now the color of Silly Putty. But I don't throw them away, because they remind me of when I first fell in love with dance. I was nine years old, and I took classes three times a week at the Boston Ballet School.

One day when we were practicing tendus at the barre, I began to imagine that I was a robot, and danced with very sharp, precise movements. I have no idea where this idea came from; I only know that as I danced, I pictured a robot in my mind and tried to move exactly as it did. I imagined my arms being made out of aluminum, my torso out of steel. When I moved, I pretended I was slicing through the air like a knife.

The teacher stopped the class and pointed to me with her impossibly long finger. I felt my cheeks flush—I was in trouble, for sure. But then she turned back to the rest of the class. "Everyone watch Hannah," she said to the other little girls. "I want you to move *just like her.*"

I couldn't believe my ears. After that day, my teacher started paying extra attention to me, and the following year the artistic director of the Boston Ballet offered to give me private lessons. That was unheard of: Imagine, the director of a premier ballet company taking the time to teach a ten-year-old girl variations from *Giselle* and *Raymonda.*

When I took them from their box, the slippers smelled like the cedar sachet I keep in there with them. They seemed tiny.

What happened to that girl who dreamed only of dancing? I wish I could talk to that girl right now. I wonder if she'd tell me not to lose hope. Because a single compliment from Annabelle can't erase the built-up frustration—not by a long shot.

I sit up in the bath and look down at my breasts. They're pretty much the same size they always were—which is to say, they're bigger than Otto would like them to be.

"It's not your fault," I say to them, and then sink even deeper into the bath.

26

"Did you hear?" Zoe asks, trying to sound calm even though she's obviously upset. "Eliza and Olivia got promoted to soloist." She slams a new pointe shoe in the door to break it in, which is also a good way to take out frustration. "Soloist!"

"What, are you serious?" I practically yell, forgetting for a moment that I'm supposed to be happy for my peers. These are girls like me — ones who have been toiling in what we all thought was perpetual frustration. It's a monumentally huge deal and, for Olivia and Eliza, the accomplishment of a lifetime. "Just out of the blue like that?" I ask. "Olivia hasn't had a solo in months."

"Actually, she has," Bea points out, but I ignore her. I'm in shock, as is everyone else. Daisy gathers up a handful of quarters and then vanishes. Zoe brushes her hair furiously for a few moments before going out for a cigarette.

"I mean, that's great for them, it really is," I say, trying hard to feel it. I close the lid of my theater case and then open it again agitatedly.

"It is," Bea insists.

Olivia and Eliza peer in the door to our dressing room. Olivia's little pixie face is glowing with pleasure, and though Eliza is smiling, she still looks dumfounded. "I can't believe it," she keeps saying. Her voice is almost a whisper. "I thought I'd be in the corps forever. I can't believe it."

And in a way, neither can I. We were Swans in *Swan Lake* together, and Snowflakes in *The Nutcracker*, and now they're getting the recognition each one of us deserves.

"Congratulations, you guys," I say. "That's so amazing." I do my best to sound sincere.

"And no more dancing Snow!" Bea cries. "You guys are so lucky."

But even Bea sounds like she's faking it.

Eliza and Olivia smile, thank us, and accept quick hugs. Then they go down the hall to their own dressing room.

I *am* happy for them — but I'm also disappointed for myself. Bea and I sit at our spots, quietly digesting the news, both of us lost in our own thoughts. After a while I feel restless, and I collect all my makeup brushes and take them into the bathroom. One by one, I wash them against my palm with some hand soap.

"Honestly," I say over the running water, "how did Olivia manage to get noticed?" The water runs pink, then brown, then purplish brown. "She's not exactly a standout."

"Yeah, she is kind of dull," Bea allows.

I lay the brushes delicately on a pile of paper towels and then carry them back to my spot.

"But she's consistent. And she's, like, always around," Bea says as she inspects her fingernails.

"And what about Eliza?" I ask as I squeeze each brush with a paper towel and place it on my counter.

"Well, she's been getting demi and soloist roles on and off for years," Bea offers as Zoe comes in, smelling like smoke.

"I'll bet it's her new, blonder hair, courtesy of Oscar Blandi. That and the fact that she started dating Sam," Zoe says confidently.

"God, you're cynical," Bea says as she picks at the label on her water bottle.

"I like to think of myself as a realist." Zoe purses her lips in the mirror and turns her face from side to side.

Leni comes in, smiling, with her yoga mat rolled under her arm. "Hey, ladies!" Then her voice drops. "Oh . . . I see you've heard the news."

"Is it that obvious?" I say. I look over at Bea, who's opening and closing her water bottle again and again, as if in a daze. Even Zoe looks defeated.

With a jerk of her wrist, Leni unfurls her yoga mat, and pretty soon she's balanced on her hands, with one leg sticking straight out behind her and the other resting on the backs of her bent arms.

"Side crow variation," she grunts, before anyone can ask her. "Nothing clears the mind like a partial inversion. Except a full inversion, of course."

Daisy enters the dressing room, her eyes slightly red and swollen, and drops a bag of Cheetos onto the floor. She's wearing Caleb's faded Mets T-shirt over her leotard. "I can't believe it! Olivia? What did she do to deserve a promotion?"

Zoe turns on her, green eyes flashing. "Why, do you think *you* should have gotten it? Because let me remind you that we were all busting our asses here while you were still in diapers. Don't act so entitled — you're sixteen years old."

"It's obvious that you're just jealous because Otto pays attention to me. And for your information, I'll be seventeen in two months, and Mai was promoted when she was seventeen!" Daisy says hotly, stamping her little foot.

Leni falls out of her pose onto her mat. "Honey, can you lower your voice? My chakras are all off kilter."

"Screw your chakras!" Daisy yells as she waves her fist in the air.

Leni stares up at Daisy with a look of concern, and then she breaks into a wide, beautiful smile. Daisy scowls at Leni, but eventually she begins to chuckle, and pretty soon she throws her head back and makes this weird choking, guffawing sound. I'm not sure if she's laughing or crying; it's probably a combination of both.

After a few moments she stops, gasping a little. "I can't believe I just ate all those Cheetos!" she cries. "I'm going to have to skip dinner for the next four days."

"Cut off an arm," Zoe suggests. "That'll knock off seven pounds, easy." She snickers, trying to stifle a laugh, and I snort under my breath.

Daisy starts to pace the room. "Or should I try South Beach again?"

Even Bea is laughing now as Daisy goes on and on about cleanses, fasts, and crazy diets. After a while, Daisy looks up, sees that we're laughing, and starts laughing again herself. "Oh, listen to me!" she cries. "I sound like a crazy person! Tell me to shut up!" By now even Leni is howling with laughter.

I look around the room — at the drying leotards and tights hung on every available hook and bar, at the pictures of celebrities' fashion mistakes, at the theater cases spilling onto the floor, and at my friends' faces. There's something kind of amazing about being able to laugh together like this when we are all so utterly disappointed and frustrated. Finding humor in the situation binds us.

But to be honest, it's not only that I feel a sudden wave of affection for these people that I've grown up with and struggle with daily. I realize that if Olivia and Eliza can be promoted, there is hope for me, too, and for all of us older girls. After all, Annabelle just told me that I was doing better. All I have to do is choose to focus. To give everything to dance again.

ॐ ॐ ॐ

The roof of the theater is a sooty, windswept place. My hands shoved deep in my pockets, I walk to the corner overlooking the plaza where the boys come to smoke. There's a single folding chair next to a bucket filled with sand. *Park your butts here*, the bucket reads, but still the roof is littered with the remains of

Camels and Marlboros. If Otto ever came up here, he'd have a conniption. "This?" he'd yell. "*This* is how you treat the roof above your heads?"

I sit down on the chair and put my feet on the edge of the bucket. The wind picks up, and I notice a few snowflakes falling slowly from the sky. I look up in surprise; snow is rare in March. I pull my hat down tighter over my head and watch as the flakes melt against the asphalt roof.

Back and forth, back and forth, I flex and point my feet. I lift my right leg and turn out my thigh. I lift my left leg, too, and feel my core engage as I balance on my hands on the cold metal seat of the chair. I can feel the tremble in my arms as I support my weight. Then I push myself up to stand and move to the edge of the roof. The snow comes down silently and more steadily.

I pretend I'm waiting in the wing — that I can hear the violins and the cello over the sound of the traffic below. I piqué arabesque with my arms circling into fifth, one at a time, and then tombé and lean backward, looking at the sky. Snowflakes melt against my cheeks. I glissade and balancé turn slowly, then piqué arabesque, chassé, tour jeté. The air loses its chill as I continue to dance. The snowflakes spiral around me as if they, too, are dancing.

I hear a creak, and the door swings open. Jonathan stands at the threshold, an unlit cigarette in his mouth. His light brown hair is flopping into his eyes, and he could use a shave. His blue eyes widen when he sees me.

"What in the world are you doing, darling?" he says, stepping onto the roof.

205

I stop short, horrified at being caught. My breath comes fast and light. "What does it look like?" I bend over and put my hands on my knees. I realize how strange I must look, dancing in tights, sneakers, and a winter coat, all alone on a rooftop.

"*Metamorphoses.* And it looks pretty good."

I can't help but smile. "Thanks."

"Suicide stick?" he asks, holding the pack out to me.

I shake my head. "No, thanks."

"Suit yourself."

I walk past him as he lights his cigarette and takes a deep drag.

"You really got some air on that tour jeté," he calls, and I wave.

On the other side of the heavy iron door, the staircase is dim and warm. I hurry back down to the dressing room. Rehearsal starts in twenty minutes.

My body hums from its exertions. I think about the adagio in *Metamorphoses* and the string section in *Tschaikovsky Suite No. 1*; I think about how thrilling performing can be. The thought of saying good-bye to it all suddenly feels awful and terrifying.

Knowing this, I feel an enormous sense of relief.

"I'm home, I'm home," I whisper.

I bump into Leni on the way to rehearsal. She opens the door for me as we enter the studio.

"You know," I tell her, "I think this is a good thing. The promotions, I mean. Am I crazy? Because I feel kind of hopeful."

Leni nods carefully. "*Immer wenn du meinst es geht nicht mehr, Kommt Von irgendwo ein Lichtlein her,*" she says.

"What does that mean?" I ask.

"Just when you think you can't go on, somewhere a little light comes on," she says. She holds out a bag of something green. "Kale chip? They're loaded with good phytochemicals."

I shake my head and smile. I *do* feel as if a little light has come on.

When Jacob calls me that night, I run to grab my phone to tell him the news. But then I hold it in my hands as it rings. There's his picture, flashing on the screen—his smiling face, with a Big Apple tour bus behind it. I count three rings, then four, then five. *Focus, Hannah, focus.* I don't press the button to answer it, and the call goes to voice mail.

27

Of course, I'm not the only one who's motivated by the promotions. In addition to beginning a new diet, Daisy has bought an entirely new workout wardrobe. She looks like a model from a Danskin catalog.

"God, she's desperate," Zoe mutters as she roots around in her purse.

"Yeah, if that tactic worked, we'd all be wearing Day-Glo Lycra," I whisper back.

Daisy is oblivious as she prances around the room, her wavy black hair shining from a recent hot-oil treatment. "Dr. Shapiro says that colors can really affect your mood and outlook on life, you know," she says.

"Yeah, that yellow really says soloist." Zoe smirks.

"What?" Daisy asks.

"Oh, nothing. I was just saying how I like the yellow of your leotard."

It's not as if Daisy's the only one to feel competitive. Zoe has begun dancing next to me again and occasionally shooting me looks — part-joking, part-serious — that are full of challenge.

Only Bea and Leni seem the same to me. As Daisy put it, "They have greater emotional equilibrium," which is obviously a phrase she learned from Dr. Shapiro.

"I'm *la ballerine près de l'eau*," Leni says.

"You and your foreign phrases," I say. "What does that mean?"

"It's French," she says, "for 'the dancer closest to the water.' It means an older dancer, one who's assigned a spot by the back-drop. In the old days that was a fountain."

"I don't get it."

She shrugs. "I'm like the scenery. But I think Otto will keep me around. I think he likes me, as much as he's capable of liking anyone. But I'll never be promoted."

And for all I know, she's right. Maybe she's just a competent, strong dancer who lacks (or sees herself as lacking) that ineffable quality that could make her a star. Bea thinks that about herself, too, though at least she has youth on her side.

ക് ക് ക്

"Do you think we'll have the cute one again today?" I whisper to Bea. "Taylor?" We're back at Bikram because now that I've rededicated myself to the Manhattan Ballet, I have to tighten my soft bits and look flat and tight for the upcoming leotard ballets.

Bea shrugs as she unfurls her yoga mat. She lies down in corpse pose. She didn't really want to come.

"I'll buy you a smoothie after," I whisper to her.

She opens one eye. "I'm going to order a large, with all sorts of extras like spirulina and stuff. It's going to cost you."

I smile and poke her arm. She tries to stifle a grin, and I poke her again. I'm on the verge of embarrassing both of us with some kind of tickle attack when the door to the studio slams and we look up. Instead of Taylor, bronzed and clad in clothes that hug every muscle and sinew of his body, *Zoe* enters the room. She's wearing tiny black yoga shorts and a minuscule purple sports bra. She walks in our direction, stepping around people, and places her mat next to mine. She sets up her towel and water bottle in silence and then turns to me and smiles broadly. "Couldn't let you get into killer shape alone, could I?"

Beside me I hear Bea exhaling slowly. She's going to pretend that Zoe isn't even here. Too bad that'll be impossible for me, since she's only inches away.

When Taylor walks in, flashing his photo-shoot smile, Zoe leans over and whispers, "Damn. As if I needed to feel *more* motivated."

I can only sigh.

And of course she gets his number. She goes right up to him after class and tells him what an *incredible, amazing* teacher he is. She says that his encouragements really *inspired* her and that he helped her get to a new level in her practice.

I almost spit out the water I'm drinking. "Her practice?" I say to Bea. "She's never even tried Bikram before."

"She's totally shameless," Bea agrees as we head into the locker room. "Remind me of that the next time I wonder how it is she has so many boyfriends."

"Taylor will never be her boyfriend," I say. "She might sleep with him once or twice, though."

"Boyfriend, fuck buddy, whatever," Bea replies. "Let's go get that smoothie you owe me."

I stare at her. "Did you just say *fuck buddy*?"

"I believe I did." Bea tries to keep a straight face, but I can see a smile dying to come out.

"I've never heard you say the word *fuck* before."

She gives in and grins. "People change."

"Don't change too much, okay? You're my rock."

"No problem," she says with a laugh.

I strip off my sweat-soaked clothes and step into the shower. The hot water rushes over me, and I feel like I might melt. "I need to e-mail him," I say, almost to myself.

"What?" Bea calls from the neighboring shower. "You're going to e-mail Taylor? What for?"

"No, Jacob. He called me days ago, and I haven't called him back."

"Better get on it," she says. "Hey, can I use some of your shampoo?"

I can't make a date with him, but I can at least write to say hi. And so that night I do:

To: jcnyu@yahoo.com
From: hannahbanana@gmail.com

Hey Jacob,

I'm sorry I didn't call you back. They promoted some older girls to soloist, and it made everyone a little crazy. Now we all think we're next in line.

I've been back on the training regime: Pilates, Bikram, etc. My friend Leni says I should try gyrotonics, but I think I take enough weird classes already.

Anyway, I was just thinking about you. I hope things are good.

Hannah

But then a few days go by, and I don't hear from him at all.

"Just let me bring you lunch," Matt says. "I've got nothing to do today."

I hold the phone in the crook of my neck as I change into a new pair of pointe shoes. "Are you sure you don't have to take a flight to Paris or whatever?" I ask. "You're not due on a chartered jet to Gstaad?"

"Very funny. As a matter of fact, I'm here for the foreseeable future. At least until after the Met Opera gala."

"Hmm," I murmur.

"How are things?" he asks.

"Busy. I didn't even mean to answer the phone."

"But you saw it was me," Matt says, "and so you had to."

"Actually, I just forgot for a second," I say.

"You're looking good up there lately," he says. "Your leaps are fantastic."

I forget that he's so often in the audience, sitting next to his father, the lanky, gray-haired banking tycoon. Even when I haven't spoken to him in a while, Matt knows where I am and what I'm doing.

"Thanks. I'm trying."

"So, what do you want me to bring you?"

"I barely have an hour," I tell him. "It's not worth your time."

His deep voice goes deeper. "How about you let me be the judge of what is and isn't a good use of my time?" Then he laughs. "Seriously. You know how this goes. I propose something, you protest, I persist, you give in. So, what do you want for lunch?"

How I wish this lunch offer had come from Jacob — but he would never be so pushy.

I find my toe separators underneath my chair. "Tuna on rye and an apple," I say.

"What kind of apple?" Matt wants to know.

"Are you serious?"

"Yes."

I think about this for a minute. "Fuji."

"Fuji it is."

And when I meet him outside the theater, I'm surprised to find myself happy to see him. He's always untroubled, and I don't know very many people like that. Plus he's one hundred percent attractive. As Zoe would say, he's runway material.

We sit on the edge of the fountain as Matt sips a coffee and I eat my sandwich. We make a funny-looking pair: He looks ready for the office in a well-cut gray suit and shiny shoes, while I'm sporting a pair of Adidas warm-up pants I stole from Jonathan, and my rattiest Tretorn sneakers.

A group of teenagers walks by, and even though I only see them out of the corner of my eye, I recognize them as MBA students. The girls walk with their feet turned out and their tights rolled up at their ankles; the boys are as thin and leggy as colts. They've no doubt just come from School of the Arts, where they napped or doodled through their classes, the girls drawing ballerinas in the margins of their handouts, the boys scribbling band names — Blink-182, Maroon 5, whatever — on the backs of their notebooks.

Perhaps their poor teacher was trying to teach them Shakespeare, but their heads were full of the combinations they learned in class that morning. Maybe one of the girls was willing herself not to eat for the rest of the afternoon, while another one was imagining taking her curtain call at the end of the performance and curtsying to the wildly applauding audience. I was one of those kids once; I know how it goes.

"Hey," Matt says, nudging me gently. "Where'd you go?"

I smile. "Sorry. Spacing."

"What are you dancing tonight?" he asks.

"I can't even remember," I admit. "Are you coming?"

"I've got a party to go to."

"Oh." For some reason I feel disappointed.

"Your friend, the one who looks sort of like you," Matt says. I roll my eyes. "Zoe."

"Right. She's got that solo now."

"Yes, thanks for reminding me." I take a bite of my sandwich and wrap the rest in a napkin.

"She's strong, but she's not as graceful as you," Matt says, tapping my knee gently with his finger.

I kind of wish he'd stop talking about her. "Tell that to Otto."

"I could. He's coming over to my father's for dinner next Monday."

"Don't say a word to him," I order Matt.

Matt laughs. "I wouldn't, but I don't have to. I can tell you're stronger and more relaxed. You look great up there, and I'm not just saying that because I have a big crush on you."

I look at him and open my mouth to speak, but he holds up a hand.

"Look, I'm only human. And you're a bombshell. But I don't have a reason not to tell you the truth. You're going to be recognized one of these days. I know it. I'm just quicker at figuring things out than your director."

My face flushes, and I can't help but notice that I feel proud to be sitting here with this incredibly handsome guy who thinks I'm a bombshell.

But it's time for rehearsal again, so I stand and brush the

crumbs off my coat. "Well, thanks," I say. "I mean it. For lunch and for saying that."

"Don't forget your apple," he says. "It's organic."

Then he stands, too, and he leans down and kisses me on both cheeks. "See you soon, Hannah Ward," he says. And he strides off toward Broadway, hails a cab, and vanishes.

28

"Doesn't Mr. Edmunds remind you of Mr. Smithers?" I ask Bea.

We're in dress rehearsal for *The Awakening*, watching Mr. Edmunds lurk behind Otto like a creepy shadow. He's wearing a puffy shirt and tight jeans (both Otto trademarks), and when Otto puts his hand on his hip, Mr. Edmunds does, too. When Otto crosses his arms, Mr. Edmunds crosses his arms, as if their postures are choreographed. It's kind of hilarious.

Bea stifles a giggle as she piqués away from me. "Totally," she says.

Later, as I'm picking up my water bottle and bag, Mr. Edmunds comes over to me, his brow furrowed. I have a momentary panic—could he have heard me?

"I can tell that you've been working much harder," he says brusquely. "You look stronger. You're on the right track, Ward, but you *must* stay focused."

"Thanks," I squeak out. I'm glad for the compliment, but Mr. Edmunds has always made me nervous.

As I walk back to our dressing room, I think about the fact that my body really does feel pushed to its limits. You know how in movies about athletes there's always a great montage sequence in which you see the main character getting into shape to the beat of some inspirational music? You see the time fluidly, painlessly passing as she goes from chump to champion. Her sweat gleams; her muscles harden; she's heroic in her efforts. Every camera angle is flattering.

Well, real life isn't like that. I want the time to fly by while I strengthen my body and my resolve. But it doesn't. It's just a ton of grueling work.

In the tiny moments of spare time I have between rehearsals, gym workouts, and Pilates and gyrotonics lessons, I try to keep up with my journal. This is what I wrote yesterday: *Ugh. Oh God. Ow. Ow. I want to sleep. Everything hurts. Ow.*

And that's absolutely all I could manage.

୨ଡ଼ ୨ଡ଼ ୨ଡ଼

That night, after a triple-header, my buzzer rings. I press the button and lean in close; the intercom doesn't work very well. "Who is it?"

The voice comes through the speaker so fuzzy and cracked it's almost unrecognizable. "Jacob. Jacob Cohen."

"Oh," I say, feeling my heart begin to beat faster. "Hi."

The speaker crackles. "Are you going to buzz me up?"

I hesitate — it's almost midnight — but then I lean my head against the doorframe as I press the buzzer and wait for him to walk up the three flights of stairs. I open the door and there he is, red-cheeked and smelling like the night air.

I'm wearing a pair of paint-splattered sweatpants and a long-sleeve T-shirt that used to belong to my dad. It says *Old architects never die, they just lose their structure.* I am sockless, braless.

"What are you doing?" I ask. I can feel a smile twitching around the corners of my mouth, but I'm nervous. Considering he never responded to my last e-mail, I'd sort of figured he was finally through with me. Why try to date a girl you can't ever see?

"Can I come in?" he asks.

I step back and he walks into my living room. Then he reaches into his pocket and pulls out a little box. "For you. A Hanukkah present."

I look at him in confusion, then take it from his hand; it's surprisingly heavy. "Hanukkah was almost four months ago, you know," I say.

"Yeah, okay, then it's a happy —" and here he glances around my little apartment. The couch, which I've obviously just vacated, has a nest of pillows and blankets and a mug of tea steaming on the coffee table. "Happy Hannah Day," he finishes.

The smile I was trying to suppress comes out. "Is that a legal holiday?"

"In certain municipalities," he says.

"Funny," I say, "because it isn't in mine."

He shrugs off his jacket, which he lays on the back of a chair. "I

219

know," he says, "you never have any free time. Save it, Ward, I've heard it all before. And I'll have you know that I've become the butt of many of my friends' jokes because I'm still hung up on you."

I'm still standing by the open door. In the hallway the over-head light flickers.

"Well, aren't you going to see what it is?" he asks, pointing to the box. He sits on my couch and pats the spot beside him.

I sit down next to him and lift the lid of the box.

Inside there is a small, carved stone figurine of a dancer. But she's not a ballerina — her body is thick and powerful, and she's wearing many layers of carved clothing and jewelry.

"It's an Iteso dancer," he says. "From Africa. She symbolizes strength and power and happiness."

For a little while I don't say anything; I just turn the figure over in my hand. It's cool and smooth, with a pleasing weight. The woman's feet are invisible underneath her skirts, but her hands are raised above her head, and on her face is an expression of joy.

"Well?" Jacob asks. "Do you like it?"

"I love it," I say. I place the little figurine on the coffee table between us. "Thank you." I'll put it on my bookshelf, right next to the agate my dad gave me when I was ten and a bronze casting of my first pair of baby shoes, which I use as a bookend.

"So . . ." Jacob's hand cups my shoulder, and I feel a slight tug toward him, which, for some inexplicable reason, I resist. "How have you been?" he asks.

"Exhausted. The end of the season is always tough, and now that I'm going for a promotion, I'm pushing myself even harder," I say.

"So what else is new?" he teases.

"I know, I know; I'm an overachiever from way back. Why didn't you answer my e-mail?"

"Sorry, I got really busy, too. I meant to, and I just kept spacing. I thought about you a lot, though."

His hand moves from my shoulder up to my neck, and his thumb touches skin. He rubs me, ever so softly, and then his fingers reach up and wind themselves into my hair. I fall against him, folding my body into the space along his ribs, and bury my face in his shirt. I sigh deeply.

I can feel myself relaxing, sinking into him, and then Annabelle's voice echoes in my head. *"Your job is not to have a life. Your job is to dance."* I sit up abruptly.

"What?" he asks, but I just shake my head.

Jacob looks at me with concern, and then he reaches down and clasps my foot firmly in his hands. He runs his thumbs under my arch. I have a split second of anxiety when I remember how ugly my toes are, but then I relax. He presses hard in all the right places. I sigh.

After a few moments, he reaches for my hands. He pulls me toward him again, and he holds me tight and close. I resist for a moment, and then I stop resisting; I put my head against his chest and exhale. His heart beats against my cheek like a drum, and I imagine it pumping the blood through his body.

After a while I lift my head and look from his lips to his eyes and back again. The corners of his mouth turn up in a little smile. I'm drawn even closer toward him.

"I know you're busy, but do you think you have time to kiss me?" Jacob asks.

"I believe that I could make the time, yes." I laugh as I lean in even further.

Our lips touch, and an unfamiliar tingling feeling washes over my body in waves. We roll over, and then Jacob is above me. I feel his weight on me, and it feels better than anything I've ever felt. I wrap my arms around him as he eases my shirt over my head. His shirt comes off, too, and soon I lose track of where my body ends and his begins.

႒   ႒   ႒

The sun wakes me, and I lift my head slowly. I realize that we fell asleep on the couch, and that Jacob's warm, bare chest was my pillow. He's still asleep; his dark hair is messy, and he looks so handsome and vulnerable that I can't help but smile. I kiss him gently on the cheek, but he doesn't wake up. I curl back up in the space by his ribs and take his arm and wrap it around me. I'm wearing only my white cotton underwear and a skimpy tank top. *I could get used to waking up to a cute guy*, I think.

After a few minutes, he stirs. "Hey, lady," he says, his voice hoarse and sexy. He runs his fingers along my arm.

"Hey," I say, sitting up. I've never been this naked in front of a guy before.

He looks at me and smiles, and little creases form in the corners of his eyes. "What are you doing today? Want to grab brunch or something and then walk through the park?"

I reach up and touch his cheek. *He needs to shave*, I think. *But he's gorgeous.*

"You're not answering me," he points out.

It takes all my willpower to respond. "I can't," I say, touching his chest. "I have to do all my theater laundry, and I have Pilates at noon, and then I'm meeting Bea for Bikram."

He frowns slightly, but his expressions eases as he props himself up on his elbows. "Okay," he says, "how about we meet up later and see *Dial M for Murder* at the Paris Theater? It's supposed to be great."

I sigh. "I'm sorry—I want to, but I can't. I have to rest up for tomorrow. I have two really hard ballets in the show."

He gets up from the couch abruptly and reaches for his pants. He tugs them on, tightens his belt, and then grabs his T-shirt from the floor.

"What are you doing?" I ask. I reach for a pillow to cover myself.

"Getting dressed. What does it look like?" His voice has lost its warmth.

"What's the matter?"

He whirls to face me. "You know what, Hannah? I'm really trying here." He pulls his T-shirt on. "But I'm about out of patience."

Immediately, I bristle. "What are you talking about?"

"Don't you ever give yourself a break? You're so damn rigid." He's standing in the middle of my living room, and he's almost glaring at me.

I stand up, the pillow still clutched to my chest. "This is my *career*," I say. "Nothing is more important to me."

"Yeah, apparently." Jacob stalks across the living room looking for his shoes.

"I told you about the promotions," I say. "How they're making everyone work harder—"

Jacob interrupts me. "Has anyone ever told you that you're completely self-involved?"

I can see that his shoes are under the coffee table, but I don't tell him. "Because I care about my career?" I say, my voice rising.

He puts on his coat and crams his hat on his head, but he still can't find his shoes. "You can't make time for anybody but yourself."

"You have no idea how hard my job is. This is what it takes! You're just jealous that I made it as a performer, and you *most likely won't.*"

As soon as the words come out, I regret them.

Jacob's eyes darken, and his jaw clenches. "I'm leaving," he says. He finally sees his shoes and he shoves them on. "See you later. Or not." The door slams behind him.

"Jacob!" I call. "Jacob!"

But he's rushing down the stairs, as if he can't get away from me quickly enough.

SPRING SEASON

29

It's still unseasonably chilly and gray when we start rehearsal for
the spring season in April. Before this we had a weeklong break,
which I spent in Weston with my parents. My mother, whom I'd
told about my off-and-on attempts to not eat animals, decided to
experiment with seitan and tempeh at every meal, which prompted
my dad to start looking for his car keys every day around din-
nertime. He'd suddenly "remember something at the office" and
drive off in his Volvo, heading for the nearest diner. When he
came home, he smelled like eggs and bacon.

At night we lined up on the couch and watched old movies,
and I tried to hide the fact that I wouldn't indulge in the buttered popcorn. Even though my parents wanted to know all
about the goings-on of the company, I didn't really want to talk
about it. And though I'd missed them during the season, there

was a big part of me that wished I was already back in the city, taking class and whipping my body into even better shape.

I called Bea to commiserate. "I've been dying for a break, but now that I'm here, I just feel restless. And I swear, in three days my muscles are already starting to atrophy."

I could hear Bea flop down on her bed. "Ech, tell me about it. I hate falling out of shape and then having to get back in shape. It's too hard."

"So you're taking classes?" I asked.

"Yeah, are you kidding me? I go back to the city tomorrow. Those dumb young girls who take the week off? You can *always* tell."

I gazed out the window at the trees in our yard, which were just beginning to bud. "Maybe I should switch my train ticket."

"Oh, just hit the gym or do yoga or something—you'll be fine."

I took her advice and had my mom drive me into Boston for yoga each day. (I'd never learned to drive, since I pretty much grew up in Manhattan.) And at night I slept in my childhood bedroom, its yellow walls still plastered with images of Allegra Kent and Gloria Govrin and glow-in-the-dark stars still dotting the ceiling. My old pointe shoes were still in a crate in my closet. And lined up on top of the bookshelf were all the stuffed animals I used to love so much—but not enough, apparently, to take with me when I left.

I imagined my mother coming into my room to straighten the covers and fluff the pillows, even though there was no need to, because I was gone. I realized for the first time how hard it must have been for my parents to allow their fourteen-year-old daughter to move to New York by herself. They must have wished I'd stay with them a little longer. But they knew how driven and ambitious I was, and so, however reluctantly, they deposited me in the Manhattan Ballet Academy dormitory and waved good-bye.

I could never regret leaving. But it wasn't an uncomplicated feeling.

And lying there in bed, I couldn't help but replay the fight I'd had with Jacob. I was sure I'd ruined things permanently this time.

I told myself he'd be better off without me. There were plenty of girls with more time on their hands, and I was pretty sure he wouldn't have any trouble finding one.

A few days later, my mom sent me back to New York with a suitcase of new clothes, freshly highlighted hair ("This'll make Otto adore you," she'd whispered), and one of her glazed ceramic bowls, which was supposed to bring me good luck. For a while I left it on my coffee table, but then I wrapped it in tissue and put it under my bed. If it really brought me good luck, then I wouldn't be perpetually frustrated at work and Jacob wouldn't have vanished from my life.

But I try not to think about him too much these days. We have three weeks of rehearsal period before spring season opens. It's a time to learn new ballets, rehearse the ones that are in the company's regular rotation, and practice ones we haven't danced since last year. The schedule starts off light, with everyone just back from break and easing into their dancing bodies again, and then picks up as we get closer to performance season. Though there are no-last minute throw-ons during rehearsal period—which, when it comes down to it, is the most anxiety-provoking part of performance season—rehearsal period isn't without stress. The ballets you're called to rehearse are the ones that you'll be performing, so you spend a lot of time worrying about where your name will be on the rehearsal postings.

One evening, after a long day of learning new ballets, Jonathan links arms with me and walks me home up Columbus Avenue. "I hardly ever see the sunset," he muses. "It's always pitch-black when we're done."

I glance up at the wispy purple clouds. It's true—when was the last time I saw a New York sunset? "It's pretty," I say. "We should appreciate things like this more often."

Beside me, Jonathan gives a little hop of excitement. "I'm just psyched to get home in time to watch *Models of the Runway*."

"How intellectual of you," I say.

"Hey, I never claimed to be a scholar," he replies.

We walk for a few minutes in silence. "I hate rehearsal period," I blurt out.

"Really?" He raises his eyebrows at me. "But don't you love evenings off?"

"They make me anxious," I admit.

"What's to be anxious about getting off early?"

I shrug. "I don't know what to do with myself when I'm not performing."

Jonathan purses his lips and looks thoughtful. "Yeah, now that you mention it, I can't wait to get back onstage, too. I'm dead sick of standing next to Caleb in *Wonder/Ponder* rehearsal. He's a total mouth-breather."

"It's weird — when our lives are just a little bit less intense, I miss the crazy intensity. What's wrong with me?"

"Dr. Jonathan knows what's wrong with you," he says. He pats my hand. "You're just what they call a *dancer*. Here, take two of these" — and he hands me his ballet shoes — "and call me in the morning."

"Oh, go on," I giggle. And I toss his shoes back at him as the sun sinks slowly behind the buildings of New York City.

30

When our spring season opens, I'm in the best shape of my life. I've lost five pounds since winter season; my breasts are smaller and pressed against my ribs (Bernadette has made me two more *undergarments*). So what if I don't have time to appreciate the pretty pink buds opening on the trees near the Avery Center? So what if I've stopped eating bread, stopped opening mail, stopped answering my phone?

My mother learns to text in desperation. *Call me sometime why dont u?* she writes. *Daddy sends luv.*

So busy, I write back. *Love u.*

One morning when I'm coming out of the elevator on my way to the dressing room before company class, I almost bump into tall, muscular Roman Fielding. Since he's a principal, I don't think I've ever exchanged a single word with him. He gazes down his aquiline nose at me.

"Sorry," I say, trying to get out of his way.

He stops, which makes me pause, too. His dark, heavy-lidded eyes search my face. "You never smile anymore, Hannah," he says. And then he gets into the elevator without another word.

As I hurry to the dressing room, I marvel at the fact that he knows who I am and that he noticed my facial expression. The vast majority of dancers spend their time noticing things about *themselves*, not other people. After all, it's our job to scrutinize ourselves in the studio mirrors so we can correct our imperfections.

But is Roman right? Have I stopped smiling these last few weeks?

As an experiment, before I walk into the dressing room, I fix my mouth into a bright and I hope sincere-looking smile. "Morning, ladies," I say.

Daisy looks up at me from her chair, where she's sewing her shoes. "What's that weird expression on your face?" she asks.

I guess Roman was right. But who cares about smiling? I can see my stick arms returning. I can picture *Hannah Ward* on the casting list, right there under the name of a big solo part.

๑ ๑ ๑

After company class I decide to stick around and practice my pirouettes. I've never been a great turner, especially to the left; it always makes me kind of anxious. (Being partnered with Luke doesn't help, either, considering he's always an inch away from dropping me.)

All around me other dancers are leaping and madly spinning, practicing tricks or going over the choreography for upcoming ballets. Luke is practicing his double tours, and Julie is doing furious fouettés, like she does after every class, her curly hair flying; she's hoping to be cast as the Swan Queen this season.

I focus on myself in the mirror as I prepare in a large fourth position, with my weight mostly in my front leg. I spring into a passé while snapping my head to the mirror, *one-two-down*, and again *one-two-down*, and again. I fall out of the turn and gasp in exasperation. When I attempt pirouettes to the left, I stumble awkwardly out of the very first rotation. "Damn it!" I say under my breath. I take a breath and prepare to turn to the right, *one-two-down*, and *one-two-down*.

"Don't rush it," I hear someone say.

Suddenly Zoe's standing right in front of me, still pink in the face from the grand allégro. "Try bringing this arm in directly to your chest," she directs. She grasps my left arm and says, "You're leaving it out there too long."

And I admit, my first instinct is to resent her for thinking that she ought to give me advice. But when I try the turn again, this time almost slapping my chest with my left arm, I do a *triple*. I smile.

"Perfect," Zoe says, nodding.

"I don't know about perfect," I say. "But it felt good. Thanks."

Zoe smiles. "Sure thing. You want to do it again?"

"I don't want to jinx it," I say. But I do it again anyway. I tell myself that this is just part of the montage sequence, and that all this additional work is going to pay off.

Pretty soon I'm doing triple after triple and my leotard is soaked, so Zoe and I head back to the dressing room for a quick change before rehearsal.

At my spot is an enormous bouquet of yellow tulips.

"Wow," I say. I rush over to look at the card, hoping madly it's from Jacob. But of course it's not: The flowers are from Matt.

"So, who's this Matt guy again?" Zoe asks, looking over my shoulder.

"He's the one in the front row who always shouts 'Whoo!' during bows. He's a total balletomane," I say.

"Doesn't ring a bell," she says.

"He's got the Patek Philippe?"

She bends down and smells one of the golden blooms. "Oh, right. The hot one who sends girls balloons and flowers. He dated Serena and Olivia last year."

I shrug; I can tell she's trying to bug me. "I guess. That's what Daisy says."

Zoe squints at the card. "'One remembers an atmosphere because girls were smiling in it,'" she reads, and then looks up at me with a baffled expression. "What in the world does that mean?"

"I don't know," I say, snatching it out of her hand. "It says here that it's a quote from Proust."

"Who?"

"A French writer. Matt's a Francophile, too."

"A man of passions. I like that," Zoe says, smirking.

"You probably *would* like him," I say.

She nudges me with her foot. "Are you guys dating?"

I sigh as I struggle out of my soaked tights. "It's complicated."

"He says these flowers match a present that's coming later."

"Yeah, I don't know what that means," I say.

"Oh, look at you," she says, nudging me harder. "Nineteen years without a kiss, and now two boys after you at the same time. You're practically like me now."

I just shrug. But I think to myself: *I'm nothing like you.*

Eventually I get the tights off and then rummage in my theater case for another pair. "I don't think Jacob is after me at the moment."

"Because you blew him off again."

I groan. "We sort of had a fight. It's hard enough just trying to get through the day here without bursting into tears or tearing a major muscle group. I don't know how to date on top of that. I mean, it's incredible that some of the older dancers are married. How do they find the time and energy?"

Zoe sits down on her chair and starts running her fingers through her glossy blond hair. "Duh, Hannah! They all married dancers."

"Well then, how do *you* have time to date and still maintain your career?"

"We all *have* time, it's just about prioritizing. If you *really* wanted to see Jacob, you would." Zoe takes the lid from a Chanel lipstick and eyes the color thoughtfully before dabbing it on the back of her hand.

"You make it sound so easy," I moan.

Zoe shrugs, then carefully applies the lipstick in the mirror. "Will you do that smudgy purple eye on me that you sometimes do? It'll go great with this color."

I sigh. "Fine."

Zoe claps with glee and carefully lays out her NARS eye shadows in a neat row.

"Close your eyes," I say. I straddle a chair, facing her and leaning forward so that our faces are very close. Zoe is quiet and still. I dab lavender powder on her lids with my index finger.

"Hey, Han?" she asks.

"Yeah?"

"Remember when we used to snoop around my mom's vanity and try on her makeup?"

I smile, thinking of Dolly's beautiful mirrored vanity and her collection of perfume bottles and silk scarves. I gently smudge on a darker purple in the outer creases of Zoe's eyes.

"And remember when you tried on her leopard Dior boots and you couldn't get them off for, like, forty-five minutes?" She giggles.

"Oh my God, they were so tight!"

"And you started to panic because we thought Mom was coming down the hall, but it was just Gladys!"

"And you almost peed your pants laughing!" I cry. "But hold still, you're making me mess up!"

Zoe sits still and tries to suppress a giggle. I sweep on a little shimmer with a brush.

"There," I say. I lean back and admire my handiwork. "You can open."

She turns to look in the mirror and turns her face from side to side. "I love it."

"You look beautiful," I say. And she does.

She smiles. "Thank you. Just what I needed—a makeover in time to sweat it all off in rehearsal. Do you want me to do your face real fast, just for fun?"

Instead of answering, I plop down in the chair in front of my mirror. I open my eyes really wide and puff out my cheeks.

"What in the world are you doing?" Zoe asks.

I grin. "It's my chimpanzee impression. It's my new face."

Zoe shakes her eyeliner at me. "Promise me that you will never, ever do that again," she says.

31

Backstage it's pitch-black, except for these heavenly pink rays of light streaming in from the stage. I'm giving myself a barre before I have to dress for my ballet. A pianist plays Debussy on a glossy grand in the front corner of the stage, and I sneak glimpses of Julie as she passes by in her furious piqués manèges stage left. Her body casts long shadows across the linoleum. When she comes off for a brief moment, she leans over with her hands on her knees, breathing heavily. Then she takes a hurried sip of water and adjusts her costume before returning to the stage for the coda. She transitions from woman to ballerina the moment she steps back into the light.

I take a break from my barre work and stand in the second wing, behind a boom, to watch. Holding on to the boom for support, I do plié relevés to keep my legs warm. Julie is mesmerizing. She seems to eat up the space as she moves from one side of the stage to the next in about three piqués. After a few minutes

I return to the barre to continue my warm-up, but I keep stealing glimpses at Julie as she passes by the wings.

When the ballet concludes, the audience erupts into applause. Some people shout and call out to her, and I think I recognize Matt's familiar "Whoo!" But I might be mistaken; it could be another balletomane.

I sit on the floor to go through my gyrotonics and Pilates mat exercises just as Julie exits the stage from her bow. She collapses next to me, flat on her back with her legs sprawled out. She's gasping for air and dripping with sweat, and her curly hair is working itself free of her bun. This is the person who only moments before brought tears to my eyes. She rolls onto her side and sits with her back slumped over. There's a pool of sweat on the floor.

"Well, that's a doozy," she says, smiling.

"You were great," I tell her.

"You couldn't hear me cursing the whole time, then," she says, smiling broadly. Her dark eyes flash with humor.

I shake my head.

"Good," she says. "Because that would sort of take some of the magic out of it."

I smile. "Yeah, I guess it would."

Then Otto appears, looming over us in the dim light. "A word?" he says to Julie.

She peels herself off the floor with a grunt, and he helps her to her feet. Before they leave, Otto turns to me and gives me the slightest nod.

My heart seizes up as I watch the two of them disappear into the dusky shadows. That was almost *friendly*, wasn't it?

Later, as I step into my costume, I try to mentally prepare myself for the coming ballet. The fourth movement has nonstop jumps that make my legs cramp up like crazy, and I can never get enough air. Just thinking about it makes me lose my breath. As Julie would say, it's a doozy.

Don't think, I remind myself. *Just do.* And then I hurry down the hall to the wings.

Normally I don't look at the casting sheet before performing, but tonight for some reason I do. I stand under the dim blue bulb, squinting as I search for my name. And when I find it, I literally gasp aloud. I'm called to learn the lead of *Rubies*! It's the second section of *Jewels*, which is one of my absolute favorite ballets.

I hold my breath, and then let it out in a long, slow, measured exhale. This is the kind of part I've been working so hard for — the kind of part that, if I dance it well, can lead to a lot of attention. Which would mean getting other great parts and, eventually, a promotion.

Might I finally be on my way?

The answer is yes, I might be — but I'm not the only one.

Because right below my name on the rehearsal call sheet is another name: Zoe Mortimer. She, too, will be rehearsing the role, but only one of us will perform it.

   ℘   ℘   ℘

After all our ballets are done for the night, Zoe, Daisy, Bea, and I, along with the rest of the corps, tiredly peel off our costumes in the Green Room and clutch our sweatshirts to our chests.

We're still breathing heavily as we swarm toward the elevator, pushing up against each other, urging the doors to close. As usual, there are discussions of missteps and miscounting, of girls out of line. "Emma was late on her entrance," someone whispers. "I danced like a cow tonight," someone else complains.

The adrenaline still courses through us, even though we've been in constant motion for twelve hours.

Upstairs, Zoe kicks the dressing room door open, and it ricochets off the wall. The hinges need to be repaired again; they get screwed up because we're always smashing our pointe shoes in the door to break them in.

I throw my leg warmers at my theater case and watch as they fall to the floor. I consider retrieving them, but the thought of bending down to get them makes me reconsider. Even before the performance, my quads were already blown out, so I leave my leg warmers where they are and slouch in my chair in front of the mirror to free my throbbing feet from the confines of my pointe shoes. I can feel my heartbeat in my bunions. I watch a bead of sweat roll down my cheek as my chest rises and falls.

Daisy collapses on the carpeted floor, her pointe shoes still tethered to her feet. She sticks her legs into the air and rests them against the concrete wall. "That was terrible. I'm so embarrassed." She sighs.

I had thought we were together, but I don't feel like arguing. I'm too excited about *Rubies*.

Bea carefully steps over Daisy to get to her own spot. "Take your shoes off, Daze. My feet hurt just looking at you."

Daisy flares her nostrils as she stares at the ceiling. Then she rolls onto her side and squats as she slides a pair of scissors through each stitch attaching the ribbons of her shoe to her ankle. The strands of pink satin are released, and they lie wrinkled on the floor. She carefully slips out of each heel and then sticks her legs up against the concrete wall again. "Better?" she asks.

Zoe returns from the bathroom bound in a peach towel, her flip-flops smacking against the floor. Dark makeup pools in the recesses of her eyes. "So we're learning *Rubies*, Han," she says, as if she's just read a casting sheet in the shower.

"Yup," I say. "It's you and me, together again." I flash her a smile.

Daisy sits up, leaning on her elbows. "Ech! And I'm still stuck in the back line of the corps. That is so unfair."

Zoe flops down in her chair. "Oh, go eat a Twinkie."

"Be nice for once, Z," I say. I uncoil the acrylic twist of fake blond hair from around my stumpy ponytail and hang it across the wire-caged bulbs of my mirror, just as Zoe reaches over and flips the light switch.

"Watch out! You'll burn my hair!" I yelp, and yank my fake hair away.

But Zoe doesn't apologize. She slips on a pair of black tights and then pulls on a leopard-print sheath that probably cost a month's salary.

I take off my eyelashes one by one and pick at the glue that held them on. It comes off in little black balls that I roll between my fingers and flick toward the garbage. Many of them land in Zoe's theater case, and inwardly I smile.

32

A few days later, at the end of my hour-long lunch break — which I actually spend outside, soaking up some of the spring sun's rays — I come across a bright red shopping bag by the stage door. Taped to it is a note with my name on it. I look around, as if I might catch the person who left it, but I'm alone.

If my overprotective father were here, he'd tell me not to touch it: *It's New York City; who knows what it could be?* he'd say. My mother, on the other hand, would assume that it's a present from an admirer. She's always the romantic.

Inside the bag is a package wrapped in brown paper — it's very light — and I hurry to the dressing room to open it. Though I want to tear the box open, I force myself to read the note first. *See you next door at the Met, next Saturday 8 PM*, the note reads. *It's gala night. — M*

I feel a shiver of excitement: Matt wants to take me to the

opera gala! And balletomane that he is, he must know that I'm free; that night is a special program with no corps ballets. As usual, his assumption is that I'll agree to his plan. (When, after all, have I refused him? Not since the night I met him, when I wouldn't go to Chloë Sevigny's party.) My only conflict is the extra class I'd planned on taking at the gym.

I remove the brown paper. Underneath is a cream-colored box that says *Zac Posen* in a plain but elegant font. I take off the lid, push aside layers of tissue, and gasp as I see yellow. I lift it up: a buttercup-colored strapless gown made from some kind of incredible fabric that slides like air through my fingers.

Oh my God, I think. *For me?*

Quickly I strip down and pull the dress on; it's a princess-cut sheath that falls all the way to the floor. It fits perfectly.

Just then the door comes flying open, and I hear laughter that abruptly stops.

"What are you wearing?" Zoe squeals, running up to me. "Where did you get that? Don't tell me you bought that with your crappy corps salary." She touches the fabric reverently.

Daisy, too, comes over to inspect me. "Wow," she says.

Zoe flings herself into her chair. "Some people might tell you that you look like a banana in that," she says, "but not me. You look great. Seriously, *where* did you get that dress?"

It occurs to me to point out that Zoe basically did tell me I look like a banana, but I can see myself in the mirror, and I know she's wrong. I look fantastic.

"It's a present," I say, turning to admire the way the V of the back hits right at the base of my spine.

Says Zoe, "The balletomane! Because I know your college guy can't afford Zac Posen. Tell me why in the *world* he gave you that dress."

"He bought it for me to wear to the Met Opera gala." I can't keep the surprise from my voice. Or, it seems, the pride: I can't help feeling proud to receive such an extravagant gift.

At this, Zoe shrieks and bangs her fist on the counter. "*I want to go to that!*"

"Get one of your boyfriends to take you," I say.

"I'm unattached at the moment, Hannah Banana," Zoe says.

"See?" I say. "You *do* think I look like a banana."

"No, I don't," Zoe says, grinning.

Daisy shoves Zoe in the shoulder. "You know Hannah looks beautiful."

"Of course she does," Zoe says. "Beautiful . . . and ripe."

"Seriously, I'm going to kill you," I tell her.

She giggles. "I'll stop, I'll stop. I'm sorry."

I slip the dress over my head and lay it gently on my chair. Zoe hands me my leotard. "If you need to borrow shoes . . ." she says. Her voice is kinder now.

"Thanks."

She smiles. "Anytime."

"Dr. Shapiro says yellow means optimism and happiness," Daisy chirps.

"Really?" I muse. "I hope he's right."

33

A week later, the tulips have exploded in the Broadway medians, and I have the almost unheard-of Saturday night off. As I slip on the outrageously beautiful Zac Posen gown for the Metropolitan Opera gala, I vow to be a good little ballet dancer. I gaze at myself in my bedroom mirror. *I'll be home by midnight*, I tell myself. *I'll still hit the gym in the morning.*

Matt's eyes grow wide when he sees me walking across the plaza to meet him. "You look stunning," he says.

He's wearing a tuxedo, and his hair is slicked back from his face. I have to admit that he looks pretty great himself.

I don't say anything right away — I just smile and let him take my hand. I borrowed a pair of Zoe's shoes: strappy Louboutins that make me three inches taller.

"Shall we go in?" He leads me through the huge glass doors into the magnificent gilded lobby. Coiffed women in feathered concoctions, sequined gowns, and fur stoles seem to float up the curved staircase, their necks and earlobes shimmering with diamonds.

I turn to him before we go any farther. "Thank you," I say. "Thank you for this." I gesture to the dress.

He reaches out and touches my arm. "The way you look? I should be thanking you."

And I smile again. Matt might be a little cheesy, but he does know how to make a girl feel special.

Even though it's next door to the theater, I've never been to the opera because our performances coincide. And as we settle into our red velvet seats, the curtain parts, and the singing begins, I can see that I've been missing something profound. The sets are ornate, like a moving piece of art, and the *music* . . . I've never heard anything like it.

"Well?" Matt whispers, his hand brushing my thigh. "What do you think of *Don Giovanni?*"

I don't respond; I'm entranced by the costumes and the sets, struck in speechless awe.

I'd thought that the Manhattan Ballet was glamorous, but the opera is a whole other matter entirely. The singers coax their voices to incredible heights, into mind-boggling trills. It seems as though their voices are their bodies, and they're making them dance. The women clutch their hearts as they sing— as if, if they didn't, they'd burst from their chests, still beating.

Once in a while I hear myself gasp at some new vocal feat. Matt smiles indulgently at me; he finds my naïveté charming, I guess.

"Impressive, isn't it?" he asks as the curtain closes for intermission.

I nod enthusiastically. "It's incredible."

He gently kneads the fabric of my dress between his fingers. "Come on, I want you to meet some friends: Charles, Will, and Madison. I know them from Trinity."

"Oh, okay," I say, standing up and wobbling just a tiny bit in my heels. I hadn't realized that tonight was going to be a group activity, but I'm curious to meet them.

Matt puts my hand in the crook of his arm and leads me to the mezzanine, where there are tables with white linen tablecloths and centerpieces overflowing with fuchsia peonies. Above us hangs a giant crystal chandelier, so brilliant and glittering it looks like an exploding diamond. Below us are the other operagoers, dressed in floor-length ball gowns and black tuxedos. All of them look wealthy and manicured to within an inch of their lives.

Maybe this *is what prom feels like*, I think. Then I laugh to myself when I realize that prom doesn't include a bunch of old people in fur coats.

"What's so funny, Ms. Ward?" Matt asks as we walk.

"Oh, nothing," I say, flushing. "Don't mind me."

Matt leads me toward one of the larger tables, where two twenty-something guys and a girl are waiting. One guy, the one with darker hair, stands when he sees me, and then the blond one with his bow tie slightly askew follows his lead. I glance back at Matt, who's grinning at them. The three of them could almost be brothers — they're all tall, lean, and tanned, with floppy hair, and they have that same confident, perfectly white-toothed smile.

The blond guy's eyes widen a little as we reach the table. "Way to go, Matt!" he says, looking directly at me. He bends over at the waist and kisses my hand with a devilish expression. "I'm Will."

"Hannah — hi." I pull my hand back, and the darker-haired guy reaches for it next.

His smile is friendlier. "I apologize for Will," he says. "Emotionally, he's still in utero. I'm Charles."

"Nice to meet you," I say, relaxing ever so slightly.

Matt pulls out the chair next to him, and I take a seat. A bottle of champagne rests in a silver bucket by my right hand.

The slender platinum blond wearing a short black sequin dress gazes coolly at me from across the table. She's leaning back in her chair and bouncing her leg up and down.

"Aren't you going to introduce me?" She raises an eyebrow.

"Madison, this is Hannah," Matt says obediently.

Madison extends her spindly left arm and weakly squeezes my hand. "Pleasure," she says with a smirk.

She obviously doesn't mean it. I can feel her eyeing my dress before she turns and whispers something to Will. She's dressed to the nines — besides the dress, she's got on a killer ruby necklace — and I wonder if her mother named her Madison after the avenue.

Waiters in white gloves serve us tiny salads with spiky, complicated-looking leaves and the bright pink petals of edible flowers.

Charles elbows Matt and says, with his mouth full of salad, "You guys should come to Ibiza next week."

"Yeah, Christmas was a bore without you," Will says, rolling his eyes. "I skipped out on George's party and took the jet home early."

Madison kneads Will's thigh and giggles.

Matt turns to me. "You wanna go to Ibiza?" he asks, leaning back in his chair and sipping his champagne.

"We're in the middle of the season!" I say. "You know I can't go." I look around at everyone at the table. "I mean, how can you guys get that much vacation time away from work?"

Matt laughs. "Charles's whole *life* is a vacation."

Charles points a fork at Matt. "Like you should talk."

"I work," Matt says, spearing a piece of lettuce.

"Yeah, for your *daddy*," Charles points out. "Who lets you take weeks off so you can enrich yourself through travel."

Matt shrugs. "What can I say? Nepotism has its perks."

I push my salad around on my plate, strangely not hungry. Sitting at the table with these people feels like some kind of social experiment. I'm learning how the rich manage to have zero responsibilities. "So, what do you do, Will?" I ask.

Will lifts his champagne glass to his lips and smiles at me over the rim. "I'm between jobs," he says. "I was in banking for a while, but it just wasn't that much fun. Madison and I might start a line of luggage together—right, Mad? She'll do the design, and I'll tap my friends for investment."

A tiny sneer flickers over Madison's face. "*Handbags*, Will. Not luggage."

Will waves his hand. "Whatever."

"You're going to be a purse CEO?" Matt snorts.

Will grins slyly. "You know the ladies love a man who can get them the latest to-die-for bag." This prompts Madison to swat him on the arm. "Ouch!" he yelps.

"I guess none of you really need to work," I say softly.

"God no," Charles says. "That would totally suck."

Suddenly, Madison sits up and points across the room. "Ooph, that's *sooo* unfortunate. Look what Bunny did to her face!"

Charles and Matt crane their necks, but I just sit back and take a huge gulp of champagne. Will seems preoccupied with Madison's right hand, which is angling down toward his crotch. *Doesn't anyone care about the opera?* I wonder. *Or anything of real substance, for that matter?*

"She should have stuck with the last face-lift," Charles says.

Meanwhile Will's hand is creeping up Madison's dress. Every once in a while she swats him, but I can tell she doesn't mind.

"Is Leo here tonight?" Matt asks, scanning the room.

"Haven't seen him," Will replies, pouring himself another glass of wine.

"He was here with that model last year. Cool people. I bummed a Nat Sherman from him outside during intermission." Matt pauses and looks around again. "Chloë, too. I would have expected her."

Madison winks at Matt and giggles.

Matt seems to have forgotten that he brought me. As a reminder, and in an attempt to change the subject, I speak up. "So, how long have you been coming to the opera?"

"Ever since I was a kid," he acknowledges.

"Really?" It's hard to imagine Matt as a child — a kid in jeans instead of a suit and a Patek Philippe. "Do you like it more than ballet?"

"How could a bunch of middle-aged, fully clothed people singing compare to a stage full of half-naked girls dancing?" he asks.

Madison snickers and snaps the corner of her napkin at Matt. "You pig," she says affectionately.

And I don't know who's annoying me more right now, Matt or his friends. "You know, that kind of makes you sound like a jerk," I say.

He laughs. "It was a joke." He reaches over and gives my hand a squeeze. "That's not really why I like the ballet better."

He goes on to explain the similarities he sees between the two art forms. Charles, Will, and Madison are busy discussing a mutual friend's most recent trip to rehab. I let my mind wander.

Matt's voice interrupts my thoughts. "How do you like the entrée?" Matt asks.

"It's great," I say. I look down at the plate in front of me. "I love scallops." I hadn't even noticed that they served the next course. I stab a scallop with my fork but I don't put it in my mouth. Instead I take a sip of water and wish that I were here with Jacob.

ᥱ   ᥱ   ᥱ

When the opera is over, we join the glittering crowd as it pours into the night. I'm walking toward the street when Matt reaches out and stops me.

"Hannah," he says softly. "You are so elegant, and my friends are such Neanderthals."

I nod in agreement. That's probably the closest thing to an apology that he can muster. I kind of think that he's a bit of a Neanderthal, too, but I'm not going to say anything.

He puts his hand under my chin and gently lifts my face. He bends down, and his lips meet mine, a hundred times warmer than the air.

I can feel myself hesitate, but his mouth and tongue are insistent. He presses me against the side of the building, and his hands find their way to my hair. He kisses me deeply. The dizziness I feel is probably from the wine — but maybe it isn't. Maybe it's the way Matt's kissing me, which feels both passionate and strangely deliberate. Expert.

After a minute I pull away. "I don't want to do this," I say.

But Matt puts his arm around me and tugs me toward his chest. "Yes, you do. Come home with me," he says into my hair. "It's just across the park."

And if I were Zoe, I'd go with him. Dating a patron of the ballet? Even Otto would approve of that. He'd look at Matt and see dollar signs, more than he already does.

"I can't," I say softly.

"Why not?"

Because I don't want to, I think. But I don't want to be rude. "I have a matinee tomorrow," I say.

"Oh, what's one night?" Matt asks. "Come on. I've got the best view of the park from my apartment."

I take a step back and look down at the beautiful dress he bought. "I don't think this is really working for me."

When I look up again, Matt wears an expression of complete surprise. "What do you mean?"

I could give him a hundred excuses about my career and everything else, but I decide to be honest. "There's someone else," I say—even though I'm not sure there is. For all I know, Jacob is finished with me forever. I take another step away. "But thank you for tonight. Thanks a lot."

And then I turn my back and hurry toward the street, where a cab seems to be waiting just for me. I duck inside and relax back against the vinyl seat, relieved to be alone.

34

"Let's begin with the solo," Otto instructs.

The pianist shuffles through his music as his glasses slide down the bridge of his nose. Zoe briskly walks toward center stage, her pointe shoes loudly smacking the floor, and positions herself with a thud. I stand a little too close to her on her right. We've been rehearsing *Rubies* for two weeks now, and we have our first run-through today.

"And——" Otto motions to the pianist to begin.

I curl my toes in my shoes and feel energy coming out of my fingertips. I exhale and step into an arabesque. I thrust my hips forward and exhale again as I brush my leg through. I stumble a bit on the swivel but quickly recover for the piqués. I see Zoe out of the corner of my eye inching closer to me, but I force myself to imagine that I am alone. I focus on making large, full movements that flow into one another. Otto is seated directly in front of me, but I ignore his steely gaze. This isn't for him.

As the music accelerates, my chest tightens, and I sip breaths deliberately through my nose. Overcoming the anticipation of exhaustion is always the most difficult part. It's a mental battle on top of a physical one.

Sure enough, toward the end I can't get enough air, and I begin to experience the familiar choking feeling. *This is temporary, this is temporary*, I think. But it feels like I'm drowning. As I come to the last set of turns, I turn off my mind and go for them. Overthinking will make me falter. *Don't think, just do.*

I float through them. I nail the final pose. I hear Zoe panting beside me.

"Okay," Otto says quietly. And then he walks away.

"You seemed a little off in the double pirouette to the knee," Zoe says, turning to me. "Is your hamstring bothering you?" On her face is a look of what can only be false concern.

"I'm fine," I answer, although, honestly, my hamstring hasn't been feeling that great.

"I hope so," she says. "Because those pirouettes are a really important part of the solo, and I can't see Otto risking the role on someone who feels shaky."

"Well, it would be convenient for you, wouldn't it?" I ask mildly.

For a moment, she looks surprised. Then she smiles, revealing a row of small, perfect teeth — the result, I happen to know, of ten thousand dollars' worth of orthodontia. "Oh, come on now, Hannah. You know I'd be happy for you if you got the role."

I bend down to gather up my sweatshirt and leg warmers. "Of course," I say. But I don't mean it any more than Zoe means what she said about being happy for me.

We walk back to the dressing room in silence, and then Zoe goes up to the roof for a cigarette. I sit down in front of the mirror and put my head in my hands.

The physical effort is hard enough; why does the competition have to make it even worse?

❧   ❧   ❧

After the run-through, I head down to physical therapy. The PT room is sandwiched between the vending machines and the laundry area, and it has all the charm and spaciousness of a utility closet. On the familiar cinder-block walls are random, aging anatomy posters, as well two large mirrors with big dinosaur stickers decorating the edges. There are two massage tables and some plywood shelves. The lower ones display a stash of Advil, Band-Aids, ice packs, and Ace bandages, while the top ones have a couple pairs of crutches and a boot.

"Hey, Hannah! How's it going?" Frannie, the physical therapist, smiles broadly as she thrusts her elbow into Adriana's calf. "Just finishing up here."

"Hey," I say. As I wait for my turn, I scan the physical therapy sign-up sheet, which divides the day into ten-minute slots for massage, adjustments, and so on. I see Daisy's name a few slots below mine; she's been complaining about her left shoulder. The sheets go up in the mornings, and they always fill up within moments.

I watch as Frannie uses the weight of her upper body to press down on Adriana's muscle. Adriana sighs in what is probably a mixture of pleasure and pain. A moment later, Frannie pats Adriana's foot, and she slowly dismounts the table.

"Is it cool if I do a little ultrasound?" Adriana asks as she squirts a mound of blue jelly onto her foot.

"Do what you need to, darlin'. You know how to set it up?" Frannie asks.

"I'm an old pro," Adriana says as she switches a lever and turns a knob on the machine. She rubs the blue goo in circles over her metatarsals with a metal handle as the sound waves travel deep into her tissues, creating a gentle (and hopefully healing) heat.

I climb up onto the table.

"So, how can I help you?" Frannie asks. Her soft, kind face curves into a smile.

"I pulled my hammy again," I say. I try to sound nonchalant, but I can hear the pang of panic in my voice.

"Oh dear. Are you on tonight?" Frannie motions to me to lie down on my stomach.

"I have a doubleheader."

Frannie just sighs as I place myself in the head cradle, which presses against my forehead and cheeks. "I need you to work some magic," I say into the face hole.

"I don't know how you girls do it," Frannie says as she leans into my leg with her body weight. It's not exactly a feel-good massage, but I can tell that she cares about me and wants to make me feel better. I close my eyes and imagine that Frannie's hands are my mother's hands and that her touch is telling me that everything is going to be okay.

After a few moments Frannie gently taps my foot, and I lift my face from the cradle. There is a pink indentation across my forehead.

"Why don't you come back for a little heat and microcurrent before the performance tonight?" she says.

"Okay, thanks," I say. "I will."

I gather up my things, but I'm reluctant to leave. It's so rare to feel taken care of in this world that every moment of kindness feels incredibly precious.

ဖ   ဖ   ဖ

As I head backstage to prepare for my first ballet of the evening, Harry intercepts me, holding out an envelope with a slightly embarrassed shrug. "It's from Mattie," he says. "She was up late last night making it, but she wouldn't show me what it is. It's pretty late for Valentine's Day, but Lord knows that kid runs on her own clock."

"I've got to do a barre," I say, hardly looking at him or the envelope. "I'll open it when I'm done."

"Sure, sure, no problem," Harry says. He ducks his head and waves me off.

But as I stretch my calves at the barre, I wonder if I've hurt his feelings somehow. Couldn't I have just stopped for thirty seconds and looked at his daughter's card?

"Did you hear about BaryshniMoss?" Jonathan says.

"What?" I bend over my leg and feel the muscles lengthen. Then I realize he's not talking to me; he's talking to Daisy, who is sitting at his feet like a disciple.

"Supposedly, Kate Moss is, like, training in ballet, and she and Baryshnikov are going to make some dance movie together," Jonathan says. He bends down to touch his toes, pronouncing the last part of this statement into his knees.

"No way," Daisy says.

Jonathan stands up and shakes his head as he makes a crossing sign over his heart. "She thinks because she can wear eight-inch heels down a catwalk she can stand on pointe. Well, good luck, Kate! That's all I have to say."

Daisy nods. "Totally," she says. "But Baryshnikov — I loved him on *Sex and the City*."

I have to stifle a snort. So that's what Daisy thinks of when she thinks of Mikhail Baryshnikov: Carrie Bradshaw? She's even younger than I thought.

Jonathan grins. "I know. He was a total silver fox." And even though he's in the next ballet, too, he skips off to spread the Kate Moss news elsewhere.

Focus, I tell myself, *focus*.

Christine hurries past, mumbling into her headset. She looks up and our eyes meet. "Costume, Hannah?" she says, making a hurrying motion with her arm. "You're in *Fortitude*, right? That's in ten."

"I'm on top of it," I say.

On the way to the Green Room, I open Mattie's card.

Dear Hannah,
Please PLEASE come to my ballet Shcool next week on May 3rd. We're having an Open House. Their will be lots of dancing!!!!!!
Love, your freind,
Matilda
PS I think your the best dancer in the company.

It's very cute, misspellings and all. I put it with my things so I can hang it on my mirror in the dressing room, and then I step into the pink tutu that Laura holds out for me.

35

A few days later in Mr. Edmunds's class, during one of the notoriously boring adagios to the tune of "My Favorite Things," I'm
blankly watching the first group of dancers promenade in arabesque when Mai seems to sit down in a less-than-graceful spin
in the center of the room. At first Bea and I giggle — we think
it's just Mai being sloppy again — but when her head hits the
floor and she stops moving, we begin to panic. The pianist stops
mid-phrase and Mr. Edmunds rushes to her side.

The rest of us, too, all instinctually swarm around her, but
Roman yells at us to get back. "Give her some air," he cries, waving his arms madly. "Move!"

I glance down, though, as I back away. Mai looks impossibly
frail, with her hair so black and her skin whiter than white.
Lying on the floor, she looks no bigger than a child.

Julie calls 911 on her cell phone as she strides nervously

around the room on her long, powerful legs. Mr. Edmunds has one of the boys carry Mai to the physical therapy room, and a crowd of dancers follows, murmuring in concern. Before I know it, I'm the only person in the studio, standing there dumbly looking at my own figure in the mirror.

What just happened? I think.

Feeling slightly dizzy myself, I sit down at the piano and touch a few of the keys lightly. I wonder if Mai's gained consciousness yet; if she hasn't, does that mean something's really wrong? I listen for sirens coming up Broadway — not that I'd be able to hear them in this fortress of a building.

I hear voices in the hall, and I go out to see who's there. It's only Luke and Emma, who turn to me with solemn faces and say that Roman carried Mai down to a cab and was taking her to the hospital.

When I get back to the dressing room, everyone is theorizing about what went wrong.

"She's obviously malnourished," Zoe says as she takes a protein bar from her bag. "I heard she only eats, like, chicken broth and spinach. God knows how she has so much energy onstage."

Daisy says, "Olivia told me Mai doesn't like to eat at all. She thinks it's overrated."

I can't help noticing that my friends seem to be in good spirits.

As I listen to them hypothesizing about what disorder or ailment Mai has, I get more and more upset. Maybe it's because I'm hungry, too (oh, how I miss carbs!), but more likely it's because I'm worried about her. "Something's really wrong with her, you guys," I say.

They look at me blankly. Then Zoe says, "Obviously, Hannah," and takes a bite of a pear.

I sink down into my chair and sip from a bottle of water. I can't help thinking about the other MB girls who've damaged themselves. Last year a second-year corps dancer named Lila was diagnosed with a thyroid problem, and one of the soloists developed a blood disorder thanks to her continual dieting. It was similar to hemophilia, Daisy had told us (of course she knew all about it), and she'd be on medication for the rest of her life.

I know that a certain amount of suffering is necessary to make art. If ballet were easy, everyone could do it, and there'd be no need for the Manhattan Ballet or any other dance company.

But still I feel like someone has shaken me by the shoulders.

A few days later Mai comes to the theater to watch some of the rehearsals and meet with Otto. It turns out that she has developed a severe thyroid disorder, too, and the medication she's on has made her face swell up to the point where she's barely recognizable. Her black hair looks stringy and dull.

As I watch Mai sip delicately from a mug of tea, I start to wonder if I'm really doing the right thing with my life.

36

On Monday night I go down to Mattie's dance studio on the Lower East Side. It's just at the edge of Chinatown, across the street from a small, paved park dotted with a few trees and surrounded by a chain-link fence. In the park, old men play chess at cement tables, bundled up in faded jackets and worn hats even though it's seventy degrees. I walk past people carrying orange plastic bags from Chinatown grocers. The air is full of language, and little of it is English.

I could probably count on one hand the number of times I've been this far south, and I realize that Jacob was right. I don't live in this city.

There's a banner above the studio entrance that says SPRING OPEN HOUSE in big purple letters. The doors are propped open, and people enter in a steady trickle. I feel nervous and out of place—I'm no one's parent or older sister. I wish I'd brought Bea, but she's nursing a spring cold.

The studio is warm and welcoming, if a little shabby. At the end of the hallway, a pair of double doors opens into a small auditorium. At one end is a stage, complete with velvet curtains (donated from an old movie theater, Harry said), and many rows of folding chairs. I take a seat in the back. For some reason I don't want Harry to see me. I just want to sit here, unrecognized and alone.

There are kids running around all over. Some of them are in costume, and some of them are just here to watch their siblings. The shrieking and the laughter echo against the high ceiling. I see a round, black-haired kid who looks very much as I imagined Jacob's Paulo; he's eating licorice ropes, and his entire face is stained with red.

I wonder how Jacob's doing and what stupid jokes he's been told by his third graders. I wonder if he's had any shows lately, and if he ever sings "Girl in a Tutu" when he gets up onstage.

I've had *Moby-Dick* on my coffee table for weeks now, but I still haven't read it. It sits there next to *Frankenstein* and a stack of old *People* magazines.

"Good evening, everyone," calls a voice through a crackling speaker. "We're almost ready to begin."

The kids reluctantly find their seats, and I look through my photocopied program, which is hand-lettered, presumably by one of the older students. *Welcome to the Delancey Dance Academy's Spring Open House—A Gala Affair*, it says. Then the lights dim, and the curtain rises.

Mattie is in the very first dance. She prances onto the stage in the middle of a line of other little girls her age. None of the costumes match, and some barely fit their wearers. Bernadette would fall off her chair in horror.

They line themselves up, then lift their hands above their heads and wait. In the wings, someone hits Play on a stereo, and the sound of a Sousa march fills the auditorium. On cue the girls begin to move. They glide to the left, then to the right, and then some of the dancers come forward in leaps while others linger in the back, twirling around on demi-pointe. They're too young to be on pointe, but no doubt they're already dreaming about it. Every young dancer does.

The joy on the faces of those girls is contagious. I remember feeling that way, back when I was little, when I had my own first recital. And before that, even, when I was dancing in my basement in front of an audience of stuffed animals.

Mattie is among the most enthusiastic dancers. Her pudgy little legs kick and leap, and all the while she's smiling at everyone in the audience. When she's through, the applause is deafening.

I can hear Zoe's voice in my head. *She gets an A for effort, but she's totally inflexible. Not to mention kind of fat.*

I sigh. No, Mattie is not a natural dancer. But she's enjoying herself and she tried her best. Why can't that be enough?

I sit through most of the rest of the program, though my stomach rumbles because I haven't eaten dinner. Mattie is in two more dances — apparently she's one of the Delancey Dance Academy's star students.

But she could leap as high as the rafters and it wouldn't change the fact that she is as short and thick as a fire hydrant. No one would ever think she could be a ballet dancer; she'd never be accepted into the MBA.

But let's pretend she *did* get in. She would spend every waking moment comparing herself to the other girls, the girls with lanky ballerina bodies, and hating her arms for being short and her torso for being thick. The teachers would tell her to lose weight around her midsection and to pray for longer limbs to sprout.

This bright, sunny child would be miserable.

Thinking about all this, I feel protective of Mattie, and just a little bit sad for the girl I used to be.

37

Zoe and I are called to rehearse *Rubies* again, this time onstage, at the end of the rehearsal day. The backstage area is vacant except for a few steel ballet barres left over from the night before, carelessly strewn across the linoleum. On the front of the stage, I can see Zoe gesturing with her hands while perched on the piano bench. I drop my dance bag by the barre and shed my warm-up pants and sweatshirt. As I approach the stage, I realize that Zoe is talking animatedly to Otto.

What is she talking about? I think. *And where does she get the nerve?*

Our elderly pianist enters through the wing with a pile of musical scores tucked under his arm. He politely asks for his seat back, then adjusts his glasses and smiles meekly. Zoe bounds up and giggles theatrically. Otto says something indecipherable as Zoe leans in so close to him that her lips almost touch his ear.

Then she skips upstage toward me and gives a quick phony smile with the corners of her mouth. I fake-smile back.

"Let's run it from the top, girls," says Otto.

We run the opening section, the solo, the coda, and the finale, all side by side. At times Zoe pushes to dance in front of me, and I respond by moving just a little too close to her. There are moments when we almost collide but narrowly miss each other.

All of this is Otto's fault, when it comes down to it; but since there's no point in being mad at him, I just seethe privately at Zoe.

And when rehearsal is over and I'm gathering my things, I see Zoe lingering onstage, pretending to stretch her calf. A moment later, I watch her walk over to Otto. She sways her hips a little as she goes, and she has a sly, almost seductive smile on her face.

I want to tell her off, but I just don't have the energy.

☙　☙　☙

"Hannah, come here!" Jonathan practically shouts to me. He's pointing to the casting sheet that Sammy just tacked to the wall. There, under the lead for *Rubies*, is my name. *My* name. Not Zoe's. My heart does a somersault in my chest.

"Congratulations, darling." Jonathan beams at me.

"Oh my God," I whisper. I bite my lip to contain my excitement.

"You deserve it, Hannah. I'm so happy for you!" He laughs and gives me a kiss on the cheek.

"I just can't believe it." It's hard to keep from squealing with excitement.

"You get to wear that hot little red number," he says.

"Ooh, I'm going to go try on my costume." Waving good-bye to him, I rush down to the basement.

When I brush back the hideous costume-shop curtain, Bernadette lifts herself out of her chair. She hurries over and nearly smothers me in her enormous breasts.

"We are so proud of you, Hannah!" she says.

Carole, the other nice costume lady, clutches me with her spidery arms next, whispering her congratulations. I'm not surprised that Glenn, the third seamstress, pretends not to notice me; she's half-buried under a pile of tulle, and she's always grouchy.

Carole takes my hand; hers feels like a pile of twigs. She leads me to a rack of costumes and selects a short red one. "Some great ballerinas wore this before you, my dear," she says.

I look at the lining and see *Harlow* written in black Sharpie on a hand-sewn tag; next to it, there's another tag that reads *Hayes*. Lottie Harlow, Otto's star ballerina, and Annabelle Hayes, my ballet mistress.

"Lottie was seventeen and so thin," Carole says wistfully.

"You should have seen her onstage. Electric," Bernadette adds. "Try it on."

I strip naked and step into it carefully as Bernadette offers me her sturdy hand so I don't fall over.

"You're taller than they were," Carole says, "but I think it will work."

I step in front of the mirror. I don't look like myself, but like a willowy, lean ballerina. The costume is a cherry-red cropped Lycra dress that hits just below the hip. The bodice is adorned with glittering ruby crystals all the way down to my belly button.

"Lovely," Carole whispers.

The costume is old and not easy to clean, and so it has a distinctly human smell. It's not BO, exactly, but it's only a few steps away from it. If I look closely, I can see where the fabric has been bleached by the sweat of other dancers, and the places where missing jewels have been replaced by ones that don't exactly match.

I'm not sure whether to be thrilled and intimidated by the history of the costume or slightly grossed out by its current condition.

"Did you lose weight?" Bernadette asks.

"Yeah, I think so," I say.

"If you ask me, you didn't need to," she says.

"But no one does ask you, Bernie," Carole says, wagging her bony finger. "They've got their own ideas up there on the street level, don't they, dear?"

I smile ruefully. "It's a different world," I say.

I slip back into my leotard and tights. As I walk down the hall toward the elevator, I pump my fist in the air and think to myself, *I'm on the right path!* Later I'll call my parents; they're going to be so excited. I'm sure my dad will tell all his coworkers how proud he is of me, and my mom will phone my grandma in Florida. They'll probably want to come to every performance.

I take the elevator up to the fourth floor to tell the girls the great news.

When the elevator doors open, I hear hysterical shrieking coming from down the hall. My heart starts to beat faster as I run toward the noise. It sounds like it's coming from our dressing room, and as I near the closed door I'm terrified of what I'll find. The noise grows louder, and my breath comes quick and hard.

I swing open the door, ready to find a shattered ankle, a positive pregnancy test, or someone else unconscious on the ground. "What?" I gasp. "What?"

In the middle of the room, Bea, Zoe, Daisy, and Leni are huddled together tightly holding each other. Someone is wailing. "Who's hurt?" I say.

Leni turns toward me with tears streaming down her cheeks.

"Zoe got promoted!" she cries. Then she turns back to the mass, and they scream and start jumping up and down in a tangle of arms and legs.

Zoe got promoted. I say the words over again in my head. The bundle of bodies parts, and Zoe is in the center, her face damp and blotchy from crying, her arms open and inviting. "Hannah!" she cries.

I go to her and hug her stick-thin body. My heart has not stopped pounding. I'm holding her, and her arms wrap tightly around my shoulders. I am shocked.

Shocked. Devastated. Impossibly confused.

"Congratulations," I whisper. I feel like I've just been kicked in the stomach.

"Thank you," she says. Her tears wet my neck. "Thank you so much." She pulls away from me and looks me in the eye. Then she turns around to the rest of the room and raises her arms up in the air. "Aaaaaaaah!" she screams gleefully. "Aaaaaaaaaah!"

I flop down onto my chair and twist my hands in my lap.

"Guys!" Daisy yelps, pointing to the clock. "We're going to be late for rehearsal!" She gathers up her dance bag and hands Zoe hers. "Hannah, get up."

But I ignore her. In a flurry of activity, everyone else disperses — everyone but Bea and me. She comes over and sits next to me, and she puts her hand on my knee.

I'd just wanted to tell her about being cast in my first solo, but now the news has been completely overshadowed.

"You okay?" Bea asks.

I open my mouth to say something, but nothing comes out. "I — I don't know what to say." I pick at my cuticle and stare off into space. I think about seeing Zoe flirting madly with Otto before our *Rubies* rehearsal. Did that have anything to do with her promotion?

"Crazy, isn't it?" Bea says. "She's a *soloist* now."

I nod my head. I'm just sitting there dumbly while Bea pats my knee. After a while I look up at her. "I got the *Rubies* solo," I mumble.

"I know." Bea smiles. "Word travels fast when Daisy's around. Congratulations. I'm really proud of you."

"Yeah, thanks," I say, avoiding eye contact.

She stands and wraps a sweatshirt around her waist. "Come on," she says. "We really should head up to rehearsal."

"I'll catch up with you in a sec," I say, forcing myself to smile a little.

Alone in the dressing room, I stare in the mirror, but my eyes won't focus. I am nothing but a pale blond blur.

38

Bea opens my cupboards one by one, trying to find something worthy of snacking on, but they're even barer than usual. I'm slumped on the couch, stabbing a pencil into a coaster. It's eleven thirty at night, and we're half-dead from the performance.

"I just can't believe Zoe got promoted," I say.

"Really? She'd have given her left arm for a promotion." Bea starts opening drawers, as if she might find something delicious next to the forks and spoons. "Don't you have any tortilla chips or anything?"

"No, I threw them out when Olivia and Eliza got promoted." I snap the point of the pencil into the coffee table. "I saw her walking over to him like she was going to jump his bones. Do you think she slept with Otto?" I toss the pencil onto the floor. "Because she's not a better dancer than me."

Bea comes into the living room and flops down on the couch

next to me. "You're right, she's not," she says, nodding. "But she didn't get ahead because she slept with Otto—I don't think even she would do that. Sure, she might have flirted with him. But come on, do you know how many girls bat their eyelashes at Otto? And Zoe will flirt with a park bench, for god's sake."

I bite my lip and don't say anything. Bea puts her hand on my knee and continues. "Zoe got ahead because she's a fixture at the theater—"

"But we're *all* fixtures at the theater," I blurt. "We might as well sleep there!"

Bea nods understandingly. "But Zoe's always going to rehearsals she wasn't called to, just to work," she says, "and she's never missed a single company class. And more important, Zoe is willing to give up everything else to be a soloist. Did you notice she stopped dating entirely? She's *happy* to give the rest of life up. And I don't think you are anymore."

My eyes search Bea's pretty, freckled face. I can't believe that she, of all people, is defending Zoe—she doesn't even like her that much. "What are you talking about? I've worked my ass off! I can't imagine dedicating myself more than I already do."

"But you're conflicted every day. I can see it," she says gently.

"No, I'm not." I can feel my face burning.

Bea sits back and crosses her arms. "Han, you know I love you, but at least be honest with yourself, if not me. I know you love dancing, but are you sure you even *want* to be promoted?"

"Are you kidding? Of course I do!" I leap up from the sofa

and start pacing the room. "What do think I've been chasing my whole life?" I knock over a stack of old magazines, but I don't care. "I didn't have a prom! I've never had a boyfriend! I've hardly seen my parents since I was fourteen! I can't even finish one damn book!" I feel hot tears burning my cheeks. "I'm exhausted all the time, every single day. What more am I supposed to do?" The tears stream down my face.

Bea looks at me, her blue eyes affectionate and warm. "But what do you think happens after you get promoted, Hannah?" she asks softly. "You have even less of a life than before. It only gets harder." She stands to face me and holds my gaze. "The *Rubies* solo is huge. And you probably *are* on your way to being promoted. But you have to make up your mind. You can either have a life, or you can dance. But you can't have it both ways."

"But I don't want to choose," I moan.

A tear sparkles in the corner of her eye as she answers. "But you *have* to, Hannah. You have to make a choice."

I feel a lump in my throat as I try to catch my breath. "Maybe you're right," I whisper.

"It's okay, Hannah. It's really okay."

I nod silently. And I realize I'm covered in snot.

Then Bea puts her arms around me and gives me a long, hard hug. "Now, I don't know about you," she says, pulling back, "but I am *famished*. Let's order some goddamn sushi, and we'll open a bottle of red."

"Takeout menus are in the kitchen," I say, still sniffling.

Bea smiles at me. "That's my girl," she says.

The next morning I go to the dressing room before class to see Daisy, red in the face, flinging things out of her theater case. Leg warmers, socks, and T-shirts land all over the room. A pair of pointe shoes goes whizzing past my head and collides with the cinder-block wall. She's cursing like a truck driver stuck in rush hour traffic on the BQE.

The reason? Caleb has kissed another girl.

Though she's not exactly a girl: Her name is Margaret, she's twenty-seven, and she's one of the Manhattan Ballet soloists. She dances Odette in *Swan Lake*, and last year the *New York Times* called her "a dancer of thrilling athleticism."

"I can't believe he found someone he likes better than me," Daisy whines. "Do you think he's been ogling her ass the whole time or what?"

"I still can't believe he's not gay," Zoe whispers.

I feel terrible for Daisy, and I try to give her a hug, but she shrugs me off.

"Do you think his mother knows he's a cheating, lying bastard?" she hisses. "I'm going to call his mother."

"Don't," says Bea quietly from the corner, where she has gone to avoid being hit by Daisy's warm-up clothes and pointe shoes. "Tattling isn't the answer. Caleb is the person you need to confront."

Daisy rolls her eyes and looks over at me. "Who invited Dr. Phil here?" she demands, picking up a shoe and then throwing it down again.

"She has a point, Daze," I say.

Daisy ignores us both and huffs over to the door. "I'm going to vending," she says. "I need a Diet Coke and a bag of Fritos."

The door slams behind her, and the dressing room is suddenly silent. Bea gets up from the corner and begins to pick up Daisy's things and fold them. I've never, ever seen her fold clothes before. "I feel really bad for her," she says.

I nod. As I bend to help Bea gather Daisy's scattered clothes, I try to will Daisy strength.

"She'll be okay," Bea says, as if reading my thoughts. "But it's funny in a way. How it takes something like this to remember that there's more to life besides ballet."

And Bea's right, of course. We forget that the world doesn't revolve around us and our pointe shoes, and that our disappointments (and our triumphs) don't all stem from casting decisions and Otto's whims.

And this makes me think of Jacob.

39

On Monday, the May sun is shining after days of rain, and the air feels almost like summer. I slip on a little cotton shift and a pair of ballet flats (it always seems weird to me that they're called that) and take the subway downtown.

I asked Jacob to meet me for coffee after his last class of the day, and because I'm early, I sit on the steps outside the building and watch the NYU students scurrying to and from their lectures, their backpacks and satchels crammed with books and pencils and laptops. Most of them are wearing jeans and tennis shoes. Some students are talking on their cell phones, some are walking with friends, and some are trying frantically to catch up on their reading while threading their way through the crowd of their peers.

Zoe's voice comes back to me, faint and faintly mocking. "*Pedestrians* go to college, Han."

A kid who doesn't look a day older than sixteen plops down on a step near me, lights a cigarette, and opens a dog-eared book. Ironically, it's *Frankenstein*. His syllabus slides out from one of the pages and blows against my shoe. Before I hand it back to him, I have a chance to see the course title: *The Feminine and the Fantastical: Mothers, Monsters, and Mad Women in Nineteenth-Century Literature.*

Jacob approaches me, squinting from the sun, but his face is otherwise unreadable. "Hey," he says.

I stand up. "Hey."

There's an awkward silence. I dig the toe of my shoe into the steps, scuffing it a little.

"Well," he says. His hands are shoved in his pockets. "So you wanted to get coffee or something?" he asks eventually.

I nod. "I wanted to talk to you. I need some perspective."

He raises his eyebrows. "So you didn't come here to apologize for being so impossible." But he smiles after he says this. "Do you want to go somewhere else?"

"Please."

He holds out his arm, elbow bent, and I link my arm with his. To touch him fills me with something inexpressible—a mixture of anticipation and longing. It feels like he's impossibly far away, even though he's right beside me. The sun shines on his dark hair, and the wind blows it into his eyes.

We walk west, past boutiques and cafés, past shoe repair shops and dry cleaners. Girls are out in their first summer dresses; they seem shy to show their pale arms, their delicate white necks. Every corner deli has buckets of flowers out front: tulips, irises, freesias.

"Where are we going?" I ask. It's the first thing I've said in blocks.

"To the river," Jacob says. He takes my hand as we cross the West Side Highway, but it doesn't feel romantic. It feels merely protective, the way he might hold one of his students' hands to keep him or her from running into traffic.

On the other side, we're right at the water. I always forget that Manhattan is an island. It seems so solid, so gigantic—how could it be one small piece of land sandwiched between rivers? You hear the word *island* and you think of sand, palm trees.

We sit down on a bench. The sun glints on the river. Depending on where you look, the water seems either brown or blue.

I have so much to say to him that I don't have any idea where to begin. The breeze whistles by us, a few gulls turning lazily in it.

"So," Jacob says.

"So," I say. I fiddle with the edge of my skirt. I don't know why I can't find the right words to begin. It's not that Jacob makes me feel uncomfortable—it's the opposite of that. He makes me feel calm; it's my own self that's making me feel anxious.

"So something happened," I say. "Zoe got promoted to soloist—"

"Wow, okay," he says, nodding.

"Yeah, and I got this really great part."

Jacob's eyebrows rise. "That's fantastic, Hannah!"

"Yeah, it's great," I say. "And I'm probably going to be promoted, too . . . at some point. But I talked to Bea about it, and she kind of made me see that I've been feeling ambivalent about that for a while now."

Jacob looks slightly confused. "It seems to me like you've been pretty damn dedicated."

"Yeah, I have been. But don't you see? Getting promoted will only make it worse. I'll have even *less* time for anything. And I'm realizing that there are just so many other things I want to do and see and learn about." I shake my head. "The truth is that I'm not willing to do whatever it takes to be a ballerina."

Jacob nods his head slowly. "So, what would you do if you left?"

"Who knows?" I cry. "But I was sort of thinking about it, and I remembered that I used to love reading, like, biographies of famous women. Helen Keller and Amelia Earhart. And I had this fantasy about spending some time in India. But right now? I'm the kind of person who doesn't even know how to make a grilled cheese sandwich." I look into his blue eyes. "I'm envious of all you're able to explore and learn. And I want that. I want to learn Italian, too, but for real, and I want to have the time to go see really amazing art. And I want to get to know my parents."

My eyes suddenly fill with tears. I stare out over the blurry river, and a few silent minutes go by. The water laps at the shore as a seagull floats above us.

"But the idea of leaving *terrifies* me," I say eventually. "Leaving would be like going into a witness-protection program or something; I wouldn't ever see the people in my life anymore, because I'd be on the outside, in the real world. It would be like

285

starting from scratch . . . like moving to Kansas or Idaho or . . . New Jersey."

"You know, New Jersey's right over there," Jacob says, smiling. He points across the river. "So *that's* not so bad."

I can't help but smile back.

Jacob puts his hand on my knee and squeezes it lightly. "But dancing will always be a part of you. There's dance outside of this particular company, right?"

I nod, but I'm quiet for another moment as the tears run down my cheeks. Then I wipe them away with my sleeve.

"Come here." Jacob opens his arms, and I sink into them. "Can I kiss you now?" he asks softly.

But he doesn't wait for an answer. He just does.

40

"Ladies, ladies," Christine says, snapping her fingers at us. She's chewing gum so quickly it looks like some kind of facial tic, which is apparently her new way of combating the stress of her job. "*Emeralds* is up. *Rubies* goes in twenty minutes. What in the world are you doing, Adriana? You're not in this. Shoo!"

"We're fine, Christine," someone calls.

"God, I hope so." Christine sighs, then turns around and heads down the hall.

Laura smiles at me as she fits me into my short, red, jewel-encrusted costume. I check my makeup and bun in the mirror. In a moment begins my inaugural performance of *Rubies*.

"*Merde*," Laura says. "You're going to be amazing."

I smile. When you think about it, it's a really beautiful thing that we do. The company is a collection of one hundred very different people, from all over the world, but we all believe in the power and importance of art. That's what binds us, keeps us together, through the effort and the intensity and the competition.

I blow Laura a kiss and then scurry down the hall to the backstage area. Harry lingers by the boom, and he mimes a standing ovation as I pass by. Then he clambers up to the flies, where Bea is waiting for the performance to begin.

My parents, who refused to remain in Massachusetts when their one and only offspring was dancing her first solo, are somewhere in the invisible audience. And Jacob is, too, with an armful of roses so big he can barely hold them (he ruined the surprise by texting me a picture).

Before the curtain goes up, I stand alone in the darkness in the center of the stage and listen to the sound of my breath. Sometimes — and maybe this is one of the magic times — the pause before the opening notes can dilate, and the seconds seem to stretch into minutes, hours.

I think about the moment I fell in love with dance as I leaped over chiffon scarves when I was seven. I think about my mom driving me to ballet lessons in downtown Boston, and my dad hand-sewing the elastics onto my ballet slippers. He obsessed over making sure they were just perfect.

On the other side of the red velvet curtain, the conductor taps his stand and raises his arms. The audience waits. I take a deep breath and imagine the air filling my lungs. I nod to Christine and step into a sous-sous. I hear the opening strains of the violins.

The curtain rises. I feel the lights hit my skin. For the first time, I'm alone onstage, as I'd always dreamed. There's no other dancer to share the moment with — only the invisible audience. There's a terrific sense of freedom, but I'm caught off guard by how lonely it is.

I take a deep breath.

Then I stare straight ahead and charge downstage.

❧   ❧   ❧

Even as kids we were warned of the brevity of dance careers. When I was in third grade, my teacher, pretty, willowy Mrs. Eaton, would say, "Dance each step as if it were your last." We looked at her blankly. What did we understand of that then? We were eight years old: A single school day felt interminable, and childhood seemed like it would go on forever.

It was another ten years before I understood what Mrs. Eaton had been saying. What she meant was: *Time is precious. And it speeds up.*

There are a few more weeks of spring season, and then it's over, all of it. I'll pack up my theater case, and I'll take down the pictures and notes tacked up around my mirror. When I leave the dressing room, it will be for the last time.

A few days ago I walked determinedly down the long hallway to Otto's office. I ignored his secretary — who told me firmly that he was busy — placed my hand on the doorknob, and turned it.

I'd never been in his office before, never approached him uninvited. He had his feet up on a massive mahogany desk, but he lowered them as he hung up the phone. He looked down his nose at me, and his dark eyes were cool and only vaguely interested.

There was a chair next to me, but it seemed too presumptuous to sit. And anyway, what I had to say wouldn't take long. I took a breath and began. "I've always dreamed of dancing *Rubies*, and now I have, and I danced better than I ever have before. In fact I had the time of my life."

"And if you keep up that level of work and dedication —"

I put up my hand to stop him. "No." I shook my head. "I don't *want* to. I've sacrificed enough already." I pointed to the window overlooking the city. It was one of the only windows in the whole theater. "There's a whole world out there that I don't know anything about. I owe it to myself to learn as much about it as I possibly can. I want to lead an extraordinary life, a life that isn't contained inside a single theater."

Otto stared at me as if he had no idea who I was, and I realized in that moment that he didn't.

So probably he didn't care what plans I had for my life, but I told him anyway. "I'm going to college," I said. "I'm going to be a part of the world." Then I extended my hand and shook his firmly. "Thank you for this adventure, but it's time for me to go explore something else."

And Otto said nothing. He merely nodded at me, a tiny, bemused smile on his lips.

As I walked down the hallway, I began to cry — not because I was sad, but because I knew my life would never be the same again. I was scared as hell. But I was also free.

❧   ❧   ❧

This morning I got the application packet for NYU. There is an undergraduate creative-writing program that I think might be perfect. In addition to my high school transcript and three letters of recommendation, I'm supposed to include an essay about an experience that made me who I am.

My name is Hannah Ward, I'll write. *Don't call me a ballerina.*

Epilogue: Fall Semester

"Here, let me help you," Jacob says, reaching over to grab a stack of papers from my arms. "What is all this, anyway?"

I shift my bag to my other shoulder and take a sip of iced coffee. "Short stories," I tell him. "From my fiction workshop."

"Is there one of yours in here?" he asks, thumbing through them.

"Mine's due next week."

"I hope it's going to be about me," he says. "I've always wanted to be featured in fiction."

I laugh. "Maybe if you write another song about me, I'll write a story about you. Although since a story is longer, you'll probably have to write two or three more songs to be fair."

"*Oh, Hannah was a dancer and not an equestrian, but then she went to college and became a pedestrian,*" Jacob sings.

"Very funny," I say, giving him a little shove.

"Wait, there's more."

"I don't want to hear it," I laugh. "Come on, I'm going to be late."

He takes my hand and we walk south to the edge of China-town, near the park where the old men play chess.

"So, remember, I'm playing at Gene's tonight at eight, if you want to catch my set," Jacob says.

"I'll be there," I say. "I'll ask Meg if she wants to come."

"Who's Meg?" he asks, looking at me quizzically.

I grin. "She's my new friend. I met her in art history class." *And she doesn't know a piqué from a bourrée*, I think but don't add. "You'll love her."

"Awesome, can't wait to meet her."

I give him a kiss and then run across the street and into the Delancey Dance Academy.

In Mattie's dance class, thirty boys and girls are all jumping up and down and yelling happily as they fling off their coats to reveal bodies of all shapes and sizes. There is one girl with the long limbs of a future ballerina and another who's as short and thick as a little bear cub. One little boy is showing off his abil-ity to do splits, while another is sitting in the corner eating a Twinkie.

I think about Leni on her Pilates mat, and Daisy gossiping with Zoe about the latest casting as Bea rolls her eyes. Last week I happened to walk by the theater, and I saw Zoe chatting with Jonathan as they returned from the deli. I waved to them from across the street, but I don't think they saw me. Above Zoe's head floated a dozen red balloons.

After dancing in the corps de ballet of the Manhattan Ballet, everything else seems manageable. It makes the difficult things of normal life seem . . . if not easy, then at least less hard. I think about the company almost every day. I'm thankful I was a part of it, and I'm thankful that I'm gone.

Beauty is everywhere, not just in the theater.

The children hush as I enter and take my place at the front of the class. "Ladies and gentlemen," I say. "Please take your places at the barre and show me your first position."

There is a mad dash for spots, and then thirty pairs of eyes are staring at me, waiting to see what I'll do next. It is an utterly different kind of audience from the one I'm used to, and I feel my stomach flutter nervously. But I straighten my spine and smile.

"Very good," I say. "Now take a deep breath. Let's dance."

Acknowledgments

Writing this novel has been an incredibly cathartic, humbling process, and it took a small village to see it to fruition.

This book would not have been possible without the guidance and patience of my dear friend and fellow writer, Emily Chenoweth. I would like to thank my incredible editor, Elizabeth Bewley, who sought me out and gave me the opportunity of a lifetime. My literary agent, Brettne Bloome, has been the book's biggest cheerleader from the inception of this project.

Thanks to my parents, Fran and Bob, who've always encouraged me to dream big and to strive for things seemingly beyond my grasp. And a big hug to my younger sister, Hannah, whom I hope to be like someday.

My partner in crime, Josh Charles, lived with me through possibly one of the biggest life transitions I'll ever experience, during which I wrote this book. Babe, if we could get through that, we can get through anything. Your generosity, support, loyalty, curiosity, and extraordinary talent inspire me every single day.

Some of the most influential people in my life rarely receive the acknowledgment they so deserve. In order of chronology, these ballet teachers had a profound impact on my dance career: Jill Silverman, Kristen Beckwith, Anna-Marie Holmes, Alexandra Bullock, Jacqueline Cronsberg, Sandra Jennings, Gloria Govrin, Patricia McBride, Suzanne Farrell, Susan Pilarre, Kay Mazzo, Suki Schorer, Nancy Bielski, and Wilhelm Burmann.

A standing ovation for the professors who influenced the way I view the world, and have given me the tools and confidence to take on this project: Professor Christian De Matteo, Professor Robert A. Ferguson, Professor Nalini Jones, and Professor Erik Gray.

I am grateful to Peter Martins and the New York City Ballet for allowing me to achieve my dream of dancing with one of the best companies on the planet. It was an adventure of a lifetime, and my experiences there, both onstage and off, helped inform the person I am today.

And I would like to acknowledge the die-hard balletomanes up in the fifth ring. I danced for you guys every night.

Where stories bloom.